THIS
TUMULT

*For Eliza and Arthur
and in loving memory of Joan, Nick,
Tony, Barbara, Mary and Peter*

THIS
TUMULT

CAROLINE PRESTON

THE LILLIPUT PRESS
DUBLIN

First published 2017 by
THE LILLIPUT PRESS
62–63 Sitric Road, Arbour Hill
Dublin 7, Ireland
www.lilliputpress.ie

ISBN 978 1 84351 659 0

A CIP record for this title is available from
The British Library.

10 9 8 7 6 5 4 3 2 1

Set in 11 pt on 15 pt Quixote by Marsha Swan
Printed in Spain by GraphyCems

AUTHOR NOTE

This novel is based on the true story of an Irish family
in World War Two. I have had to imagine how they
coped with what befell them and how they battled
with separation, fear and deprivation. The people
they encountered and who helped them survive are
also entirely fictional.

THIS
TUMULT

Nor law, nor duty bade me fight,
Nor public men, nor cheering crowds,
A lonely impulse of delight
Drove to this tumult in the clouds

W.B. Yeats

One

Nick Tottenham was reluctant to leave the warmth of his bed. Watery sunlight broke through the cracks in the shutters and dust motes floated sluggishly in the narrow beams. A muffled, busy clatter rose from the bowels of the old house. Lilly was in the yard chasing the scrawny brown hens from their nests. Martha was baking in the basement and the smell of the sweet dough had already reached his room. It was 20 May and Nick's sixteenth birthday although he felt none of the giddy excitement that birthdays used to bring. He lifted his nose above the sheets while the despair that had been consuming him for months settled on him once again.

Perhaps today would be different, he told himself as he dressed. Today his father might stop treating him as a child. He was at an age when boys went to the front not very long ago. He walked purposefully down the stairs for his first breakfast as a man who might do such things, crossed the hall and entered the morning room. His mother sat in the window, engrossed in the paper. Gold glasses were perched on the end of her nose and strands of her chestnut hair fell onto the page from the loose knot at the nape of her neck. A cigarette rested between her lips. As the morning light struck her face Nick could imagine the beauty she must have been before bearing six children.

'Morning Mother.'

'Hmm, yes darling.'

'Lovely day.'

'Hmm ...' The minutes ticked by.

'Mother, you do realize it's my birthday.'

He briefly regretted his tone. He knew he was being disagreeable. His mother was not, after all, in the front line of those whom he believed were conspiring to ruin his life. Besides, she was not going to change and he understood that she buried herself in crosswords and puzzles to avoid the wreckage around her. He wondered why he had bothered to remind her that it was his birthday. Now she would try and make up for forgetting it and he would not be able to relish his grievance and fatten it all day as the hours passed and no one wished him well.

'Oh darling, I'm so sorry – I thought of it earlier but then I forgot.' She stood up, all lavender and grey. 'Come, give me a kiss.'

He dodged the curl of blue smoke and found her powdered cheek. She had six birthdays to remember after all. He supposed that she was exhausted. It wasn't just that there was never any money for things like birthday presents; his mother seemed to have grown tired of the business of motherhood. The Little Ones, Maggie and George, ran wild most of the time since there was no one to take them to school. His mother had taught the eldest three at home – Rose, himself and Tony – at least until Rose went off to her posh school in England thanks to Uncle Geoffrey's money and the boys were dispatched to Queen's Hospital school on the other side of the country. She seemed to have given up with the youngest three. Poor Kate, his next-youngest sister, did her best to look after Maggie and George, to teach them the arithmetic and poems she was learning at the school to which she had to cycle ten miles every morning. As the eldest boy and still at home, he received most attention from his parents but it was always critical. It seemed to him that he couldn't do anything right. And yet they expected him to make his future here, farming in Westmeath and a life tied to mounting debts while watching his parents routinely dulling the pain of their disappointment with whiskey. The crushing weight of their expectations shadowed him like the masonry of the old house.

He stared morosely into the empty hall. The ceiling paint was peeling and the doors leading from each corner were warped from lack of use. Grim-faced portraits of his forebears, all in military uniform, hung on thick brass chains. They too seemed to radiate disapproval of him. The house was closing in on them as one room after another yielded to dust sheets and the cold and damp rose from the wormy floors. The family was also in retreat – his father with whiskey, his mother in her crosswords. Tony had his model airplanes and dreams of flying, Kate her wild flowers, and the two Little Ones, Maggie and George, built playhouses in the woods. And where could *he* get away from them all? The morning room was strewn with the mess of family life: his mother's sewing, games of Snakes & Ladders, dusty accounting ledgers, bits for bridles and stirrups for saddles, fishing rods, tennis rackets, books of pressed flowers, glue and pieces of tiny Tiger Moths and Sopwith Camels waiting for Tony to fit them together, but none of it was his.

The paper on which his mother had scribbled her anagrams lay on the table. The headline was from a world far away from the morning room by the lake in Westmeath: *Czechoslovakia orders a partial mobilization of armed forces along the German border.* He wasn't exactly sure where Czechoslovakia was, but wherever it was, it wouldn't disturb life here. Nothing would. There was talk of war on the wireless but there couldn't possibly be another one; his father had only just come back from the last. Even that would not provide an escape for him.

He heard a rhythmic clip on the hall floor and his father entered the room. As always his father seemed to fill the space and Nick imagined himself physically shrinking beside him. It was not just his impressive size and straight back but the way that he assumed that he was the most important person in the room. Nick saw the slight stiffening of his father's shoulders and a tightening of his fine features when the older man realized Nick was at the table and then, just as quickly, as his mother caught her husband's eye, the immediate softening of them. He smiled at her and Nick's chest squeezed with resentment.

'Good morning, Father. You're up early.' He searched his father's face but there was no smile for him.

'That bloody cattle dealer is coming to rob me blind again. He is a rogue.' He sat down at the head of the table.

'Tea, dear?' His mother simply didn't appear to notice when her husband was out of sorts. Gerald Tottenham's hand shook as he lifted the porcelain teacup to his lips. He peered at Nick over the rim with his reddened eyes.

'If you were any good you'd take over the cattle.'

'It's Nick's birthday, Gerald,' his mother said, using the velvety voice she saved for mornings such as these. 'He is seventeen today.' She paused for a second, unsure. 'That is right, isn't it Nicholas?'

'Sixteen,' Nick corrected her. He didn't trust himself to say any more.

'Whatever he is, Eleanor, it's time the boy took up his share of the work around here.' His father was glowering fixedly at Nick as he snatched at the paper. 'That bloody corporal will have us at war again. You wait and see. We should have polished off the Hun when we had a chance,' he said as he cut himself a slice of bread, dipped the spoon into the jam pot and tried to spread Martha's marmalade but it slid off, dripping over his hands. 'This marmalade is too damned thin,' he snapped. Throwing his napkin on to the table, he pushed his chair back and reached for the decanter on the sideboard.

Nick stood up. 'I promised Kate I'd join her by the lake this morning. She has something she wants to show me. I won't be long,' he said. He could not watch his father drink at breakfast this morning.

Nick shoved open the kitchen door, which swung open on its rusty hinges, and stormed out into the yard. He pulled his head into his pullover like a turtle, lit a cigarette from the yellow packet and drew hard, his eyes narrowing. 'Bloody fool,' he muttered aloud. It would always be like this. Even on his birthday his father had rounded on him. Why should he stay for this? Heading down the path to the lake, he kicked a stone into the reedy grass. Take over the cattle? If only he'd bloody let me. He turned and looked back at the black bulk of his home. The shutters were closed on most of the upstairs rooms and the house looked asleep. Spring weeds grew in the cracks of the sills. A rotten cedar in the garden had split down its length and its limbs lay on the ground, white and jagged. Cornicing from the west side of the house lay in lumps on the ground below, moss already creeping over them. A wig of bushy ivy topped the wall around the kitchen garden and thin cattle stepped gingerly over the gaps, lured by the smell of uncut and rotting cabbages.

I can't do this, Nick thought.

The water of the lake was black and still, with only a small fishing boat breaking the line of the far shore. Cinnamon sedges hovered above the water, daring the trout to break its oily calm. Nick threw the butt of his cigarette into the water. A gentle puff of wind rippled the surface of the lake, cooling his temper but doing nothing to shift his unhappiness as he walked along the shore towards the boathouse. He liked to come here to get away from them all, to listen to the slap of the water and watch the light dapple the arch of the roof. He reached for the slimy rope and stepped into the boat. Pushing off the limestone walls, he plopped out on the lake and leaned back against the bow of the boat, his arms resting on the oars, and stared at the gunmetal sky. He was sixteen, for God's sake. Something had to change.

'Hey Nick.' The hollow echo of his younger sister's voice crossed the water.

'Hello Kate.' She was sitting on a lichened rock by the shore, head bent over the sketchbook on her knees. In the black fug of his resentment he had forgotten that he had meant to meet her on the shore. She was, as always, barefoot. Her cotton dress, white with sprigs of forget-me-nots, was tucked up to resemble shorts. She had been paddling, moving the minnows with her feet in the sand.

'Come here! I'm making something for you.'

He guided the boat onto the sandy shore, and clunking the oars into it, stepped out.

'You'll never believe what I found,' she said. 'It's a bee orchid, Nick. Isn't it wonderful? They're so rare! Look, I'm drawing a picture of it for your birthday. Its striped body is so yellow it almost glows and look at the lovely purple wings. It is just like a bee, although of course Tony says it's like an airplane.'

Nick leant forward to view her prize, parting the wiry grass to get a better look.

'You must never pick them because then there will be no more of them.'

He squatted next to her, reached out and ruffled her mop of russet curls. 'Well done you. It really does look as though it is about to fly away, doesn't it?' Lucky bee, he thought. 'Are you drawing it for me? For my birthday?'

'Yes. I'm sorry. I would have liked to buy you something.' A frown had creased her brow.

'But I love your flower pictures, Kate! I've kept them all. Let me see. I think I like the yellow ones the best, the marsh marigold and the yellow iris. I wonder why they call it a "flag" here? Oh, and then there is that lovely ... the one with the funny name. What's it called?'

'The creeping Jenny,' she answered. He smiled. She was always able to melt the anger in him, if only for a moment. She picked up the purple crayon and started to colour the wings of the orchid on the page.

He stood up, restless, and skimmed a flat stone across the water.

'Tony is better at that than you,' she said.

'Tony is better at everything,' Nick said without any sourness. Kate's words were rarely intended to wound and he understood only too well that Tony was fair and sunny and he was dark and brooding. They were inseparable, he and Tony, but it was hard being Nick. One day Kate would grow up and leave and so would Maggie and George. Rose, his glamorous big sister, had gone off to England already. There was not enough here for both Tony and him, so Tony would be allowed to go too and Nick would be left behind, endlessly mending holes in the roof, pulling ivy off walls, negotiating credit from local traders and fighting with his father.

Nick took a deep breath. 'I'm thinking of going away for a bit. Next year probably.' He fixed his eye on the distant fishing boat, afraid to look at his sister. Kate's head snapped up.

'How long?'

'Oh a year or so, and ...' he hesitated and still he could not meet her eye, '... Tony too.'

'Both of you? I mean, how will we manage? We need you here. Where're you going? Is it far? How will Poppa manage? What will we do here on our own?'

'I don't see why I can't have a life of my own, Kate. Father expects me to stay here as some sort of unpaid farm hand. It's not fair.' He stalled again. 'Australia.' He had given it no thought until this moment.

'Australia? It's so far away. Tony will only be fifteen this September!'

'Tony needs to get away too, Katie. There's no point in him going back to school,' he said, knowing that this was not the whole truth. He felt a rush, unsure whether it was the excitement of seeing a way out or the idea of doubly hurting the old man by taking Tony with him. He could see that he was upsetting Kate but all the frustration he had nurtured for so long drove him on. Talking to her made the idea possible so he ignored his sister's crumpled face and grey eyes now filling with tears. The bee orchid forgotten, she pulled at the quicks of her nails as she always did when she was unhappy.

'What are you going to do there?'

'Jackaroo.' He looked at her as she miserably contemplated the unfamiliar word. 'It's rounding up sheep and cattle on horses, that kind of thing.'

'But you hate horses.'

'Look Little One, I know this is hard but Father won't give me any responsibility. I can't just hang around here and watch him drink the place away. I might actually learn something in Oz that'll help me when I have to run the farm here.'

'He doesn't drink *every* day.'

'I know, and he's had it tough, in Flanders in the war and all that. It's just that there can't be two people in charge, Kate. We simply don't get on. When he's ready to hand over then we can come back.' He would not tell her that he didn't think the old place could survive, that it was too far gone. He would leave her that dream. They sat in silence. Nick thought about the idea, mesmerized by the swallows swooping for midges and making rings on the surface of the water. His father would never let him go, he told himself. It was just a pipe dream.

'Poppa loves you. He just doesn't know how to show it. It's all that stiff upper lip stuff.' Kate paused and looked squarely at Nick. 'He doesn't know anything about this, does he?' As usual, she had seen how things really were, that courage had failed her brother and that he had not raised the idea with either of his parents.

'You'd best start with Mummy,' she added miserably.

'I wish things were not as they are,' his mother said later that day to both boys, 'but actually I think it is a good idea. God knows there is no money to send either of you back to school and you in particular need to spend some time away from your father. Honestly, Nick, you really must learn not to fight with him so much. You will have to leave it to me to bring him round.'

He was surprised by his mother's tone but was also comforted by it. Maybe she had understood him all along. To his horror, he thought that he might cry. Despite his mother's diminutive stature, gentle voice and absent ways, here was strength and something resolute. He felt strangely humbled by her, as if he were seeing her clearly for the first time. Who might she have become had she not walked into that teashop in Aberystwyth and met his father when she was nineteen? The clever daughter of a rural doctor with her heart set on teaching mathematics and the first woman ever to graduate from the university. Everything that she had once been or could have become had been buried in the stories of his parents' chance meeting, the spicy hint that their marriage did not have the blessing of their families and the glamour of them heading out to make their life in the Far East. She could not resist his handsome father with the row of medals on his uniform on his way back from the front. He had promised her a life of plenty here in Westmeath with the prize herd of shorthorns that he would fatten on the magnificent farm he was going home to. She had given up everything for a life in a grand old house with manicured gardens and gravel paths on which she could push her children in prams like carriages.

The babies had come, six of them, but in every other way her life had turned out to be very different.

'Of course it mightn't be for very long. After all, Father went off to Malaya before he came back to farming. And it will be great experience for me to learn all about agriculture ... and Tony also,' he added.

'It will be such an adventure, Mummy,' Tony said. 'Of course, Nick hates horses but he will have to put up with that. I will be fine though. I mean, not that I am any good at riding or anything but I have just done a bit more I suppose ...' His words tailed off as his mother's eyes hardened.

'Tony you need to be very careful what you say to your father before I manage him about this. He spent four years in the trenches in Flanders before we went to Malaya. Your grandfather would not contemplate our coming home at all. It was hardly the gallivanting that this appears to be. Malaya was no picnic either. Home was in the jungle miles from anywhere. For months we lived in a tent with no shelter against the endless rain.'

'Why didn't you come straight back here after the war?'

Eleanor hesitated and fixed her eye on the lakeshore through the window. 'I never knew why your grandfather wouldn't have us. I think perhaps he had hoped for a rather different daughter-in-law with – how shall I put it – more blue blood and less blue stocking?' She smiled. 'Isn't it just as well I love your father as much as I do. Otherwise I might not have forgiven him. But even I cannot make the books balance here so you should go and see what the world has to offer. We'll find the fare somehow. It won't be like the grand ship Poppa and I travelled on.' Her eyes glazed over again. 'Oh my goodness – those banquets every night.'

She sighed. 'I didn't know which knife or fork to use. Poppa had to show me and I was so afraid of letting him down. I was such a ninny really.'

'How did you cope with the jungle after all that?' Nick asked.

'Oh you know, as I do now. Arithmetic.' She looked apologetic. 'Working out the square root of sub-prime numbers in my head. It distracts me from any unpleasantness.' She looked up at her sons and smiled. 'Yes, dears. I know you all think I'm a bit odd like that. Your father has not had it easy either. I only hope that you will match up to him one day.'

The door opened and Kate stepped into the room. Her face was blotchy and her dress was still tucked artlessly into her knickers. She held out the bee orchid.

'You picked it?' Nick gasped.

'Everyone is going to fly away anyway,' she sobbed. Turning around, she fled, banging the heavy door behind her.

Two

It was September already, and his mother had said nothing. Nick was alone, his head bowed over the *Westmeath Examiner*, when Kate found him.

'There you are. I've been looking everywhere for you,' she said brightly.

He ignored her, then grunted, threw the paper on the floor and left the room. Kate was not to be deterred because she bounced behind him down the stairs to the pantry and out into the kitchen yard, keeping up her chatter.

'Will you partner me in the mixed doubles?' Nick flicked the ash from his cigarette at the hens pecking at the moss on the cobbles of the yard. 'It's the end-of-season friendly tournament. Please Nick. Will you?'

'I *am* going to town but I have things to do. I don't know how long it will take. Ask Tony.'

Kate's shoulders slumped and she looked away across the lake with her top tooth pressed into her bottom lip. She lifted her chin as she turned back to face him.

'You don't do anything with me any more. You just float about on the lake on your own. And you talk to me all the time in the same voice you use for Maggie and George. And you and Tony are always huddled in a corner.'

'Go and play with the Little Ones, Kate. Tony and I have things to do.'

'What things?' Her expression was crushed and curious at the same time.

Nick regretted being mysterious with her. He should have known better. She had sharp antennae and now he needed to divert her quickly. 'Oh nothing, just some school stuff. Look, I'm sure Tony can play this afternoon if it's so important to you.'

'Your backhand is better than his and anyway Tony doesn't *want* to win like you do.'

'That's because he usually does,' Nick said. He was not in the mood for humouring Kate today. He could hear Tony whistling and moments later his stocky brother appeared, striding up the hill from the lake. His cap was set on the back of his head and his round face was flushed pink from his climb. The tips of his ears, which stuck out a bit too much, were bright red. He had been swimming and his fair hair was still wet. It made him look even more fresh and eager than usual. Tony vaulted the gate, and the chickens, alarmed at the commotion, stuck forward their heads, flapped their useless wings, and took refuge in the corner of the yard. He always makes an entrance, Nick thought.

Nick knew that if his mother failed to persuade the old man to let them go, booking the passage would be a declaration of war. It had to be a secret but Tony was guileless. Nick needed to warn him to be careful what he said to Kate and the Little Ones. He followed him across the cobbles to the big barn and stepped into the gloom behind him. Nick felt uncomfortable in there. It was Tony's special place, and, as the boathouse was for him, his sanctuary. He hoped that Kate might respect that and leave them alone but she was right there behind him. The two workhorses, Dolly and Daisy, heavy bay Irish draughts with loose muzzles and thick silky legs, stood in the stalls. Nick walked in a wide arc behind them. He could not understand how Tony had no fear of these huge animals with their unpredictable teeth and feet. Even Ben, the grey cob who pulled the trap, had a mind of his own and made Nick nervous. And Tony's pride and joy, a wild-eyed thoroughbred called Firefly that he had saved from the knacker's yard, was simply terrifying. The mare trusted no one but Tony and now she stamped her feet like a diva to demand his attention.

But it was not only the horses that bothered Nick in here. Unlike all the other buildings the barn was spotlessly clean, its windows sparkled and the wood was freshly painted. Tony had fixed the latches on the stalls and put new mangers in each of them. Shining saddles were mounted on racks and labelled bridles hung above them. The four animals stood in their stalls, tugging gently at the hay and blinking their bog-pool eyes. Tony had been up at first light as he was every morning to groom and feed them, muck out the stalls and polish the harnesses. For Nick the very order and cleanliness was an affront given the state of the rest of the place.

'Dolly and Daisy look very smart today,' Kate said, smoothing the hefty rump of the former with the flat of her hand.

'I've been out with the currycomb this morning. Every girl needs a hairdo now and then, isn't that right?'

'Why are you and Nick going to town anyway? It's not market day.'

'We're going to see about our passage to Australia.' He was backing the cob out of the stall and slipping the harness over his dappled neck, and so he did not see his sister's face collapse or the look of thunder that Nick threw him. Jesus. Tony, have you no wit? Nick thought.

Kate swung around to face Nick. 'What? You're not still thinking of going away are you? I thought all that stuff last spring was just you having a bad day, Nick. You've said nothing about it for months.' She looked from one brother to the next. Nick felt a stab of guilt that he had kept her in the dark. It had been cowardice, of course. Kate was the only person who would make him feel that he was abandoning a sinking ship.

'Who's going to look after the horses when you're gone?' she snapped. 'Nobody else will do it, you know. This barn will go to rack and ruin.'

She could find everyone's Achilles heel, Nick thought. He moved to the door and lit another cigarette. Even Tony was avoiding his sister's eyes by reaching down to pull at the grass growing through the cobbles to give to the cob.

'Well?' Kate insisted.

'I think Father will let the tillage land for a bit so they can have a good rest out in the fields,' Tony said eventually. The only sound came from the bit in Ben's frothy mouth clinking as the pony worked the grass through his bridle.

'Look at Ben – he's covered in great dollops of green slobber. We're going to turn up at the tennis club looking like bloody tinkers,' Kate said, her voice rising.

'Hey, easy now Kate – it's not like you to mind about a silly thing like a dirty pony,' Tony said.

'Nothing is ever the way it should be here. Everything gets spoilt. Even bloody Ben can't keep himself clean when you've gone to all the trouble of brushing him.' She tugged at the rein roughly and the animal stepped back in alarm. She picked up the brush and slid her hand through the strap, then threw it roughly into a corner of the stall. Nick looked at her in surprise. He didn't think he had ever seen Kate do anything so violent.

'What's it going to be like when you're gone?' She paused as if she were afraid to say more, and paced up and down the length of the barn behind the swishing tails of the two carthorses. 'Lilly's brother went to America and they all said he was coming back, but he never did. You won't come back either. I'm right, aren't I?' Tears slid down her face.

Tony lifted his sister on to a bale of hay so that his face was level with hers. 'Don't be crying Kate,' he said wiping her cheek. 'We'll be home in no time.'

By the time Ben had clopped his way as far as Dalystown, Tony was whistling again, and Kate, sitting between her brothers on the front bench of the trap, had regained some of her gaiety.

'Hello Dan,' Tony hollered at the publican as they trotted past his shop. The man, in a collarless shirt and braces, his trousers huge around his waist and worn at the knees, sat outside on the bench for most of the day and in all weather. His hand was, as always, cupped around the glowing tip of a cigarette, a pack of Sweet Afton beside him on the bench.

'Does Dan stop smoking to eat, do you think?' Kate asked as she and Nick followed their brother's lead and waved at the old man, who raised a lazy finger at the passing trap without adjusting his face at all. 'Poppa says he's an old robber, that he charges too much for everything.'

'Father thinks everyone is robbing him, Kate – that's because he hasn't enough money to pay them,' Nick said.

By late afternoon the matches were over and Nick had finished his errands and joined them at the club to catch a lift home in the trap. Tony was standing outside the changing room with Fergus O'Dowd, a pale, thin youth with carroty hair and angry spots on his chin. His father was a solicitor and Nick didn't like him. The boy swaggered with self-confidence because his father knew every-one's business.

'So you're not coming back to school?' Fergus said, throwing a narrow-eyed look at the other boys ranged behind him.

Tony shrugged and Nick looked away. He would let Tony answer for them both. He didn't trust himself not to say something that would make Kate's life in the tennis club intolerable. 'I suppose I know enough to earn a living. I was never much good at schoolwork anyway.'

'But Australia! That's a long way, isn't it? I never thought of people like yous having to emigrate,' Fergus persisted, his mouth twisting as he lifted his chin to emphasize his challenge. His friends looked on eagerly and moved in closer.

'It's not emigration, for heaven's sake. We're just going to learn some farming, that's all.'

'Sure, people like you get other fellas to do the work for them, don't they?' Fergus's lip curled unpleasantly.

Tony let his breath out slowly. With some effort he resumed his habitual smile. 'Yeah, that's right, we have hundreds of people, all with shiny buttons on their coats, to fetch and carry for us up there in the big house. We're only going to get away from feckers like you.'

Nick had had enough. 'Come on Tony, you don't have to explain yourself to these fellows. Let them stay here and rot.' He pulled at Tony's arm to lead him towards the trap.

Ben trotted along the road in the lengthening shadows. The trap jigged as the pony spooked at the blackening bushes at the side of the road.

'What's up Kate? You're very quiet for a girl who just won a medal,' Nick said.

'Why did Fergus say those things to Tony about us having lots of servants? I don't think he was being very nice.'

'He thinks we're newcomers and have it all easy – the big house and all that. He feels we don't belong here,' Nick replied, his voice tight. He tossed the end of his cigarette into the ditch.

'But our house is cold and damp and we have to live in one room! We don't even have electricity! I bet Fergus's house has it and his roof has no holes in it. His family doesn't have to eat only what comes out of the garden and he doesn't have to spend all his holidays picking fruit. He goes to Wexford for his holidays,' she said, as if Wexford were the most exotic location in the world.

'It doesn't really work like that, Kate. We'll always be outsiders,' Tony said cheerfully, putting his arm around her.

'Why?' she asked.

'It's our own fault really. Because we insist on doing things our own way, going to a different church, staying in the old house when it is falling down around our ears. We're oddballs, I suppose.' He shook the reins over the pony's back.

Nick pulled in his breath sharply, and felt his temper flush his face.

'Jesus Christ, Tony,' he said, rolling his eyes towards the sky. He turned to his sister. 'They think we're bloody English or as near as damn it. Not because we are, but because hundreds of years ago we were, and we keep doing things to remind them of that, like going off to war for the English, like Father did. We're never going to belong here so we should get on with a real life somewhere else and the sooner the better.' The pony's feet clipped along the road, and the curlews cried over the lake. 'I sent the wire to the steamship company and I posted the letter to Uncle Herbert to tell him that we're coming out. The rest is up to Mother and how she brings the old man around,' Nick added. His temper had fuelled his courage, and his cruelty. She's got to hear it sometime and now is as good a time as any, he thought.

'Is that why you're going away? Because we're, what did you call it, *oddballs*? Is that why Dan never waves at us when we pass his pub?' She looked down at the medal she and Tony had won that afternoon and flung it in the ditch. 'I don't understand anything any more.'

The next morning clouds hung over the lake and the wind drove sheets of slate-grey rain towards the house. By noon the wind had dropped but the rain continued to fall and water dripped relentlessly from the trees. Martha clambered stiffly up from the kitchen from time to time to place her pans under the latest leak. With all the family in the morning room, it had become crowded and stuffy. The gas fire hissed orange and blue in the grate. It was that time of the day when the rooks began their clatter over the trees and his father would soon ask what had happened to his afternoon tea. That was the cue for George and Maggie to be sent to the kitchen to eat with Martha and Jim. It didn't seem that long ago when Nick had done the same thing. And he would prefer to go with the Little Ones now. He missed having tea with Martha, listening to Jim talk about the fish he had caught that day or the frogspawn he had found in the mill race. Nick was restless and nervous. Still his mother had said nothing about how his father might react. He wanted to go so badly. Had his mother managed to turn his father around?

Maggie and Kate were sitting on the floor surrounded by paper, paste, scrapbooks and pressed flowers. Maggie was already taller than his mother and bigger than Kate. She was going to get her size from their father, Nick thought. Poor girl. She was interested only in nursing small animals and broken-winged birds. Doe-eyed and trusting, she lived in a make-believe world in which she was always the attentive mother. Poor George had to 'be baby' for hours every day and did so without complaint, apparently understanding that this was his lot as the youngest in a family of six. Nick thought that he didn't know his youngest brother very well – a serious boy with his mother's mathematical brain who was happiest playing a game of bridge or working out a puzzle.

'I don't see the point,' George said as Tony took the sticky model from him. Once again, he had made a mess of the Airfix. Nick wondered why the child volunteered to help Tony when he was so bad at it – perhaps it was a relief not to be making grass soup and feeding it to Maggie's army of dolls.

'Well, because then we will know all about the machines we're flying when we are pilots.'

'But they're not real.'

'Oh, for God's sake, why don't you go and do some bloody sums with Mummy then!'

He would miss all of this. Doubt was creeping into his excitement for the first time. He was so close to getting away and maybe it wasn't what he wanted at all. He shook his head, as if that way he could rid himself of any second thoughts. 'I don't suppose the postman will come in this weather,' Nick said, to no one in particular.

'You expecting a love letter or something?' His father's voice rumbled from behind the paper. Clearly the old man was in great form today and the paper shook in his hand as he laughed to himself. Today was a day when Nick could risk talking to him. The photograph on the front page was of Neville Chamberlain addressing the London crowd the previous day. *Peace in our Time* read the headline.

'That was close – I mean the agreement with Hitler, don't you think, Father? Only last week they were digging up the parks in London to be used as air-raid shelters. I heard on the wireless that the zoo keepers in London had plans to shoot the animals in case bombs broke open their cages.'

'Oh that's awful,' Maggie said, her eyes filling with tears.

'Now look what you've done,' George said, looking blankly at his sobbing sister.

'I don't know. I think it is time to give the Germans a lesson,' Tony said. 'I'm up for it.'

Their father lowered the newspaper and looked at his two older sons. 'War is not the adventure you might think it is, boys. This fellow Hitler is quite simply mad, and I'm afraid the Germans think he will make amends for their humiliation the last time out.'

He glanced at his wife sitting in the window seat. 'Actually, your mother and I have been talking. If you're off to Australia we think you should get going fairly soon. There's a real possibility that this will not settle down and then there could be all sorts of disruption to shipping. I can't imagine that it will actually amount to war. It's unthinkable that we could do it all again' – he seemed to shudder – 'but you never know where trouble can break out.'

Nick glanced at his mother. Eleanor seemed to be warning him to be careful, but there was also something slightly triumphant in her expression.

'You mean we can actually go?' Nick stammered, his voice reaching an almost girlish pitch.

'A year or two away will do you both good. I mean, I was in Malaya and South Africa before I came home so I think it's a good idea. I can manage here for a short time.'

'Actually Gerald, there is a sailing of the *Jervis Bay* in March. Is that too soon do you think?' Eleanor said.

'In fact, Poppa,' Tony jumped up excitedly, swinging his right arm in an arc through the air to make one of his model aircraft simulate flight, 'we have already been in touch with Aberdeen and ...' Nick shot him a fierce look and his brother's mouth snapped shut.

Kate emerged from behind her father's chair. 'Poppa, I'll help you with the farm,' she said, twisting her hands in front of her. 'After all, I am fourteen now. I am not a Little One any more.'

Gerald turned stiffly, his face registering a mild astonishment that she was there at all.

'We'll cope, won't we Poppa. They're not emigrating, are they?'

Nick could not remember ever seeing his father at a loss for what to say to his children. Fascinated, he stared at him.

'Come and sit beside me. The boys are growing up. It's only for a short while and they will be back. And don't forget that one day you too will go off and get married and live away from here.' Gerald reached his long arm awkwardly to gather her to him.

'I shall never leave you and Mummy,' she sniffed.

'Be a brave girl – the boys will write, won't you chaps?' Her father smiled and kissed the top of her head.

'Every week, I promise, and so will Tony – isn't that right?' Nick was still trying to process what was happening.

Kate turned her face into her father's chest, breathing in the smell of tobacco and damp wool. He smiled at his wife. Nick saw the look that passed between them, an unfathomable understanding of each other. He had never seen that before.

'Right Kate,' his father said briskly. 'As you are my right-hand girl now we must take the dogs out and check the cattle, even in this rain. Will you come with me?'

There was a knock at the door and Lilly peered in, mobcap askew. 'Willie Fitz is here, Mam, with a telegram. He cycled the whole way from town in this wet. He's drowned, so he is. I'm thinking I'll give him some tea, maybe with a drop of the Major's decanter in it ...' Before she could finish Nick and Tony had shot out of the room and bounded down the stone steps to the kitchen, three at a time. Nick snatched the brown envelope from the table and tore it open: *Booking confirmed. Shared Cabin. Vessel Jervis Bay departing Southampton 17 March 1939. Destination Freemantle /Melbourne Australia.*

'Jesus, Nick, we're really going then?'

'We are.'

Three

AT SEA

By the time they boarded the *Jervis Bay* in Southampton, the two boys were into the swing of things. Having made the journey across the Irish Sea they now considered themselves seasoned travellers. Nick felt a pinprick of hope that for the first time in his life he might at last blend in with the hundreds of young people hauling suitcases up the gangway and pushing to the rail of the ship to wave to their families. He and Tony found a spot amongst them and strained to pick out Rose, who had come to see them off. It was easy to spot their sister.

'Cor, she's a cracker,' said a fellow beside him. Nick had to agree. His eldest sister had blossomed in the two years since she had left home, and everywhere heads turned to get a second look at her. She wore a crisp cotton blouse tucked into her tiny waist, and a full red-and-cream-checked skirt swirled above her pretty ankles. The outfit was the height of fashion and she tossed her bouncy blonde curls with effortless poise. She looked like a softer Marlene Dietrich. She had all the polish of an English private school as well as her own beauty. Perhaps things would have been different for him if he had had a start like Rose. He was more like the rough lads pressing against the rail beside him and crowding onto the decks around its central funnel. Nick felt an irrational dislike for them only because he knew that he would suffer from the same acute shyness with them that he had endured at school, when Tony's popularity had melted some of the icy barricades around him. He had to admit that local schooling didn't seem to be holding Tony back. He understood that it was unlikely that he would get to know any of his fellow travellers or make new friends and Tony would have to do that for both of them.

A uniformed sailor barked directions, telling them that they had to find their beds. Another, holding a list on a clipboard and ticking off names, stood at the heavy cast-iron door through which they had to stoop to enter what looked like a huge steel box and where they and 200 other young men and boys would sleep for the next two months. They wandered along identical rows of bunks trying to find their names.

'This will be where they put the meat and butter on the return journey,' Nick said.

'Not the way Mummy and Poppa did it after the war, is it?' Tony said, laughing.

'No, I don't think we'll be asked to dine at the captain's table somehow. You know poor Mother did not have anything like the life that Father promised her. She thought she was being taken out to Malaya for a grand life in the colonies. She even brought her dinner service! And she ends up living in a kampong. That's where Rose was born. I've seen a picture of it. It was just a shack. No white person for hundreds of miles.'

'She never complained.'

'It must have been hard for her, especially after all the banquets and finery on the ship ... Imagine. When they arrive in Singapore Father puts her on a cart pulled by an ox and they trudge through the jungle for five days. I don't know how she ever trusted him again.'

'At least we are starting off at the bottom. Nobody could call this "grand". I think it'll be great fun – just like school really.'

'And just as damp,' Nick replied.

The next few days went by just as Nick feared they would. Tony made friends and joined groups to play soccer, French cricket, table tennis and badminton while Nick hid out of the wind behind the funnel. Running races were organized around the upper deck and the captain handed out prizes as if it were a regular sports day. Many of the third-class passengers were children even younger than Tony. The ship's playroom was always full and when they sailed into Valetta, Nick was horrified to see a white sign fluttering on the pier with the words 'Welcome Youth Ship'. He retreated to his place behind the funnel, his face in a book he wasn't reading. For the next two weeks Nick could be found there whereas Tony outshone everyone in the games, just like he had done at school.

'There are some chaps I want you to meet. They're from Germany. They speak better English than the other Germans. They're a bit older and I think you'd like them,' Tony said. Nick wanted to be left alone but in some corner of his lonely mind he recognized that this was what he had expected Tony to do – to pimp friends for him – and the fact that they were a bit older was some solace. Besides, Tony had scampered off to fetch them before Nick could stop him.

'This is Zach.' Tony pointed to the smaller of the two boys, a slight fellow with narrow hips. He had dark good looks and an easy, fluid smile. 'Zach, this is my brother, Nick.'

Nick felt a familiar hot burn flush his cheeks and neck and ran his finger around his collar to soothe it.

'Hello Brother Nick,' the boy said with a grin.

'Zach? What's it short for?' Nick mumbled, belatedly holding out his hand.

'Zachariah. Zachariah Schmitz. What's Nick short for?' the boy asked, looking steadily at Nick, his dark eyes fringed with thick long lashes.

'Nicholas. Nicholas Tottenham,' Nick said, rubbing the back of his neck again and realizing too late that the boy had been making a joke. He let out his breath as if he didn't want to.

'And this is my friend Yitzhak, but he is not called Yit,' Zach said, pulling a silly face. The second boy put down the fiddle he had been cradling to shake Nick's hand.

'Can you play that?' Tony asked him, miming the strumming of a guitar.

'Yes a bit, but not like that,' Yitzhak replied pleasantly.

Nick had an uncomfortable feeling that he and Tony were being slow, and that these fellows were making a joke at their expense. He wasn't sure that he liked the way the one called Zach was looking at him so intensely.

'He is very good. Not just a bit, like he says. He played in big orchestra in Vienna,' Zach said. Nick's unease grew. He and Tony could have nothing in common with such boys.

'Gosh,' said Tony. 'Do you know jigs?' And he started to throw his arms about above his head and hop from foot to foot in a lamentable imitation of the dancing he had seen the tinkers do on fair days at home. The other three laughed and Yitzhak tucked the fiddle under his chin and started to play. Nick wished he could do something like that or at least goof around like Tony, making people laugh. He tapped his toe against the deck self-consciously while Tony continued leaping about on the deck and the German boys laughed and Zach clapped.

'Why are you boys going to Australia?' Nick asked when Yitzhak put down the instrument.

'Like everyone else here, we go to farms, *ja?*' Zach said.

'Are you going to family?'

'No we are refugees. We were rescued by the British German Aid Society. They are *gute Menschen*,' he said simply.

'Gosh, I didn't think there was a British-German anything these days. Rescued from what?' Tony asked brightly, his eyes shining and his face pink from his silly dance. Zach's eyes emptied of light and the corners of his mouth dropped. He seemed to be embarrassed and looked away over the ship's rail to the horizon.

'I don't know how to explain you,' he said. He searched for his words in a way he had not done at first. 'It was very bad for us in Austria since the Nazis came. Storm troopers took my father away in the night and he never came back.'

'Sorry. What did you say? What do you mean? Taken away? What are storm troopers? Where did they take him?' Tony's words were colliding into each other and his voice rose with each question. Now it was Nick's turn to be embarrassed and for once he wished Tony would shut up.

'They told us he had gone to a camp in the east,' Zach said quietly running his long fingers through his black hair.

'What camp? Had he done something wrong?' Nick asked. The thought crossed his mind that there might be a reason why he would not want to know this boy. He was already disconcerted by the way Zach lunged from being a clown to a tragic wretch in seconds.

'Nothing, unless being Jewish is something wrong. *Vati* is a heart surgeon. Yitzhak's is – I mean was – a concert pianist.' Zach threw an apologetic look at Yitzhak. 'His father drowned in a moat at one of these camps. There are many stories,' he added quietly.

His face seemed to cave in on itself and all the chirpy self-confidence of a few moments ago was gone. 'I think maybe both my parents are also dead now.'

Nick did not know what to say but it was shock not shyness or embarrassment that dried up his words this time. In all the discussions at home about what was happening in the Third Reich, in all the information that he and his family devoured from newspapers and the wireless and in all the thundering roars from his father on the subject of the 'bloody corporal', there had been no whisper of any camps. He wondered if anyone in Ireland knew what was really going on at all.

'Do you play chess, Nick?' Zach asked, breaking the heavy silence.

'Yes, a bit,' Nick said numbly.

'Actually, he's pretty useful,' Tony said.

The two older boys became a familiar sight strolling around the decks, deep in conversation or playing chess together. Tony made friends with everyone as always but especially with a group of cheeky Scottish lads with blue-white skin and freckles who were destined for church-run homes in Melbourne and Sydney.

'There's a bunch of fellows from Scotland,' Tony told his brother who lay on the bunk above him, 'who get a year in technical school in a place called Wangaratta, all paid for by the Aussies. I wonder could I do that do you think?'

'Those chaps are from poor homes, Tony – that's why they're getting help.'

'Same old story, isn't it? We haven't a brass farthing either but because we are who we are I'll stay totally uneducated. Oh well. Something will come up I suppose,' Tony said, rolling over to sleep.

Nick lay staring at the steel ceiling above him. Uncle Herbert was giving them work in Victoria, but what then? He wondered if they were doing the right thing and if he should have brought his younger brother away from home before he was half educated. He thought back to the morning they had left home when he had brought the Riley around to the front of the house for their journey to Dublin.

The day had been crisp and the sky as clear as gin. Nick had washed the old motor for want of something to do and then waxed her running boards and polished the lamps. The tartan rugs were stacked in the back and his own case was already in the boot. Tony emerged from the front door, awkwardly propping it open with one foot as he levered through the suitcase, festooned with stickers from his parents' sea journeys to countries that no longer existed.

'When was the last time this door was opened?' Tony complained. 'The wood has swollen with all the rain I suppose.' And no one will do anything about it, Nick thought. Eleanor followed Tony out onto the porch, looking up anxiously as if she were expecting to be hit by falling masonry.

'Hurry up, Kate. No, you can't bring the dog. Buster will have to say goodbye here. Where's your father?'

Gerald appeared at last, wrapped in a huge tweed coat that Nick had never seen him wear before but thought he recognized from the dog basket in the kitchen. His mother was also dressed in tweed, in the coat and skirt she had worn on every high day and holiday since he had been a small child. The hem was coming down on one side. On her head was a black felt hat, the one she wore to funerals, with a pearl-topped hatpin. Kate looked dishevelled too: her favourite blue cardigan was thinning at the elbows and the buttons stretched across the new swell of her chest. Her hair, as always, tossed about her head in a wild halo of disobedience. Lace-up shoes with white ankle socks under a bawneen skirt, which, in contrast to the cardigan, was too big for her, made her look awkward and clumsy, but there was the possibility of the beauty she might become. Next time he saw her, Nick thought, she would be all grown up. He was overcome by an unfamiliar wave of affection for his odd family, all dressed up for their day in Dublin. He pushed it down and chivvied them into the car. He leant forward to kiss Maggie and gravely held out his hand to George.

'You'll have to be the man around here now, George. Do you think you'll be up to that?'

'No, not until I'm twelve,' he replied, poker-faced.

'Send me a postcard of a kangaroo, one with a baby in its pocket,' Maggie bawled, hardly able to get the words out. She reached up and flung her arms around Nick's neck as if she would never let go.

'Oh. I've forgotten something. Sorry, I'll just be a minute,' Tony said and he raced off towards the yard.

'What did you forget?' Nick asked crossly, as his brother, breathless, returned a few minutes later.

'I wanted some of Firefly's tail to remind me of her.'

'Jesus! What the …'

Nick was about to tease him but he had heard the catch in Tony's voice and stifled it. After all, he had put Kate's wildflower pictures into his breast pocket. His brother climbed into the back seat beside his mother and Kate and closed the door. His father, hunched over the wheel, head grazing the roof of the car, pulled and released the throttle, needlessly revving the engine. As the car rolled slowly away from the house, Nick turned and waved at Maggie and George standing with Martha, Jim and Lilly on the front step as Martha blew her nose again and again. Behind him he saw that his brother had no room to wave and had to make do with waggling his fingers at them. Buster the terrier stood sniffing the air importantly as though he had been given responsibility for those left behind. The thought crossed Nick's mind, as he contemplated the brave little dog, that this was exactly what he was not prepared to take on himself.

And now he asked himself whether he should have come on his own. Perhaps Tony was too young. He recalled painfully their ship leaving the harbour in Dun Laoghaire. The boys had found a place at the ship's rail and waved wildly at their parents and Kate. Gone was the day's earlier forced jollity, when his father had pompously ordered 'his usual' claret from the thin-lipped waiter in the Hibernian who then ignored him.

'This is just the beginning, Tony. Exciting, isn't it?' He needed to remind himself of that.

'It's hard saying goodbye,' Tony had said.

As he lay on his bunk staring at the steel ceiling above him, Nick's unease settled on him like a cold fog.

The following day, Nick and Zach stopped to watch the younger boys playing an improvised game of rounders. They had slung a net from the flagpole on the forward deck to stop the ball sailing out to sea. Tony was batting. He leant over the bat gripping it tightly and then swung it a couple of times in an exaggerated circle as if testing its weight, leaning back on his heels as he did so. His brother's face was tight with concentration. As Nick knew he would, he struck the ball hard and it pinged off the pole.

'Good man, Lugs, that's put us ahead. Double points for hitting the pole,' yelled a stocky, black-haired boy with a sunburnt face sitting on top of one of the ship's ventilation shafts, like a gnome on a toadstool. 'He's good at sports, your brother,' Zach said.

'Yeah, he was on the first team in rugby and cricket as a junior. Actually, he's pretty good at anything he does. Sometimes it can be quite annoying.' Nick couldn't believe he had said it. He didn't think that he had ever owned that thought before but Zach pulled these things out of him. Perhaps it was because he was sharing confidences with Nick in such a way that at home would have been considered, well, unmanly.

'Have you ever kissed a girl?' Zach asked him.

'Sort of,' Nick said. He laughed to cover his embarrassment as he thought back to the toothy embrace with Fergus O'Dowd's sister behind the clubhouse.

'Did you like it?'

'I think I will the next time.' They both laughed this time.

'You must learn to court a girl in as many languages as you can,' Zach said, and Nick reddened again.

'*Ich liebe Dich*,' Nick said slowly, trying out the words. 'It doesn't sound very loving, does it?'

'It's worse in Yiddish. Today is *Shabbes*. I must go to pray. I must recite the *Kaddish* with my friends and read the Book.' Zach's face lit up. 'Last night I sang *Lecha Dodi* with them.'

'You're going to church? Here?'

'No, but if there are ten of us when we come together to pray, God says we are in synagogue and we will be forgiven for not doing *Shabbes* properly and for eating food that is not *kosher*.'

'What's *kosher*?'

'We are supposed to separate meat and dairy ... that sort of stuff.'

'Sounds weird to me.' Nick looked at Zach. He was afraid to ask another question. It made him uncomfortable that his friend was so odd. He feared that Zach, and then he by association, would not be accepted when they got to Australia. If Nick could hide his embarrassing background could Zach not do the same?

'You and the rest of the world, I think,' Zach said.

And yet the incomprehensible rules about eating also intrigued Nick about Zach and his 'kind'. He had heard his father use that word to describe anyone who was not a member of his own self-de-fined tribe and Nick fell upon it now. Zach was obsessed by food, and by food that sounded disgusting to Nick.

'*Gefilte* fish,' Zach explained. 'The head of a carp is stuffed and we eat it cold. And *krupnik*. It's a soup made from oatmeal, pota-toes and fat. And what about *schmaltz*? It's rendered fat that we eat on bread.' Zach was clearly enjoying the effect he was having on Nick.

'Tell me about something that is not going to make me seasick,' Nick begged him.

'I have been dreaming about *Sachertorte*,' he said. '*Oy* ... that was good. Thick black chocolate that you could stand a spoon in. And *mein Gott*, the *rogellach*. They are sweet pastries. Not that my mother made them of course. The cook did.'

Nick looked at him in surprise. 'I ... I thought everyone on this ship was ... a bit strapped,' he said, reddening.

'Ah Nick you are such a *schmuck*. We were rich in Vienna. Big house. Lots of maids. A gardener. My father was a very good doctor and he made lots of money. He treated all the *goyim*.'

'I suppose some people might think we have a nice house too. It's big, anyway, and Martha makes the best walnut cake. But we are not rich. Truth is my father is just useless with money. The farm is a sucked lemon now and one day we will have to sell it. It's one of the reasons I want to go to Australia. There is nothing at home for me.' He waited for Zach to say something but for once he had little to say. 'Why can't you go back to Vienna?'

Zach looked at his feet. 'There's nothing there for me either,' he said. 'Vienna is not my home. I now know that it never was. I told you that my father was taken away to work in the camps after *Kristallnacht*. Some of our friends, all Jews, were sent away too, loaded onto trains. We were told that they were going away to work ...' Zach sniffed sharply and pulled in a long shaky breath.

'*Krist* ... all ... *nacht*?' Nick asked, trying to make the word sound the same way it had done when Zach said it. 'What's that?'

'Last November all our homes were broken into, the shops smashed, and they ... the SS, beat people with sledgehammers. They burnt our synagogues. They dug up the graves in our cemeteries. My father was arrested but he did not know why. Then they put him on a train ... a cattle truck ... with many other Jewish men, to Dachau. You know what that is?'

Nick shook his head.

'It's a work camp, a prison. The next day I watched my mother as the Nazis made her scrub the blood from the street outside our home. Imagine my poor mother on her hands and knees. She did not even know how to dust before that.' Zach was agitated now. 'Our neighbours did nothing, Nick. Nothing. After that my mother got me away on the *Kindertransport*, the train to England, but she could not come. It was for children only, *shnippsy* fellows like me. I did not want to go ... I didn't want to leave her.

She made me go. I went with many other children. She said she would be right behind me but she did not come. She wrote to me and said that she could not come yet because she was afraid that my father would not find us when he came home and then in the next letter she told me that our home had been taken, and all our things stolen from us. I have heard nothing from her in months now. I suppose she has been put on the train to the camp by now too.'

Nick could say nothing. He found the story hard to believe.

'How could I call such a place home?' Zach said. 'Nobody tried to stop the thugs. They let it happen. Imagine what it is like to know that all the people you thought were your friends, your neighbours who you say *A gutn tog* to every morning, all the shop-keepers, everybody and all that time they were thinking that we were just *schmutzig* Jews.' Zach's hands were shaking. He leant his head back against the metal funnel and closed his eyes.

Nick thought he knew what it was like to feel like an out-sider, but nobody had dispossessed the Tottenhams; they had not been thrown out of their home. An ugly thought occurred to him that it had been *his* ancestors who had done the evicting and that some sort of genetic memory of that wrong survived in the likes of Fergus O'Dowd and Dan who sat outside the pub. With their pompous ways and cut-glass voices his family and others like them had made sure that the rift had never healed. No wonder some of the neighbours at home did not think too much of the Tottenhams. Zach had thought that he was as Viennese as the next man. He was happy there, growing up in comfort with friends and neighbours who liked and respected his family.

Now he had lost everything, and had to live with the knowl-edge that his people were not his people after all and that they had stood by, or worse, while his parents were robbed and sent off to camps like criminals. Being considered an oddball by the people of Mullingar was not so tough.

'Would you like to be a doctor like your father?' Nick asked eventually.

'I dreamed of that but no chance now. I must go where my rescuers send me. These Aussies want farmers, don't they?'

'Did you like your father?'

'*Mein Gott*, Nick. What a question. I never asked myself that. We Jews *respektier* ... how do you say, honour our parents. That is all we know how to do. He is – was – a good man. Do you not like your father?'

'It was difficult. That's all.'

'Maybe for him too? Huh?'

His reply irritated Nick. 'Do you know where you'll be placed after Wangaratta?' he asked, his voice tight.

'No, it's not decided yet. I think we have some choice where we go but I suppose the Australian Jewish people will have to agree, as they're paying for us.'

'Does that mean you'll have to go to a ... Jewish home?'

'No, I don't think there are enough of those,' Zach said, laughing.

'Maybe you could come and work on my uncle's place or we could get a job somewhere else together. What do you think?'

'I'd really like that ... mate,' he said, and they both smiled self-consciously because it was the first time either of them had spoken like an Australian.

Four

VICTORIA, AUSTRALIA

A s the train crept into Natimuk junction, Nick leant forward to see where the line divided. They would have to change here to catch a smaller train to Balmoral.

'It'll start to get a bit more remote from here I expect,' he said.

Tony was staring out the window at the parched landscape. 'Is this the main station? For the junction, I mean?' he asked, peering over Nick's shoulder to get a better view. 'God – it's a shack! What the hell is Balmoral going to be like?'

They gathered their suitcases and stepped onto the empty platform. A single clapboard hut stood beside the line, its outline stark against the dry treeless plains behind it, and a hot wind whistled through the cracks in the timber.

'This is a mournful sort of place, isn't it?' Tony's voice was light but he scanned his brother's face anxiously.

'Don't worry, it's just the place where the line divides – it's not like, er, Mullingar.'

The train rattled down the track in the relentless midday sun. The station house at Balmoral had a galvanized rust-red roof and a veranda that faced towards the track. Dry acacia bushes and gum trees with peeling bark sheltered the building from the sun. It reminded Nick of one of the country cricket clubs he and Tony visited on away matches at home, except that here the dirt was red, giving a rosy tinge to everything, like an old sepia photograph. The boys were the only passengers to alight and when the train with its two paint-chipped carriages lumbered away through the dusty trees, Nick felt that they had come to the loneliest place in the world. He cleared his throat. 'Hello. Is there anyone there?' He stepped into the hot building. Black flies buzzed furiously against the slats of the window.

'Howya. You must be the Tottenham boys.' A small man with a stoop emerged from a side office buttoning up his flies and rubbing sleep from his eyes. 'They wired me from Twin Oaks to say you'd be here. They may be a bit late comin' to get ya. There's bin rain up there and the road's a bit crook. This your first trip here?'

'We arrived in Melbourne only yesterday. I'm Tony.' He thrust his hand out.

'Glad to meet ya, Tony,' the man said, and turned to Nick expectantly.

'I'm Nick, how do you do?' Nick knew he sounded stiff and formal. He felt the line around his collar grow hot again.

'You boys are Poms, right?'

'No, no, we're Irish,' Nick replied, more smartly than he meant. He felt the thump of disappointment that the Australian in front of him, like so many at home, assumed him to be English.

'We've come to jackaroo for our uncle,' Tony said, apparently unperturbed. 'The Commander ... do you know him?'

'Lovely fella,' the man said immediately. 'You'll work hard, no doubt. It's a fine big place. He'd have 10,000 sheep and a lot of cattle. Not many places around here can do both. You have to have water you see. Twin Oaks is under the mountains. It gets the runoff and that's why he can farm the two.' The throaty sound of a truck engine grumbled from the distance. 'That'll be them,' the man said. 'They made good time.'

A young man in dusty shorts and heavy work boots, a bush hat pressed firmly down on his head, jumped out of the cabin of the pickup. 'You the lads for Twin Oaks?' he asked unnecessarily, tilting back his hat with his index finger to reveal a wide smile. 'Hop in and throw your gear in the back. It'll be a bit tight in the front but the dust is fierce back there. I'm Tom.' There was a strong smell of rancid mutton from him.

'You boys stayin' long?' he asked as he threw the gear stick forward.

'Yes I think so. It's pretty indefinite,' Nick said at the same time as Tony also answered, 'Just a year, maybe.'

The truck bumped along the dirt road through yellow grass. Thick-bellied gum trees with heavy green canopies smudged the line of the gentle hills in the distance. Closer to them, spring bark trees stood bright against the cornflower sky. Beside the road the trees were twisted and gnarled, their trunks soft and pulpy as if they had been salvaged from the sea. As the truck climbed out of the valley the vegetation changed and trees stretched into steely columns that tossed heads of spidery leaves.

'Can you fatten cattle on that grass?' Nick asked raising his voice over the engine. 'It looks very dry.'

'You'll see a big change as we get close to the property. Green as Ireland there,' Tom replied and he swung the truck to the right on to a narrow road, which ran along the top of a wide ridge.

'There – all that is Twin Oaks,' Tom said after a while, pointing to a sunlit valley to his left. 'She's a beaut', isn't she?'

A pink-bricked farmhouse with plumbago climbing its walls stood in the middle of the valley, through which an inky river snaked its path. A ridge of indigo mountains framed the property. The grass running down to the river had been eaten close by dusty sheep with faces like bad-tempered poodles, kept together by bleached wooden fences. Frothy-headed eucalyptus with papery stems shaded them and a small number of fat black cattle.

'Aberdeen Angus?' Tony asked with surprise.

'They're just a hobby for the Commander,' Tom said in a tone that Nick thought said *well for some*. 'They remind him of home. The steers are away over that ridge. That's where the stock pens are too ... and the bunk house where the rest of us ordinary fellas live.'

'How many chaps work here?' asked Tony, his eyes searching the valley greedily.

'About twenty, give or take, and there's always a few visiting jackaroos – you know, fellas like yourselves from Europe, come to learn the ropes and grow up a bit.'

Nick glanced at Tom, fearing a put-down, but Tom was smiling amiably. Pulling a cigarette packet from the pocket of his shirt, he offered one to Nick.

'Thanks, mate,' Nick said, and then blushed. Maybe he was trying too hard.

A tall, grey-haired man with a handlebar moustache stood on the porch of the house beside a thin woman in a high-necked blouse. As Tom pulled on the handbrake in the wide gravel sweep in front of the house, the man drew a gold watch from the pocket of his waistcoat and glanced at it briefly. The woman fingered the pearls around her neck. Uncle Herbert looked so like his father that for a moment Nick thought crazily that the old man had got there before him and he swung from being irritated to find him there to disappointment that he was not. He climbed out of the truck, followed by Tony, who scampered after him like Buster might have done.

'Welcome, boys – welcome to Twin Oaks. You made good time. You are the first of the family to visit from home. Well, my home anyway,' his uncle said, throwing an apologetic glance at his wife. 'Splendid.' Uncle Herbert pumped the hands of the two boys. 'Come on in chaps. This is your Aunt Virginia.'

The lady turned her dry face to be kissed, and, squinting her eyes against the sun, backed into the shadows of the hall behind her as if the light pained her. 'You'll have some tea after your journey, won't you? Joshua here has it all ready,' she said, waving her hand distractedly at a black man who wore a tailcoat and stood in bare feet in the gloom of the hall.

They followed their aunt into a large room. The floor, rich and polished, matched the panelled walls. Persian rugs softened their footfall and calico blinds and chintz curtains saved the room from the worst of the harsh mid-afternoon sun, which dappled the floor through the trees swaying beyond the windows.

'Tell us about your journey, boys,' Uncle Herbert said with a jovial bellow while Aunt Virginia poured tea from a silver teapot into china teacups. An iced cake sat on a high plate. Nick felt numb with disappointment. How far had he come to be met with tea just as it was at home? Could he make a new start here? He listened to his brother recounting all the fun of his shipboard games while hoovering cake from his plate into his mouth. Life was such a lark for Tony. He envied him.

After tea, Joshua brought them upstairs to show them their room and closed the bedroom door with a soft, deferential click.

'Isn't this great?' Tony said. 'Did you see your man? At first I could only see the whites of his eyes. No shoes and big black feet! Did you see the tailcoat and stiff collar and all?' Tony bounced on to the second bed. 'This is nice, isn't it? I wonder are there any fish in the river?'

Nick lay quietly on the other bed, as his brother's chatter washed over him.

'Let's go and explore.'

'I'd like to find the bunkhouse that fellow Tom told us about. That's the life I came for,' Nick replied, lifting the lace curtain and peering across the ridge.

'Don't you want to stay in the house?'

'No, not really, it's too much like home.'

'Jesus, Nick, this is a palace compared to home! I don't see bits of it falling onto the lawn or patches of damp on the walls.' Tony laughed.

'I just don't want to be the boss's nephew, that's all.'

'There won't be any cake in the bunkhouse, I bet.' Tony linked his arm through his brother's and squeezed it. 'Sure, give it a try and see how you like it.'

Nick leant on the stockade and watched his brother neck rein with one hand and crack a whip with the other. Tony was the horseman in the family. Nick was not surprised to see how quickly he adapted his riding style. He could turn the animal on its haunches at a gallop. A few days later Tony was given a brumby to break. Nick thought he saw a sly look pass between Tom and some of the other cowboys and he worried that Tony might make a fool of himself. But Tony seemed to know that he had to abandon the way he had broken horses at home. No running reins or mouthing bits here.

He watched nervously as Tony threw a saddle on the wild pony's back and Tom legged him up. The mare lunged forward and Tony had to sit out the bucks and the dives as best he could but he made it look effortless as he anticipated the twists and vicious fly kicks from the animal underneath him. Tony pulled up the horse's head and squeezed her body between his legs. Within minutes the creature seemed to know who was master and was trotting politely around the fence with Tom and the others cheering and clapping. Nick despaired that he would ever learn to ride. Although taller than Tony he did not have his extraordinary core strength or his athleticism, and he looked on the battle between his brother and the mare with a curdling mixture of admiration and desolation. He would never be able to do any of this, he thought. When he climbed cautiously aboard an old and sleepy nag he bumped uncomfortably in the heavy saddle, and grabbed the unfamiliar pommel like a drowning man clinging to a log.

'Take it easy to start with,' Tony said as he pulled up the girth under Nick's leg. 'This fella is as quiet as a mule. We should have got you started on Ben before we left home,' he said and slapped the rump of the old horse. 'You'll soon learn to trust him.'

Nick did not believe that day would ever come. These animals are just as unpredictable as the ones at home and less schooled, he thought. But ten days later he realized with surprise that he was getting out of bed and no longer feeling as though he had slept with his legs around a barrel. The ache in his groin and thighs was easing. A few days after that, when he was riding behind the herd of over a hundred beasts, he found that he was not thinking about the horse underneath him at all, so hard was he concentrating on the cattle in front of him.

'Watch the right flank,' the foreman yelled. 'Easy now. Go at their pace. That's it. If you rush them, you'll lose 'em.' Nick saw out of the corner of his eye a cow break loose, crying for her calf in the mayhem of the moving cattle. Nick swung the rein across the horse's neck and the animal wheeled underneath him. He raised his right hand and cracked his whip.

'There you go girl. Back this way,' he said as he nudged her back into the throng. He loved the music of the lumbering beasts, the moans and bellows punctured by the higher notes of the lost calves, bleating for their mothers, and the earthy, tangy smell of them. He grew used to the clouds of dust the animals threw up behind them that stung his eyes and the back of his throat. He wrapped a cloth around his face, pushed his bush hat down hard and felt that he was at last indistinguishable from the other men who had been doing this for years. He sat tight in the saddle when swamp hens spooked his horse, fluttering up from the water lilies, and steered expertly through the blue gum plantations of the Grampian foothills. He spent long days on his horse moving the herds to the high ground where the air was chill and thin, and volunteered for the jobs that would keep him away from the home farm for weeks on end. He lived in the open on his swag, shaved without a mirror, and could kill, gut and cook a sheep for himself and the other hands. On his return from the second of these longer trips, he threw his kit onto an empty bed in the bunkhouse as if he had always lived there.

'Welcome back, Nick. Good trip?' Tom asked him. 'Cold up in the mountains, was it?'

'As a witch's tit,' Nick replied. 'Lost three calves but they were crook when we started out. Two cows with mastitis and a lame bull. Not a bad trip.'

'Hand of poker starting over there, mate. You in?'

'Yeah and a cold beer would be bonzer too.'

Zach wrote to him. He was on a place near Bannockburn. He told Nick that he was missing his Jewish friends on the *Jervis Bay* and the fact that he could not sing the '*Lech Dodi*' with anyone. He said he missed him and Tony too. He liked farming well enough but the other fellows on the farm were a rough lot. He had bought a harmonica and was practising 'Waltzing Matilda' as they liked that better than Austrian ballads.

Nick felt that he had grown up and moved on and that Tony wasn't ready yet to join him in the bunkhouse with its bawdy talk and drinking games. Tony was doing fine in the old house where Aunt Virginia was spoiling him and that would be a new experience for him, God knows. Several afternoons a week Nick saw his brother and his aunt climb into the trap and set off to the cricket club in Coleraine or the tennis club in Balmoral.

On the few occasions when Nick went up to the house Aunt Virginia was full of stories of Tony scoring a century or winning a tennis match and, of course, just like at school, Tony made friends easily. He had slipped into a life of tennis teas and cricket-club hops and escorting his stiff English aunt to her social engagements like a royal equerry. Prompted by his wife's example, towards the end of July Uncle Herbert brought Nick to his club where they drank strong scotch and played bridge, and Nick silently thanked his mother for the hours of card-playing he'd had to endure at home.

'Is there going to be war, Herbert?' a neighbouring farmer asked his uncle.

'Germany doesn't look like she's going to back down,' Uncle Herbert replied, pulling a queen from his hand and laying it on the table. 'Two of her battleships, the *Graf Spee* and the *Deutschland*, are making ready – not a good sign, but it is inconceivable that we could go to war again. My trick, I believe.'

That night, Nick went back to the bunkhouse and Uncle Herbert did not ask him to the club again. He and Aunt Virginia seemed to accept that he was where he wanted to be.

'You want to come to the Sheepvention?' Nick asked Tony. 'It's next Tuesday. Pay day. Hard to believe it's the end of August already.'

They set off at sunrise, a spring chill still clinging to the ground. As they crossed the river a heron heaved itself into the air, its cold eye scanning the black water below. A family of ducks waddled busily in the rushes.

'The birds remind me of the lake at home but they're not the same, are they? Nothing is really the same here,' Tony said. He sounded unusually wistful and Nick thought he heard a catch in his brother's voice. 'I hope the family are going to be all right if this mess in Germany gets going.'

'I very much doubt the *new* Ireland will get involved,' Nick scoffed. 'Anyway, Father is much too old now for any of his old heroics. He's over fifty, for heaven's sake! And we're better off here being the people we can be.'

In Hamilton they stopped the pickup outside Brady's General Store and bought two cups of tea, a couple of rock buns and a newspaper that lay unopened on the table between them. Absently Nick flattened it out, stirring sugar into his mug. *Germans invade and bomb Poland. Britain mobilizes. Military age 18 to 41.*

'Christ, is this really going to happen?'

'At least it counts you and Dad out ... and Uncle Herbert too.'

'Well, you're not eighteen yet either,' Tony pointed out.

'Yeah, not till May but I'm sure it will all die down in a week or two. Do you remember Czechoslovakia last summer? And we're a long way from Poland out here. Come on ... let's go find Zach.' He threw the newspaper into the bin on his way out.

Sheep of assorted size and colour were crammed into long lines of makeshift pens: Scottish black-faced with mean eyes; merinos with tight curls; English Leicesters, their coats skirting the ground, seeming to move on wheels; and Texels with wool matted like the shrunken jumpers the boys had worn as children. The animals set each other off, bleating and jostling in squashed and ill-tempered discomfort. The three boys watched the judging of the hoggets, the first lambs, the seasoned rams and for good measure gave some laddish support to the Beautiful Baby competition. It was clear that Zach had little interest in any of it but it was a welcome distraction as Nick found that his crippling shyness had come back to life. He and Zach seemed to have lost all the spontaneity of their conversations on the *Jervis Bay*. Nick was not a great man for writing and now he found it difficult to talk of anything beyond his beloved cattle. It had been clear from Zach's letters that he did not share Nick's enthusiasm for the farming life. When they were on the *Jervis Bay* Zach had been looking forward to it all but now Nick couldn't picture Zach in a bunkhouse. Tom and the lads would not appreciate the poetry or the singing of Old Testament verses. Nor could he imagine Zach's delicate fingers tying a sheep's feet together or roping a calf. Perhaps he had just forgotten how foreign Zach was. Of course, Nick had changed too. He had moulded himself on the likes of Tom and the others in the bunkhouse and that was bound to make things different between him and Zach. But he was finding it difficult to recognize anything familiar in his friend. For once, Tony's easy banter was doing nothing to help.

'Do you know what? I've seen enough sheep for one day. And enough fat babies too. How about a beer?' Zach suggested.

'Great idea. Aunt Virginia keeps a rather tight rein on the booze,' Tony said. 'You buying?'

'Sure – whoever said Jews are mean?' Zach's eyes danced at last and he broke into a goofy smile.

This was more familiar to Nick. 'You'll be in good company with all the Scots around here.'

They fetched the beers and sat at a table in the sun. 'So tell us about your station, Zach.'

'Oh it's fine. They're very good to me – the family, I mean. But that makes it harder because it reminds me of home and then I remember that I don't have a home any more. The mother makes great cake. But it's not really the life I want. I am not made to be a cowboy. I'm sick of sheep, to tell you the truth.'

'How long do you have to stay there?' Nick asked. Here at last was something of the ease that they had known on the ship. 'Maybe you could come to Twin Oaks? They're always looking for more hands. You'd like the cattle better than sheep.' He was not sure that he believed this: Zach would be happier entertaining Aunt Virginia on the piano in the drawing room.

Zach smiled. 'I just don't think there is any point making new plans. War is coming.'

'Surely it'll all be over in a week or two. Isn't everyone saying that no one, not even the Germans, has the stomach for another big show?' Tony asked.

'I don't think that's right, Tony. These people have been pre-paring for a big fight for a long time. They have many tanks and planes.'

Zach looked at him in that intense way and Nick remembered what he had said about Vienna. 'It will take everything we have to stop them. I have to be a part of that. Maybe I can save some of my family, if any are still alive. Remember, I have seen how bad these Nazis are. We cannot let them win.'

Nick was at a loss for words. He recalled the conversation with Tony in the general store only an hour or two ago. They had been so sure that it would not affect them. Zach's quiet but firm assertion that war was coming was chilling, and so was his certainty that he would go back to Europe and fight the war against Germany. He tried to imagine what it would be like if he were to watch his friend go off to war and he stay behind at Twin Oaks. He looked at Tony, at his bright, enthusiastic face, and dismissed any idea that he would have to stay in Australia to look after him. Tony would be fine, and a new war couldn't last very long. If he went to fight he would no longer have to worry about whether he would go home or stay at Twin Oaks. And what would his father think of him then? If he came home with a row of medals on his chest, that would show him, wouldn't it?

'Well, Nick, will you come with me?'

As Zach's words crashed through Nick's mind the thought that he might wave a flag at a departing troop ship, one with Zach on board, tipped him. He felt a hot twist of excitement and smiled broadly. He would go.

'Of course I'll come with you, Zach. You will need someone to keep you under control,' Nick said firmly. He and Zach lifted their glasses.

'*Viel Gluck*,' Zach said.

'I'll be right behind you,' Tony added.

Five

Nick and Zach met up in the small town of Vasey. There were about twenty other men and boys waiting in the street outside for the doors of the recruiting office to open. One by one they stepped inside and swore an oath of allegiance to His Britannic Majesty George VI. Zach was clutching his brand-new Australian passport, which he handed to the man behind the desk.

'Glad to see you're an Aussie now,' the man said, winking at him and fingering the pristine document. Nick was jealous. He had thought that he might tell the recruiting officer that he was Irish because suddenly it seemed important that the records would show that, but his passport was British. He also wasn't sure that being Irish was the right thing for this business. He put down his father's name as his next of kin and had to spell Mullingar for the officer. He gave Uncle Herbert's name as well. Zach asked Nick if he could do the same.

'Course you can,' Nick said, surprised at how good this made him feel and realizing with a thud that the poor fellow had no one else.

'We'll be in Europe in a few weeks,' Zach said, his eyes shining.

'Yeah we'll drive those bloody Krauts back where they belong. Didn't we do it before? We'll do it again. And this time we won't be floundering around in the muck as my father did. We'll be in France by midsummer I'd say.' Nick felt an emotion he didn't recognize, standing beside these people who had come from all around Puckapunyal to fight.

'They won't be a pushover you know. This man Hitler has possessed them. He is like the devil. You British have no idea of what it is like in his gutter.'

'I'm not ...'

'I know, I know. You're not British but you're the only person who notices.'

Anger now infused Nick's excitement. And you sound like, and were, until a few days ago, a German, he thought. He turned and walked off. Zach could be insufferable at times. Most of the other new recruits milling outside the office looked as though they were from farming backgrounds, with hard, sinewed limbs, suntanned faces and deep wrinkles around their eyes from a life in the outdoors. As he looked at them closer he realized that he and Zach were probably younger than most and he felt self-conscious about his boy's body, his narrow shoulders, skinny legs and the fluff on his upper lip. Zach's small frame and pianist's fingers were especially out of place here amongst these farming folk. But Zach seemed to share none of Nick's awkwardness and was sitting smoking and listening intently to a huge man who was talking about the five children he had left back home in Coleraine.

Like Nick, each of the new soldiers outside the office was quietly sizing up the men and boys with whom they would be spending the next months on the biggest adventure of their lives. Many of them were staring at Zach, clearly finding it difficult to imagine how the slight foreign boy in front of them would cope with the job they had just signed up for. Zach turned to address an older man, pushing forty perhaps, and he sparkled with animated confidence.

'What age are you, son?' the man asked.

'Eighteen,' Zach answered.

'Christ, you're only a baby.'

Zach was unperturbed. 'What age are you?'

'Forty. I teach history to kids your age,' the man replied.

'We'll call you Prof then, shall we?'

A man emerged from the door of the recruitment office. He had thick brown forearms, his khaki sleeves rolled neatly to his elbows. His shorts had a sharp crease and the noon sun reflected off his polished boots.

'Right then, you fellas. You're with me and the 2/2 Pioneer Battalion and it's my job to turn you lot into soldiers.' His accent was Irish. He scanned each of them from head to toe and back up again. 'Most of you won't make it. I've never seen such a shower of gombeens.'

The men around him clearly had no idea what this meant, but Nick smiled.

'My name is Maloney. Sergeant Maloney to you. Though, in time, if we make a soldier of you, you might get to call me sarge.' Everyone laughed nervously but the sergeant remained deadpan.

'Who are you?' he asked a plump, red-headed boy standing beside Nick. He had an early beer gut and soft white hands and hovered from one thick leg to the other.

'B ... b ... illy Mac ... Macdonald,' the boy stammered. He blushed scarlet under his ginger hair.

'Where from?'

'Coleraine, sir.'

'And what do you do in civvy street?'

'I'm a clerk, sir.'

'First rule here is, I am not sir. I am sergeant. Got it?'

Billy nodded, his face crimson.

'You?' the sergeant said, jerking his head at Nick.

'Tottenham, sergeant. Nick Tottenham, Vasey, jackaroo.'

'Now what do you take me for Tottenham? I know the gentle tones of Westmeath when I hear them, which just ... *just,* mind you, softens your West Brit accent?'

'Yes sir ... I mean sergeant.'

'Right,' he barked, 'we have a posh Protestant from me neighbouring county here. He'll have to learn the same as the rest of you.' The sergeant locked his eyes on Nick. Here we go again, he thought. When he could look up he saw Zach was watching him, laughing noiselessly. Nick allowed the muscles in his jaw to loosen.

'Next?'

'Jim Lightholder, sergeant,' said the boy beside Billy. He was tall and gangly. His head poked forward and the lump in his gullet made a jutting knot at the front of his neck. He stood with his back curled over his belly the way a man does when he has been too tall all his life.

'You're well named, Shorty,' the sergeant said and chuckled, apparently well pleased with his wit. 'Right. Uniforms over there. On the truck in thirty minutes.'

'Hello Billy,' Nick said, thrusting his hand forward. 'Your man seems a right bully, doesn't he? I think it's the uniform. Makes all of them think they can act like they're a curse sent from God. This is Zach. We came here together – in fact, we came to Oz together last year.'

'Hello. And this is Piper. He's my friend from Pucka. He's a butcher. He's going out with my sister, see, so we're more like brothers.' Nick thought they looked like brothers too. The two boys were the same height and shape, short stocky lads with square chins and flat foreheads, but Piper was dark and his chest hair fought to escape over the top button of his open-necked shirt whereas Billy's skin was like a woman's and his hair was almost luminous orange.

'What do you do, Zach?' Billy asked.

'I'm a philosopher.'

They all laughed politely and Nick rolled his eyes to heaven.

The training wasn't strenuous despite what the sergeant had said. At times it was hard to believe that any of the drills would prepare them for real fighting: endless kit inspections and roaring NCOs complaining about skewed bush hats and loose puttees. Compared with the sergeant majors on the parade ground, Maloney was a pussycat. They marched backwards and forwards. Eyes right. Left, right. Left, right. Occasionally they practised handling rifles but were rarely issued with any ammunition.

'How do we know if we can hit anything?' Nick complained. 'All this fixing of bayonets went out with the ark.'

'Sure we'll only be diggin' ditches to support the engineers. We won't have to hit anything or anyone,' said an extraordinarily thin man from Pucka called Tubby.

'You are not in the front line and never will be,' Prof said. 'So you can forget trying to be heroes, lads. You want to be thankful for that.'

Zach's face darkened. 'What would he know?' he muttered.

The Australian winter came and went with interminable parades. Square bashing, they called it. All of them thought that it was a waste of time, a way that the army filled in time while they waited to be sent to a war that seemed to have stopped. No orders came for them. Summer passed in the same way. Nick was profoundly bored again but it was not the same as it had been back at home. Here he was with people he liked, whom he dared to think might now be his friends. They were as frustrated with the rules and the waiting as he was. He didn't have to face down his father every morning although he had to deal with Maloney instead, who continued to make snarky remarks about him being a West Brit. It rankled but being picked on lifted his standing amongst his friends.

Zach found it more difficult to ignore the taunts and jeers of the NCOs and when one of them called him 'Pretty Boy', Nick was afraid that Zach might hit him.

'They do it to test you,' Prof said, putting out his hand to restrain Zach. 'If you snap they'll throw you out. It's all part of the fucked-up psychology that the army uses.'

It wasn't just the NCOs and their endless pointless military drills that got under Zach's skin. None of them had joined up to spend months learning how to march in time and they were all disappointed that their enthusiasm for fighting Germans had been misplaced. Zach was growing more and more sullen with every morning that brought no news of a posting. Nick reluctantly understood that his own surly behaviour the summer before he left home must have looked like this and, just as Nick had been then, Zach was poor company. It wasn't only authority that Zach resented. He wasn't able to go along with the everyday teasing and ragging from his fellow recruits that was the lot of every new soldier. He simply didn't see the humour in it and was obsessed with getting back to Germany to rid his people of the Nazis. He was becoming unpopular and Nick caught his new mates looking sideways at Zach, eyeing him narrowly. They too had joined up to fight Germans and Zach's accent, and his Yiddish asides, confused them. Far from the others getting used to him they were finding it increasingly difficult to square this angry, odd boy and his graceful good looks with the tougher men they were becoming. Worse, he had overheard some of the older men muttering darkly about Zach being a liability, a fellow who might not follow orders, a Jonah. Nick understood that the war was a personal crusade for Zach because of the awful things that had happened to him, but his friend's frustration and strange habits were going to land him in trouble and he embarrassed Nick.

'This bloody war will be over and we'll still be pissing about here with toy rifles,' Zach grumbled.

'The trouble is there's nowhere to send us,' Nick said. 'After all that mess in June at Dunkirk when the boys were driven out of France, everyone is waiting for a new push. It's the same for the chaps in England.'

'And in the meantime those Nazi bastards strengthen their positions and my friends and family die.'

'We all want to get going,' Piper said after another petulant outburst from Zach. 'Sure, my poor Dad is minding the shop in Pucka and I was supposed to have taken it on by now. He's too old for the killing and stripping the hides, you see. I come from a long line of butchers.' He lifted his chin. 'Me granddad started the business.'

'You save your butchery for the fucking Germans,' Shorty said, 'you can make sausages out of them,' and they all nodded. Shorty's frame had filled out in the ten months they had been there and his back had straightened. All that standing to attention had made him four inches taller, he said. Muscle now bulked out the awkward hollows of his young body and Shorty, although still a man of few words, had earned their respect.

Billy had lost his paunch and his hands had grown strong and brown. He had no natural flair for soldiering but he followed orders to the letter and Nick was sure that he would be like a pit bull in a tight spot. He and Piper were inseparable. Piper did not seem to tire of his friend's childish chatter and if he ever found it irritating he showed no sign of it. Nick wanted Shorty, Billy and Piper to like him and so he instinctively put distance between himself and Zach and then struggled with the disappointment in himself that he could not be more loyal like Piper was to Billy. He tried to focus instead on what it would be like to come home from the war as a fellow who had done his bit, and a man who might share his experiences with his father.

In the middle of March 1941, a jubilant officer, a black-haired captain with a pencil moustache called Smyllie (and naturally known as Smelly), announced that they were to report for embarkation on the HMS *Queen Mary* the following week. Cheers erupted, hats were thrown in the air and fellows punched each other on the arm. The long wait was over. The battalion was being shipped to Syria, they were told, where the Vichy French were holding the territory to ensure oil supplies from Iraq for the Germans.

'Syria?' Nick said. 'Where the fuck is that? Who are the Vichy French? I thought we were trying to liberate France?'

'The Vichy are Frenchmen who have sided with the Germans,' Prof said.

'Useless soldiers, the French. Piece of cake,' Tubby followed, slapping Nick on the back.

'Hardly the main game, is it?' Zach said. 'I wonder if we will we even see a Nazi.'

Tony came to see them off and they met for tea in a café near Flinders station. Nick thought that his younger brother had not changed at all in the year he had been in Australia.

'Jaysus, look at the two of you. Proper soldiers. I wish I was going with you,' Tony said. Despite his bright smile, his voice had little of its usual brightness. 'I'm just wasting time here. I can't go home because there's no way of getting there. I want to be a pilot but they won't take me until I'm eighteen, even for training, and that's another six months. The war could be over by then. I wish there was some way I could get started.' He sounded just like Zach.

For the first time, Nick thought that perhaps the Prof had been right and that they should all be careful what they wished for. He and his mates had pushed the disaster of Dunkirk last June out of their minds. They had not talked of it because no such thing was going to happen to them. Now that they were finally heading off to some part of the war, even though it was an insignificant one, it was time to think about what that might mean for them. They had been naive to think that they could join up and go straight in and Nick was glad that they had some training, even if it was mostly on digging trenches and making roads. The boys at Dunkirk had none. Tony was thinking the very same way as he had done a year ago. He thought that he would be able to jump in an airplane and start shooting Germans out of the sky in a matter of days.

'Look, it's going to take time to prepare for a landing in Europe. We're in this for the long haul. I think this war is going to be as long as the last one,' he said. 'And Tony, you'll need basic maths if you want to fly – you left home with no exams done.'

'Good point – maybe I could put the time in doing that,' Tony said, his face brightening. 'Oh I nearly forgot, I had a letter from Mummy yesterday. Poppa has fiddled the system again and has a commission in the Royal Norfolks.'

'What the hell? He's far too old! What does he think he's doing, the bloody fool? And why the Norfolks, for Chrissakes?' Nick registered Tony's reaction to his torrent of words and struggled to control himself. Perhaps this was just his default reaction to any news of his father, or maybe it was something else. 'He's over the military age. Well over.'

'He just changed his birth cert. You know what he's like. Never one to let the rules get in the way. I think it's rather splendid of him, really.'

'And what about the farm? And Mother? How is she going to manage?'

Tony's face showed his surprise. 'That's not like you, I mean, you've never ...' Tony swallowed hard. 'They've offered her a commission as well, in the WAAF. All those sums had to come in useful sometime. In fact, Mummy was the one they really wanted. She's to be based in England – in Lincolnshire, I think she said. It's becoming one enormous airfield with all the bombing raids. Exciting, isn't it? I can't wait to get back home.'

'I suppose you're going to tell me that Rose is in uniform too?' Nick said.

'Yes, actually she is ... with Mummy in the WAAF.'

His parents and Rose would now be in the real war while he was being sent off to a sideshow in Syria. The thought would not leave him that he should have tried to get home and, as the time loomed for him and Zach to heft their kitbags on their backs and get to the docks, he remained in a fug of anger and resentment. He knew that he was sulking but he could not pull himself out of it and, as the unhappiness caused by the pending goodbye etched deeper onto Tony's face, Nick ignored it.

'I'll see you soon,' Nick said stiffly as they left the café. He managed to give his brother a small squeeze around his shoulders and threw his hand in the air behind him as his goodbye wave, but he did not look back.

Tony stood in the street as it milled with uniformed men and stared at the backs of his brother and his odd friend. Both were adjusting to the weight of their kitbags. The flaps of their trench coats danced rhythmically at their calves and their heads had a curiously lopsided look with one side of their bush hats pinned up. Just like his mother's funeral hat, he thought. And then the crowds of other Diggers heading towards the ship swallowed them up. He did not think he had ever felt so alone. He should not have mentioned Mummy's letter. The news about Poppa was bound to agitate Nick and put him in bad form. Why didn't he just button his big mouth for once, and engage his brain, before opening it? Now the goodbye had gone badly and he would have nothing to hold onto in the months of waiting ahead of him. What were the Diggers heading into?

He reminded himself that they would be in a support role and therefore in no real danger. And besides, they would probably be home in a few months as Syria was just a mopping-up job. If they were sent on to Europe for the big push, on the other hand, he might catch up with them there. He would join up the first day they would let him. He would stay up in Melbourne tonight and go and see what the RAAF needed him to do to get in the air as quickly as possible. The new plan and the thought that he could be following Nick in six months eased some of his misery. He would have something to focus on in the months ahead, arithmetic probably, he thought. How he wished he had his mother's help now!

The dark flower of his loneliness bloomed again as he thought back to the times when she had painstakingly tried to teach him the theory of *Pi*. He missed home. That was the long and the short of it. Aunt Virginia was good to him, God knows, but she was not Mummy, and Uncle Herbert for all his physical resemblance to Poppa was not his father. The birds on the river were likewise only cousins to the ones on the lake. Nothing in the stables matched Firefly.

He had been away for two years and he ached with missing Kate and Maggie and George and with wanting to be a big brother again. He wanted to be in the morning room with them all, with Maggie and Kate sitting on the floor behind his father's chair with their scrapbooks and pressed flowers. He wanted to be getting cross again with George for getting his fingers sticky.

Six

EGYPT

Here was the port of Suez again, which had seemed so exotic to Nick and Zach when they had sailed into it on the *Jervis Bay* two years ago: a year as a jackaroo and a year playing soldiers, Nick thought. Not exactly what I had planned. The boys sat smoking on the deck of the *Queen Mary*. The engines of the old ship began to slow to a low grumble, while her sister ship, the *Queen Elizabeth*, which had sailed alongside her from Freemantle, growled back. As they made ready to go alongside, sailors shouted instructions to men on the wharf, and huge chains with links the size of a man's thigh clunked out from where they had been stowed. The ship groaned to a stop and the men began to button their uniforms, pull up their socks and collect their kit bags.

'Who's got my pixie blanket?'

'Hey, my boot's got a bloody hole in it already!'

The ship throbbed with a new energy. Nick assumed that the men on the deck were as nervous as he was and that this banter was a false heartiness designed to mask it. Zach was the only one who seemed calm, whistling quietly to himself as he gathered up his belongings.

He stuck close to Zach as the ship bumped off the wharf. The men stood in the white heat of the midday Egyptian sun until the gangway was lowered and the ship's company could disembark. Camels and donkeys carried goods to the smaller boats tied up at the *Queen Mary's* bow and stern. Coolies wearing white *jelabias* over baggy pyjama trousers and moving like forest ants carried fresh fruit, sacks of flour and rice, fodder for horses, barrels of cooking oil, and sides of beef and mutton into the holds. Huge cranes heaved machinery onto the deck of the *SS Ethiopia*, the ship that would take the Pioneers north to the border with Palestine. As they shuffled up the gangplank of their new ship an armoured car hung over the deck above them, swinging precariously from the scaffolding.

'The old *Queen Mary* looks a bit palatial compared to this bucket, doesn't she? Just as well it's only seven hours up the canal to the next camp.' Nick wasn't at all sure that he was looking forward to that. The sight of military equipment and supplies being loaded onto the rusty ship unsettled him.

'Seven hours closer to where my people came from,' Zach said quietly.

As the old steamer chugged its way up the canal, an eerie silence descended over the ship. On either side, the desert stretched as far as they could see. They passed a sunken ship jutting out of the still canal waters like a broken tooth. The paint was still fresh, not yet rusted, a recent casualty.

'This is the real thing now,' Nick said and swallowed hard.

El Katani, where they would camp for a couple of days, consisted of an untidy line of ramshackle huts either side of a pitted desert road. Carts and wagons, most of them broken, were dumped along it like discarded toys. A train of ten heavily laden camels loped towards the minaret of a small mosque, which jutted into the cloudless sky at the far end of the town. Arab men, their heads bound in swathes of cotton, led donkeys pulling carts of watermelons and cauliflowers, and dirty children played in the dust. None of the locals paid any attention to the hundreds of men in filthy shorts with jangling dog tags around their necks and bush hats or tin helmets shading their hot faces.

'So this is where your people come from?' Nick said to Zach, giving him a nudge in the ribs and scrunching up his nose at the smell of drains.

'I hear there are places in Ireland that are not much better,' Zach said, pushing him back. 'And we're not across the border yet – we're still in Egypt.'

The military camp where they would rest up was the far side of a single railway line from the town. Canvas tents flapped in the desert wind and soldiers sat smoking and playing cards. Trucks and armoured cars were parked in tidy ranks, many with their bonnets open, and mechanics tinkered under the hoods and lay under the engines, their legs sticking out into the sand. As Nick and Zach and their company crossed the track to find their quarters, a black engine blowing thick smoke chugged out of the shimmering sands. As the train hissed to a stop, the doors of the cattle wagons behind it clattered open and disgorged more khaki men in varying states of undress.

'They're on leave from Syria,' someone said. 'That's the train that'll take you lot north to Gaza tomorrow.'

Zach grabbed Nick's arm and gripped it hard.

'What's wrong, mate?' Nick asked him, but his friend seemed unable to speak and his chest was heaving. Eventually Zach's breathing slowed.

'They put my father into a wagon just like those, pushed him in like an animal. There were people screaming. In a dark box like that. I have always bad dreams about this. I cannot go in, Nick. I cannot.'

'This is different,' Nick said helplessly. Zach had been distraught when he had first told him on the *Jervis Bay* about the night his father had been taken away but nothing like this. Now he had a wild look that Nick thought was like poor Firefly's when Tony first rescued her. Perhaps the prospect of what was ahead of them was affecting him? It was like lighter fuel thrown on his own fears and he struggled to find any words of comfort.

'I don't want to go in those wagons,' Zach mumbled. He was trembling.

'Remember we're going to Palestine, where you've always wanted to go. And we get a few days' leave before we start training again. We can go to Jerusalem like we said, okay?' He searched the pitiless skyline for something that would make Zach feel better. 'I'll be with you in the wagons, Zach. We can leave the doors open,' he said in a tone he imagined was like the one his mother had used with him when he had nightmares.

Zach shook his head and took a deep breath. 'Thank you Nicky, that might help.'

They spent a month at Hill 69, which lay in the middle of a vast barren plain with not a hill in sight. The men dug holes, laid pipes and mended craters in a treeless moonscape. It was hot and dusty. They worked without their shirts and their chests and faces became black with sweat and grime. Rifles were thrown carelessly in the corner of the truck every day. They were prison rock breakers, not soldiers, and Zach grew sour again. 'All this bloody making of roads ... why can't we just go into Syria and shove the fucking Vichy into the sea? We're supposed to be soldiers.'

A week or two later, the monotony of camp life and smashing rocks was broken by a posse of horsemen galloping into camp out of the desert in a flurry of dust. They rode fine horses with wide nostrils and heaving flanks, wet with sweat. Rifles were slung across their backs and Arab headdresses flowed behind them.

'Who the bloody hell are they?' Shorty asked. 'They look like they've come out of the circus.' To Nick they might have galloped out of the painting of the Battle of Waterloo that hung over the fireplace in the hall at home.

'Free French,' explained Sergeant Maloney. 'Very dashing, aren't they?'

'They sure as hell won't be heaving pickaxes or shovels like us,' Zach murmured, apparently entranced by the spectacle. '*Shön*,' he added with a deep sigh. Zach was right. The horsemen looked very different to the tired and dirty fellows they had become. All of them hoped that there would yet be some glamour in going to war after the endless boring training but the reality was proving to be very different. Nick felt a prick of resentment: he couldn't see what men like that could contribute to a modern war. They belonged in the painting. The five friends and the sergeant stood staring at the horsemen as they dismounted and threw the reins to some grovelling Egyptians before striding into the officers' mess tent. 'I wonder how they feel about taking on their own when we move north? My old man didn't think much of it in Dublin in '16 that's for sure,' the sergeant said.

Nick knew about what had happened in the rebellion. His father had been apoplectic about the rebels taking advantage of the British having their backs to the wall. But even he had said that he was glad he did not have to give the order to the troops to fire on them. The sergeant's father and thousands like him had come home from fighting the Turks to a war against fellow Irishmen, men who were their friends and neighbours before they had left for the Dardanelles or Flanders. And when they returned for good, when the war was over a few years later, the Ireland they had known was changed utterly. The returning men were not heroes but despised by those who had not gone. His father never spoke about the war he had survived. And Nick and the sergeant, like their fathers before them, would probably also be shunned if they ever got back to the runt of a country that they had called their home.

'Hey Tottenham, I'm sure you had thoroughbreds like that where you come from. Big house and all that,' the sergeant said. Nick felt his stomach lurch. Here was another jibe. But the sergeant's face was benign and there was no remnant of the contempt that Nick had seen there when they first met at the recruiting office in Vasey all those months ago.

'No sarge, not at all,' Nick stammered. 'My family was always soldiering so there was nothing like that. The farm was squeezed dry already by the time my father came home from Flanders.'

Sergeant Maloney glanced sharply at Nick. 'My lot were soldiers too, the Dublin Fusiliers ... my father and my uncles, in Gallipoli they were ... and before that my granddad was in the Leinster Regiment. He was in South Africa. And then my dad worked on a big place for some gentry in Carlow when he got home ... like your lot, I expect. They were often the only people to give the old soldiers a job. Strange, isn't it, that you and me end up as good mates in the Diggers?' The sergeant winked.

His words seeped through Nick like sweet tea. Perhaps the sergeant was able to look beyond the big house and the resentment most Irishmen felt about that. Nick hoped that his family history didn't matter to these rock-breaking men. The sergeant and he had had very different childhoods and the Carlow man had gone to Australia because he had no alternative, the few miserable acres on which he had been born not able to support him and his eight brothers and sisters. There had been no shortage of acres in Nick's case. His family had simply squandered them. But they both came from a long line of soldiers and the two of them had volunteered immediately when war broke out. Neither had questioned their duty to do so but acted instinctively as their fathers and grandfathers had done. Very few back at home would understand why.

'My uncle was lost on the *Invincible* in '16,' Nick said.

'Yeah, I know, son – it's been a bad century so far,' the sergeant said quietly and turned to wander back to the mess.

'There'll be a right Irish mafia now,' Shorty said. Zach was still gazing at the dark hole of the opening of the mess tent entrance, waiting for the French horsemen to reappear.

'Come on Zach,' Nick said, 'I've organized a truck so we can go to Jerusalem. I've heard there's a great place to get Jewish food near the ... what do you call it ... the Wailing Wall. Falafel and stuff I've never heard of. You can tell us what's what.'

'I want a pint of bitter,' Billy said.

'Steak and chips,' Piper said, 'none of your foreign muck.'

There were hundreds of soldiers on leave in Jerusalem, bargaining in the shops on King David Street for toy camels and silk scarves to send home to their children and their girlfriends, but Zach was the only one here at the Wall where his ancestors had worshipped. As Nick watched Zach get in line to take his place at the Wall, fervently clutching his black book, he wondered again how they had become friends at all. The other pilgrims wore long black coats, knee breeches and wide-brimmed hats, and had ringlets framing their faces. Zach, on the other hand, in his shorts and his socks pulled up, looked like a child going to Sunday school. His head was nodding towards the wall and his lips moved in prayer, engrossed in the book he held open in front of him. When Zach pulled out a note from his breast pocket and tucked it into a crack between the ancient blocks Nick felt a surge of affection for his friend as he sent his special prayer heavenwards.

Nick left his friend alone at the Wall. He told himself that he didn't want to intrude on Zach and his prayers, but the truth was that he found the sallow people who were lining up to sway and chant alien and disturbing. He couldn't understand what this remnant of an ancient temple could possibly mean to them. His own childhood devotions in the sparse church at the end of the drive at home were very different, a knot of people in tatty tweeds tunelessly bellowing the only four hymns that old Ethel Duffy knew how to play. No one said a prayer out loud. The hour of Sunday morning worship was something to be endured, no enthusiasm tolerated, and devotion a black mark. It was a tribal ritual, which marked their difference from their neighbours, and God did not mean much to them.

While Nick waited for Zach he sipped the thick sweet coffee that he had come to like. He had been back several times to this café in the last few days. Sayid, its elderly owner, now hailed him as a friend and kept some honey-drenched cakes behind the counter for him. Nick congratulated himself that he was now the sort of chap who could make friends and eat strange food in a foreign city. He wondered what his father would make of him now.

'Howya, Sayid,' Zach called to the old man as he threw his hat on the table. 'Please can I have some of your *baba ganoush*?' He rolled the glorious word around his tongue.

'Hey, you're in good form,' Nick said, delighted at the lift in Zach's spirits.

'To be a Jew and say my prayers in this place – I am blessed,' he said simply. 'You my friend have no hope of reaching *das Himmelstor*, how you say – the pearly gates. And we may be there sooner than we think.' He grinned. Nick said nothing. He was mildly shocked that his friend had said such a thing when they had no idea what was ahead of them.

'What did you ask for ... in the note I mean?'

'You know Nick, I think God will forgive me,' he said quietly.

Seven

Zach was still in good spirits as the Company, almost a hundred men, marched away from Hill 69 and towards the frontier fence with Syria. After two hours they stopped in the lee of a small hill for a smoke.

'Right men,' the captain, Smelly, said. The man had seemed foppish to Nick and his friends back in training, a fool with pre-war Sandhurst notions about himself and his elevated rank. But they had been with him a long time now and even Zach reluctantly agreed that, like all of them, the captain had changed. He had removed his silly moustache, abandoned the swagger stick, trained hard with his men and all of them now had a grudging respect for him.

'The fence is a mile away at Al Malakiya,' Smelly said, consulting his map. It meant nothing to the soldiers, as they had no idea where they were anyway. 'It's barbed wire and iron picket,' the officer continued, 'and it's our job to breach it and then build a road across the fields.'

This is a routine back-up Digger operation, Nick thought, and Smelly has managed to imply that the success of the Syrian campaign depends on it. But some of the captain's enthusiasm rubbed off on Nick because he was disappointed when the breaching of the fence turned out to be an anticlimax: they had simply cut the wire and moved inside Syrian territory where the work they then did was no different to that they had been doing the other side at Hill 69, making roads and laying pipes. The terrain also looked exactly the same as it did the other side of the border and there was no sign of an enemy Frenchman anywhere.

A few days later, on 15 June, the captain again drew the men around him and excitedly announced that new orders had been received. Their company was to join up with the others in the battalion who had been scattered over the region and engaged in similar engineering projects.

'We are to meet up with them at the Litani river and hold it against an advance by the Vichy French. They have taken Fort Merdjayoun.'

'Seems these Frenchies are better than we thought.' Zach was delighted with the idea of seeing action and shouldered his rifle across his narrow shoulders as if he had been killing Frenchmen since he joined up instead of breaking rocks.

They could smell the river before they saw the bright green gash in the rubble of the rocky outcrop through which it ran. A large waterwheel turned on the far bank, dwarfing the houses underneath it, slurping black water into pipes made from the trunks of thin young palm trees. Like their brothers in El Katani, the local men, their tunics tucked up like baggy shorts, ignored the massing soldiers on the bank opposite them. They led donkeys to drink and washed buffalo in the shallows.

As the railway line had done in their first camp, the river divided that old world from the place where, like a disturbed ants' nest, soldiers were rushing around erecting tents. The dull thud of heavy mallets driving posts echoed against the rocks of the ravine. Mules bellowed. The men from Victoria, who had not met since El Katani, hollered greetings to each other and engines revved as trucks became stuck in the sand. The noisy business of setting up camp helped divert Nick's thoughts from the possibility of a French attack.

For two nights they waited for an attack from across the Litani river. Nick slept little and when he did doze off he was visited by confused and terrifying dreams. In the early hours of the third morning, they were rallied and Sergeant Maloney organized them into lines as the sky brightened. When the sun appeared like a broken egg yolk over the hills, they were ordered to cross the river. No one explained why the position had changed and that the job was no longer to hold the Litani river but to march beyond it and retake the fort. There were no bugles or bagpipes, nor any surge of excitement, and this time Nick did not even feel a buzz of adrenaline. He simply felt sick. Hundreds of men, holding their rifles above their heads, followed each other silently into the water and waded towards the creaking water wheel. Nick looked to his left and there was Zach, smiling serenely and pushing the water away from his thighs with big exaggerated strides. The river boiled with soldiers. They regrouped on the far bank amongst the donkeys and the buffalo, the sergeants shepherding each wet platoon to its place in the line.

'We're actually going to do something today. Can you believe it?' Zach said, his eyes shining. 'We're going to retake the fort.' Nick's stomach heaved. They marched for an hour. Zach stepped out smartly beside him, enthusiastically looking to his left and right for the enemy he was so anxious to find. Absurdly Nick thought of Tony looking for frogs in the reeds beside the lake.

By the time they arrived at the foot of Merdjayoun hill, the Australian guns were already in place, pointing up at the old fort, black and jagged against the brightening sky.

'Glad to see those boys are here,' Nick said to Zach with a nervous laugh, nodding his head towards the guns. His throat tightened. How many might die here in this game to win an ancient pile of stones left behind by the crusaders?

'Right lads, you lot with me to the left of the road,' the captain said. Nick kept his eyes on the fort, now less than 200 yards above him as they circled it, creeping slowly over the crumbling rocks. They dodged behind a wall topped with thorn bushes, using it to give cover until they reached higher ground, almost level with the fort itself. Nick looked down towards the valley from where they had climbed and saw the artillery and their friends from 'B' Company together with the Free French on their horses. How had his company ended up as the advance party with the job of taking the fort? They were Diggers – the mop-up chaps – weren't they? There was a barbed wire fence between them and the fort in which Nick could occasionally see men move like spectres across the windowless black spaces. So this is the enemy, he thought. A pulse throbbed in his forehead. The guns below them would provide cover for the attack, he told himself, looking anxiously over the open ground between him and the old building.

'If we can't bag a Kraut, a Vichy frog will have to do eh?' Zach turned to concentrate on the fence before him. Billy and Piper were to his right, fervently talking to each other. Shorty was on his other flank, checking his rifle. 'Good luck, mate,' he said.

'You too,' Nick mumbled. He turned to Zach. 'You be careful.'

A man was on his belly in front of them cutting the wire. The captain raised his revolver above his head and, with an almost nonchalant wave, ordered them forward. Nick stood up and there was an explosion of sound. He had never heard automatic gunfire before and the cracks from the French guns were deafening. He winced as each round went off, expecting that he would fall. Bullets pinged off the wall behind them. They inched forward. Tubby fell in front of him and a crimson flower grew through the khaki of his shirt. One foot, then the other, Nick said to himself. Just do it. He thought that every minute was to be his last and each of them seemed endless so that time had no meaning. He had no idea how far he had gone or how long he had been under fire. A boom then burst the world and sucked the air from all around them. A blast of hot air stunned him and he hit the ground. He could hear nothing. He was winded and the breath seemed to stick in his gullet. The scene in front of him was dreamlike and in slow motion. As if an unseen hand propelled him, he got up again and took another step forward.

But he knew something was wrong. It was too quiet. He shook his head to try and rid his ears of the ringing silence. A large black shape emerged from the back of the fort, its growls now the only sound, its tracks clambering over the brittle rocks and crushing them like shortbread. Tanks. They were walking into tanks. No one said there would be tanks, he said out loud, but no one could hear him. He knew that the Australians had no artillery heavy enough to deal with them. He looked to his left where Shorty was curled in the foetal position and then to his right where Billy and Piper were prone against the yellow rock with their arms around each other. The dirt started to explode all around them and Nick fell again to the ground. He lay, trying to make himself as small as he could. A shadow fell across him blocking the sun and he felt the coolness of it. Zach was standing beside him, a rigid set to his chin.

'Get down you fool!' Nick pulled Zach's arm roughly and his friend's face loomed towards his own as he fell on top of him. 'We're trapped – the French have fucking tanks. We have to get back.'

'We have to take the fort.' Zach spoke as if there was nothing whatsoever going on around him. 'I will go on.' This was what they had feared back in training. Panic gripped Nick. In the corner of his eye he saw the captain, dragging a bloody leg and waving his revolver uselessly above his head back towards the broken wall.

'Look, Zach, we have orders to retreat. Orders,' he hissed, twisting Zach's collar in his fist. He felt Zach's body slacken, his moment of madness over. Nick pulled himself forward on his elbows and beckoned Zach to follow. Mercifully he seemed inclined to do so and they slithered on their bellies back through the hole in the fence.

Hours later, as the vicious sun began to lose its sting and the day melted into an amber evening, Nick sat with his back against a wall. Goats wandered down the hill, the bells around their necks innocently breaking the deadly silence of the desert. He counted thirty-two men under the olive trees just ahead. He had seen people falling around him, and recalled with horror the big man with the five children from Coleraine searching the ground for his missing arm. Over a hundred of them had made the attack. Where were the others? He sat still, his head hanging between his knees. His legs ached. He had been running, it seemed, but he could not remember how he had got here. He had slept, he thought, but the difference between being asleep and being awake was not clear to him. Some of the others, including Zach, who had his head on Nick's shoulder, were sleeping now. One was crying, calling for his mother. Smelly was lying on a rough mattress of thorn bush and his pixie blanket. There was a dark stain on the ground beside his thigh and his face was ashen.

Night fell and morphed into a long slow day and once again the disappearing sun backlit the rim of the desert. No one moved. Nick was very hungry. He drained the last of the water from his canteen and then, dimly remembering something they had been told in Hill 69, sucked on a pebble to ease his thirst. He dozed fitfully through the second night. At dawn a man with three stripes on his sleeve stood up and cleared his throat. With a relief that made him want to weep, he recognized Sergeant Maloney. 'Look fellas. I'm afraid the captain is dead. We're out of water and cut off from everyone else. We could make another go for the fort but it looks like we're on our own.'

'Sergeant?' A lad from Balmoral raised his hand, looking for permission to speak. 'My ammunition is for an American rifle. These aren't going to fit into a bloody Lee Enfield!'

'Christ,' the sergeant said. 'This is a bloody shambles. We've had it. There's nothing for it but to run up the white flag.'

Eight

Twenty-nine of them were packed tightly into the basement room. Some lay on stretchers, and Prof was one of them. He was barely conscious. Nick recognized a fellow called Jimmy lying beside him with an oozing hole in his right calf. The air was stale, heavy with the smell of old sweat, fresh blood and urine. Occasionally Nick and the others still standing tried to shuffle tighter together to give the injured some space but also instinctively moved to put some distance between the living and the dying. A shaft of dirty sunlight pierced the room through a small window high in the wall behind them and a soldier's boots moved across the light, causing it to flicker as the guard paced the ground above them. Nick felt dazed and punch drunk with fatigue and fear. He wished he could sleep like some of the others propped upright against the bodies of their friends but terror gnawed at the edge of his mind. They had been forbidden to speak and now even the dry whispers that had earlier escaped the notice of their custodians had stopped.

Nick was profoundly shocked at the way they had been treated by these Frenchmen. He had expected some recognition that they were all soldiers, a brotherly camaraderie like in the bathhouse after school games, an acceptance that it could have gone the other way. He recalled the story his father often told about a fellow officer in the last war who spent a brief spell as a prisoner of the Germans in Ypres. He had shared a brandy with his captors after a dinner of braised pheasant and an exchange of wildfowling stories before reluctantly escaping back to his own lines. But here it was not like that at all. Zach had been kicked down the stone steps that led to the basement and Shorty had been hit over the head with a rifle butt when he asked for water, his bony legs buckling underneath him like a newborn giraffe. They had been given nothing to eat or drink. Their jailers appeared to be drunk, holding their index fingers to their thumbs and shaking their wrists violently.

'Wankers,' they spat. The Australians did not return the offence as their tormentors were armed, angry and unpredictable.

An African with blue-black skin in desert fatigues stood apart from his French colleagues. He alone did not indulge in the spitting unpleasantness of his comrades and had earlier helped the exhausted men carry the stretchers down the steps.

'*Si jeune*,' he said in a soft voice, looking from Nick to Zach and then to the inseparable Billy and Piper, shaking his big head from side to side.

'What did he say?' Nick asked Zach in a hoarse whisper.

'So young,' Zach translated. 'Foreign Legion, I think, not the same as the other bastards anyway,' he added, cupping his hand over his mouth to smother his voice. Nick looked at his friend. His face was so like those of the men pointing bayonets at their bellies, with his dark skin and Semitic features. This was not the war he had hoped to fight and a far cry from a heroic return to Germany to save what was left of his family. None of them had thought back in Vasey that they would be sitting on a filthy floor as a prisoner of the Vichy French and their Arab allies. Where were the Germans? Not far, Nick supposed, but he was confused as to who was fighting who at this stage. There had been those glamorous Frenchmen on their horses who had fought alongside them two days ago. Arab guides had brought them to the fort. Did they go back to their villages and sup with the angry men in front of him now?

After several hours, to the accompaniment of more scornful shouting and thumps from rifles and truncheons from the French guards, the men were herded into an adjoining room. A desk stood against the far wall. The new, larger space alarmed Nick after the closeness of the smaller one. Shuffling stiffly, he pressed up against his mates, backing away from the hissing men who prodded and poked at them. The door opened and a squat bald man with waxy skin entered. He ignored the prisoners and sat heavily at the desk with a ledger in front of him. Two Arab soldiers with dirty turbans stood behind him like guardians of an ancient tomb, legs wide apart and bodies rigid. The face of the man at the desk trickled sweat and his small round spectacles slipped quickly and repeatedly to the end of his nose. He pushed them up to the bridge with his left hand every few seconds, as if he had an uncontrollable tick.

Sergeant Maloney stepped out, pulled up his shoulders and thrust his chin forward. 'We need water and food,' he said to the man behind the desk. 'We are entitled to proper treatment.' His words sounded confident but his eyes darted nervously from the man to the soldiers standing motionless behind him.

'Who are you?'

'Sergeant Maloney, 2/2 Battalion, The Australian Pioneers. I insist my men have food and water.'

The fat man leaned back in his chair. 'And why should we comply with the codes of war when you use our own countrymen against us? You can expect no *chee-val-ree* here.' He squeezed the word through his teeth.

'But your countrymen, the men who were with us out there, they don't want to be German.'

'*Ferme-la!*'

'Where are our officers?' Maloney persisted. Nick was proud of the sergeant. He was going to get answers for them.

'They will go to Germany to answer for this sacrilege.'

'And what is to happen to us?'

'We have not yet decided what to do with you. Now you will give me the name of all these men.'

'Nick!' Zach grabbed urgently at Nick's sleeve. 'Call me Jack. Jack. Understand?' Although the sentries behind the desk could not see who had broken the rule of silence or hear what was being said, one of them lowered his bayonet and lunged. Inspired by the sergeant's courage, Nick returned the angry stare and held the Arab's eye but it was too much for a plump barber from Coleraine, who started to shake violently. A dark stain appeared at the front of his trousers and the guards erupted again into coarse taunts.

The man behind the desk tapped his pencil on the desk to restore silence and mopped his brow with dabs of a white handkerchief, a strangely feminine and delicate gesture out of place in the male stench of this room. He licked the lead repeatedly and carefully wrote the date at the head of the left-hand page of the ledger. The man, with his glassy eyes and darting tongue, reminded Nick of a gecko he had watched on a log behind the bunkhouse.

'We'll start with you, sergeant. First name? Nationality?'

'Eamon. Australian,' the sergeant replied firmly.

'Tottenham. Nicholas. Private soldier, British,' Nick said when his turn came. That is what he had told the recruiting officer over a year ago back in Australia, and he would have to swallow his confused heritage again now.

'Smith. Jack. Private soldier. Australian,' Zach said and looked the man straight in the eye.

'Next!'

Nick had been holding his breath and now let it out slowly, thanking God for his friend's musical ear and gift of mimicry. He was relieved, too, that here was evidence that some of the rules of war were to be observed. Names taken, a record kept. But his tongue stuck to the roof of his mouth and his lips were cracked. They had been given no food and no water. No medic had come to treat the injured. He thought of the cool peaty water of the lake beside his home in Westmeath and imagined it sliding down his raw throat.

The grey dawn seeped into the room and the slumped bodies of his companions took shape. Nick had slept fitfully. He was no longer hungry. He supposed that his stomach had simply got used to being empty. The door opened and a barefoot Arab with fearful eyes in a filthy *jelabia* shuffled in, carrying two pails of water slung on a pole across his bony shoulders with two tin mugs hanging on a string around his neck. A French soldier followed him and threw five round cakes of flatbread on the ground. Nick rose stiffly to his feet while Sergeant Maloney divided the loaves meticulously, handing each man his share. The two cups were passed first to those on stretchers and then from man to man. Nick slurped greedily at the tepid brown water.

'Easy lad,' the sergeant said to him. 'Sip it ... take it easy.' He turned to Zach. 'You all right?' The sergeant glanced nervously at the French soldier at the door as he spoke. 'Jack?' he said theatrically and Nick thought for an absurd second that the sergeant might wink.

'I'm fine, sarge,' Zach said loudly. Turning his back to the door he whispered, 'Do you think they'll check our dog tags?'

'No, son, it'll be fine ... they're not the Gestapo. Just keep working on that Aussie accent.'

Nick dozed, leaning against Zach. Men on both sides of them were moaning. They had been below ground now for two days and the hard bread ration of yesterday had simply alerted their tortured stomachs to the need for food. A sharp prod to his buttocks woke him and a yelp from Billy as his slumbers were disturbed in the same way. He stood in behind Shorty to climb the stone steps out of the basement. He smiled weakly at Billy and Piper in what he hoped was an encouraging way but saw their eyes reflect the terror he felt. Was this the end? His guts felt weak and he tried to think of a prayer but couldn't remember any.

'Oh God, oh God. Help me,' Billy muttered.

'It's all right mate,' Piper said but his voice cracked. The sun beat down on the chalky masonry and the glare was painful when they emerged blinking from the basement into the small square within the old walls of the fort. The French soldiers had their rifles by their sides and were leaning against the walls sucking on cigarettes and watching them narrowly. This was no firing squad. Nick heard a gasp of relief escape from his own mouth and it sounded almost like a laugh. As the last man came out, one of the guards jabbed his rifle towards a hole in the ground in the corner of the square.

'What's he bloody want now?' Nick muttered, emboldened by his deliverance. Led by Sergeant Maloney he edged nervously towards the hole and peered in. The stench was almost visible.

'Jesus, that's the shithole,' Piper said, his own relief swelling his voice. He broke into nervous giggles. Billy looked into the hole, his bright ginger hair providing the only splash of colour in this hot and arid square. He withdrew as if he had been stung, bent over and retched. Nick felt an urgent tug on his arm.

'God Nick, I can't ... they can't make us ... there, in the open, I mean ...' Zach said, his words lifting in pitch. His eyes were locked on the disgusting hole. Nick thought Zach must be joking. This was nothing compared with the horrors they might have been about to face. They were not going to be shot as they had feared, coming up the steps, and he should be giddy with relief and not fussing about shitting in public. But then again he had been like this before with the cattle trucks. Zach's face remained stricken, awash with panic. He is just a fastidious little Jew, Nick thought irritably.

'They won't keep us here for long. There'll be a proper camp somewhere,' Nick said, struggling to keep his voice even. 'They have to comply with the convention.' He took Zach's arm to lead him away from the reeking hole and they walked around the square to ease the cramp in their limbs. He was running out of cigarettes and so they shared one and smoked it to the butt. Then they withdrew into the shade and sat down with their backs against the wall.

'At least our families will now be told that we have been captured. I don't suppose anyone will tell them that the assault was a bloody crazy idea in the first place. Or that we were given no training for that kind of thing and the wrong ammo.' He hoped that he was helping Zach to believe that they had been through the worst and that everything could only get better now, but Zach seemed to have broken.

'There'll be no one waiting for news of me.'

'I'm sorry mate, I didn't ...' Nick mumbled, embarrassed. He lit another cigarette and handed it to Zach.

'I have to get back to it, Nick. I can't sit out the rest of the war somewhere like this.'

'We'll be moved to a better place. We're a long way from Europe. Even if you could escape you'd never get that far.'

Nick felt a wave of exhaustion. He and Zach were so different. He knew with a sense of disappointment in himself that he would never be a man to consider such a daring exploit but Zach was being foolish. As he leant back against the wall, he pictured Willie Fitz puffing his way up the drive with a telegram and everyone at home would know immediately that something had happened because it was the wrong time of day for Willie to bring the post.

The picture comforted him. He wondered who would see Willie first: his father perhaps, as he drove about the farm on his old Massey, looking important but losing the battle against encroaching weeds and debt. His mother might look up from her crossword through the window of the morning room or, God forbid, Kate could come across Willie as she picked the wildflowers that grew in the unkempt grass at the edge of the drive. His mother and Kate would cry and this might even be forgiven for once but he was sure that his father would call him a bloody fool anyway.

The men huddled in small groups, smoking and trying to make some sense of what had happened to them. Outside the walls the desert shimmered in white-hot silence. It was rudely shattered by an agitated shout from a soldier on top of the wall enclosing the square. Guards and prisoners raised hands to shade their eyes and looked up to see him pointing out over the desert. Three Frenchmen carrying rifles ran across the square from the guardhouse in the corner and bounded up the steps to join the gesticulating man on top of the wall.

'*Que ce passe-t-il?*'

'*Un cavalier! Regardez là-bas! Un drapeau blanc. Ils veulent parler.*'

'It must be one of those French horsemen,' Zach whispered to Nick. The man who had written down their names the previous day waddled out of the guardhouse and climbed slowly up towards the activity on the top of the wall, pulling himself up on the rail as his short legs struggled with the big steps. This time it was the Australians' turn to mock.

'Look at your man,' Sergeant Maloney said. 'Too much foie gras. Fat bollocks.' The others laughed nervously and eyed the guards posted around the perimeter of the square. The French officer, sweating and puffing as he reached the top, removed his glasses, wiped them with his handkerchief and said something to the men on the wall that the prisoners on the ground could not hear. The soldiers to whom he spoke froze and their jaws dropped.

'*Mais il est français!*' one of them wailed eventually at the retreating back of the senior man.

'*Il est un traître. Tuez-le!*' the officer said firmly as he reached the bottom of the steps. '*Montrez-lui çe que c'est d'etre libre,*' he said, curling his lip over the last word, and retreated back through the door from which he had emerged without a backward glance.

'What did he say? What was all that about?' Piper asked. A rifle shot cracked across the desert. Its echo clung to the hot white air and sang across the sands. The Australians stood fixed as statues.

'What the fuck?' Shorty said and they all looked to Zach because he was the only one who might understand what had been said.

'He was carrying a bloody white flag,' Zach said unsteadily.

'What do you mean?' Nick asked. 'What's going on?'

'What did he say, son?' Sergeant Maloney asked.

'He was coming to parlay. *Mein Gott,*' Zach said, forgetting himself. 'He was coming to rescue us.' There were now tears in his eyes and he looked wildly about him as if begging his friends to get what only he had understood.

'They've shot one of those French fellows who were with us since Katani. The fat man told the lookout up there to show every-one what it means to be "free" … to kill him. These people are worse than the fucking Germans.' He lunged towards the foot of the steps. Nick caught him with a high arm tackle around his neck.

'Shut up you fool,' Nick hissed at his ear and dug his fingers into Zach's arm. 'Don't draw attention to yourself. For Christ's sake, calm down!'

'Hey you. What you doing?' A tall thin man in an Arab head-dress and wearing a *jelabia* emerged from the shadows. 'Who are you? What is your name? Show me your dog tag. You are dog maybe?' he said in broken English, smiling crookedly at his clever-ness. He had a gold cap on one of his front teeth and was smoking a cheroot. He walked slowly towards them, reached forward and took the silver disc hanging at the base of Zach's throat into his hand.

'Zachariah Schmitz,' he said slowly struggling with the pronunciation. 'Not Australian, I think.' Another cruel smile cracked his face. 'Let's see. Who might you be then?' He licked his lips. 'I think the Gestapo in Damascus will be very interested in you, my friend.'

'Leave him alone, you bastard.' Nick shoved his hand into the man's chest. He had time only to register the hungry anticipation on the faces of the guards who had been skulking in the shadow of the walls as they rushed towards him before he felt the thump to his kidneys; a rifle crashed over his head and the ground came up to meet him.

Nick awoke on the floor of a truck, pain jolting through his ribs with the movement of the vehicle underneath him. Some of the men from 'A' Company sat on benches along both sides of the truck. The sergeant, Shorty, Piper and Billy stared silently down at him, their bodies rolling together in lazy agreement with the lurching motion of the truck.

'You all right, son?' Sergeant Maloney shouted to make himself heard above the growling engine.

'I think so,' Nick croaked. His right eye was gummed shut. One side of his head was cold and sticky and he felt a sharp pain when he tried to move his left arm, which lay crookedly by his side. 'Zach? Is he ...?'

'I'm right here, Nick,' said a voice from behind his head. 'It's OK ... they lost interest in me when you took them on.' Zach shuffled forward so that Nick could see him, gripped his good hand and, gazing at his face, began to stroke it gently. For a moment Nick felt soothed. It carried the echo of something his mother might have done when he grazed his knees but he was suddenly acutely conscious of his mates staring at this theatre on the floor of the truck. He pulled his hand slowly out from underneath Zach's fingers and closed his good eye to blot out the hurt on his friend's face.

But Zach stayed by his side when they arrived at the next prison, by which time Nick was barely conscious. Somewhere in the dark labyrinths of his pain over the next few days Nick understood that his friend was nursing him and that any dignity that he might have left was in his hands. He was embarrassed that Zach had to feed, wash and wipe him when he soiled himself. He hoped fervently that Zach was doing the same for the other wounded men. He had seen the look on his friends' faces when they saw Zach stroking his hand but he was helpless. As he improved he was relieved see that Zach fussed over, chided, wiped and scolded them all equally and he told himself that he had imagined the scene on the floor of the truck. He is being the doctor he always wanted to be, he thought as he watched Zach holding up a man as he emptied his watery bowels into the bucket, and then turned to mop up another's vomit. In the darkest hours of the night when a man called for his mother, Zach went to him and held his hand.

'Now don't be such a pussy,' he said to one of them. 'You're not going to die tonight.' Over the following days Zach bathed his forehead to bring down the fever and used his puttees to strap Nick's arm. Boils erupted along Nick's back in the places where it met the filthy floor and Zach lanced them for him. 'The things I do for you, you black Protestant *goy*,' he said.

Slowly Nick appeared to heal. Over the next three weeks the swelling in his face subsided, and his ribs and his arm improved. He could lift himself from the floor and his ribs throbbed less vigorously. But a violent gripe still tore through his abdomen, a white-hot lance slicing relentlessly into his gut. He left blood in the bucket every morning. He didn't want Zach to know that. It was hard enough to get through this humiliating exercise and there was always another man waiting to use it, so he said nothing. What was the point? There was no doctor and there were others who were worse off than him. Jimmy's leg had grown hot and swollen and he became delirious, laughing and crying in his sleep. Zach could do nothing for the infection that was rotting his body. Sergeant Maloney again demanded a doctor but none came and

Jimmy died. The plump barber just gave up and didn't wake up one morning. Nick began to think that he would be next. There was something badly wrong and he was oozing blood all the time now. When Zach asked him several times a day how he was feeling, to his shame, the question irritated him. In fact, the cheerful busyness of his friend grated and he just wanted to be left alone.

'Grand, Zach, I'm grand,' he replied in a monotone.

'That's good, Nick. You are looking much better,' Zach said, and Nick knew he was lying.

The truck had brought them across the mountains and the sergeant guessed that they were now about twenty miles south of Aleppo but he could tell them nothing about what was going on outside the walls of the jail. The French soldiers had been replaced by the gendarmerie and the policemen didn't seem to bear the same grudge against them as the Vichy military and their Arab comrades had done, which was a mercy, but they had no news of the war. The fear that they would be taken out into the hot square and shot had receded but the men were starving and most had severe diarrhoea. A tasteless soup with a few carrots and some flatbread was the only food slopped into them twice a day. Nick did not feel hungry any more and he no longer tortured himself with thoughts of going home. When the Prof died he felt inclined to give up altogether.

'Do you think anyone knows we are here?' Nick asked the sergeant.

'Our families have to be told. Them's the rules,' the sergeant replied, but he did not seem to be convinced and Nick wasn't either.

'But sarge, they don't give a fiddler's cuss about the rules. We're dying like flies in here. Of course they haven't informed the Red Cross, or whatever it is they have to do to let our families know we're alive.'

Nick supposed that by now his own would believe him dead. They would want to know how he died, and would hope he had been brave. Perhaps it was just as well that there would be no record of it, he thought, given that it looked like he would die here like a rat in a sewer. Not exactly a hero's death, he brooded. Maybe it didn't matter that his family already thought he was dead because the wrench in his gut told him that it was only a matter of time. How would they take the news of his death? Tony would be trying to get into the air force, made more determined, he supposed, by the fact that Nick was gone. No doubt he would have some silly notion that it was all up to him now. He conjured up the faces of his mother, Rose and Kate, and wondered what they might be doing now. Tony had said that his mother was going to England, to Lincolnshire somewhere, an officer in the WAAF, perhaps in a control tower looking over the plains of eastern England. She would be doing sums wherever she was. Rose might be with her, and his father, not far away, at a desk job. He imagined Kate at home, drawing the wildflowers now in bloom and looking after Maggie and George, perhaps having a picnic tea at the lake's edge with Martha's soda bread smeared thickly with country butter, and flapjacks and walnut cake.

As the days passed and the pain in his abdomen grew worse, he became used to the idea of no longer existing. He wanted all this to be over. It surprised him that he was not afraid: he had always suspected that he would not be a man to leave much of a mark on the world and now the pressure on him to do so, that he had felt for as long as he could remember, would be over. Tony would do all that for them both as everyone had always expected he would. His father would have an extra drink and his mother would putty up another sadness inside her. But Kate? Oh God. Poor Kate. He had been so cruel to her before he left.

The men, as before, were imprisoned in two adjoining rooms, one in which they slept and the other they used for the tiresome business of living. With no bedding in it, there was some space for them to move. The stinking bucket stood in the corner of the day room covered with poor Jimmy's battledress jacket in an attempt to keep the flies off it. It depressed Nick that he no longer noticed the smell and he wondered, should they survive, whether any of them would recover from the baseness to which they had sunk. At sundown the long night dropped over them like a black blanket and during the day the sergeant, with a heartiness that was wearing thin, encouraged his men to make the most of the light. He had demanded paper from the French.

'Aw sarge, our letters are not going out, what's the point?' Shorty said.

'Make playing cards,' Maloney commanded. So Billy, Piper and Shorty sat in dusty corners drawing kings, queens and knaves. At first they were enthusiastic and the early drawings were ingeniously pornographic, but this just seemed to remind them of life beyond the walls and the activity was soon put aside. They played 'jacks' using a small pile of pebbles and a golf ball, which Sergeant Maloney had produced like a magician from his breast pocket, but time passed excruciatingly slowly. Each day felt like a month. Perhaps that's a good thing, Nick thought bitterly, as this could be my last. He was not the only one to be losing heart and soon even Billy and Piper lay curled in a ball on the floor night and day. Zach seemed to be the only one who held on to a chirpiness that grew, to Nick's mind, increasingly absurd. In the oppressive heat of one late afternoon when even the flies had no energy to buzz around the bucket, Zach was bouncing the ball with his right hand in the day room and scooping the pebbles off the ground with his left.

'I'm winning,' he said, a lone voice of enthusiasm.

'My arm is broken,' Nick said sullenly. No one wanted to play these games any more. There was a distant crackle from the window.

'What's that?' Shorty asked, cocking his ear towards the window. The men who had been dozing in the sleeping room crowded through the door and looked expectantly up at the light, straining to hear.

'That's gunfire,' Sergeant Maloney said. 'The Poms must have made it through.' Nick recognized something change in him. It was almost painful. Hope.

Nine

VICTORIA

Uncle Herbert opened the breakfast room door as he did every morning at precisely 8 am. He held a buff envelope in his hand and his face was grave.

'Tony. I have some distressing news. 'A' Company has been cut off. At Merdjayoun. I'm sorry, son. Nick has not been accounted for.'

It was as though a harsh surgical light had been flicked on, and the silver on the breakfast table in front of him brightened like those new neon lights he had seen in Melbourne. Tony imagined that he could taste the metal of them in his mouth. He looked up at his uncle.

'Now listen son, this is not necessarily the news that you think it is. There are rumours that prisoners were taken and Nick may have been lucky. He's a boy that learns quickly and has a strong instinct for self-preservation. Communication is a shambles, I'm afraid. To be honest the whole thing sounds like a mess.'

Tony swallowed. He knew that his uncle was trying to sugar the pill. Even Tony could not know how Nick would cope in those conditions. 'He was a Digger. How did he come to be in the thick of it?' Tony managed.

'That's what the other fellows around here are saying. There are a lot of boys from these parts in 'A' Company. Maybe they got caught in a retreat. These things happen in war, I'm afraid. You're right though, it's hard to believe they could have been used in the main assault. That is not their job. Let's hope they find him soon.'

Tony understood just how carefully his uncle had chosen his words. They needed to know one way or the other. As his heart slowed and the room returned to the pastel shades of the morning he dared to think of the worst. Life without Nick, his other half? He didn't know what sort of person he would be if he lost Nick. Tony was able to be Tony because Nick was Nick. He could feel panic scampering up into his throat. The words *never again* slushed through his mind like dirty flood water. His uncle put his hand on his shoulder and then Tony thought that he could not bear it.

He walked over to the barn where the horses were and lobbed a saddle on the young mare that reminded him of Firefly. Down at the river he dismounted and threw the reins on the ground where she started to nibble contentedly at the grass at the water's edge. He sat watching the herons standing stock still with one leg aloft. He knew that life here would become suffocating. It had been a fairy tale, the crooked pink house, the butler with his bare feet, the polished silver on the table and the cakes for tea. The time had come to cut the apron strings that had tied him so pleasantly to Twin Oaks. If only his birthday was tomorrow, but it was three months away.

A swamp hen fluttered out of the reeds. He would go to Melbourne. Maybe he could fiddle his age like Poppa had done. After all, there were plenty of fellas in the last war who went to Gallipoli when they were only fifteen. Died there too, he thought.

If that didn't work he would try and get in as a cadet. He could use the time to do the maths exams Nick had told him to do. His throat tightened as he remembered the last time he had seen his brother outside Flinders Station and he twisted his hands together roughly and blinked to distract the tears.

Since Nick left he had been working on his maths but he wasn't sure whether he was ready to enter for the Leaving Certificate. His mother's schooling would get him through the basic arithmetic, algebra and even quadratic functions and logarithms, but if calculus came up he was in trouble. Maybe he should write to her for some help. What was she going through today as Willie Fitz delivered the dreadful news?

When the time came that autumn for him to march into the office in Russell Street in Melbourne he was armed with his certificate, and impatient. It had been a long three months and there had been no news of Nick. An officer in his late forties with a grey moustache stained yellow by years of smoking sat behind the desk.

'You will have to start in the Reserve,' he said, his voice gravelly and bored. Tony's face must have registered his disappointment. 'Everyone has to begin there,' he added. The questions he then asked were simple enough but Tony's answers clearly confused the man.

'I have a British passport,' Tony said. 'I was born in South Africa.'

'Why are you in Australia?'

'I'm a jackaroo. For my uncle.'

'Religion?

'Church of Ireland.'

The man looked exasperated. 'I take it you will have no trouble swearing the oath?' he asked.

'Of course not,' Tony said, lifting the Bible in case the man might have any further doubts. 'I swear that I will well and truly serve our Sovereign Lord the King, so help me God.' Tony felt he would have liked to shout it from the rooftops even though the words seemed like something from another era. He wondered what those oafs, Fergus O'Dowd and his friends at the tennis club, would think of it.

'A bit on the small side, aren't you?' the officer asked.

'Five foot eight and a half,' Tony said. 'Look, it says here,' he added, pushing his medical report under the man's nose. 'And I'm to be aircrew – it's good to be a bit of a squit for that, isn't it?' At last the man smiled and signed the page. Tony looked at the form in his hands as he emerged from the office into the street. *Enrolment of Person in the Reserve*, it said, *Aircrew*. Now he could get on with it.

Ten

'I didn't think we would ever get back here, to tell you the truth,' Zach said as the train screeched into Katani. The wagon doors squealed open. A medical orderly with a red cross on his arm put his hand on the side of the wagon door and peered down at Nick on a stretcher. Nick thought he smelled very much of soap.

'These fellas are for the hospital. Quick as you can,' the orderly said, recoiling. His face was backlit by the brightness of the desert behind him and his features were in shadow but Nick could not mistake the look of disgust in his eyes. 'Christ, did you see that lot? They're filthy,' Nick heard him say.

There were eight of them from Aleppo in the ward and Zach was in the bed beside Nick. Despite protesting that he didn't need attention, the medical officer had insisted that Zach stay. The Aleppo boys could see, now that they could be compared to healthy soldiers in Katani, that they had become shrunken and emaciated. Their beards had disguised their hollow cheeks and a hard-wired self-preservation had blinded them to the fact that the rest of their bodies were skeletal too.

'We have to feed you boys up ... think we got you just in time,' the nurse said. She had a freckled face and bright green eyes, her hair a bonnet of happy red curls. She walked with an athletic step. Her legs were brown and she wore no stockings. Nick wondered what age she might be. 'You've had a bad time, Private Tottenham,' she said as she lifted his wrist and held it between her thumb and her index finger. She smelt of the lilac in the garden at home. 'How are we today?'

He couldn't answer because there was a thermometer in his mouth. He felt something well up in him, so he grunted to mask it, hoping that she had not seen the wetness of his eye. The down on her cheek caught the sun from the window behind her and framed her face like a Madonna. He stared at the plump curve of her arm. How could it be so soft? She dropped his bony wrist once she'd checked his pulse, tucked the sheet under the mattress, and smiled.

'Look at you, you old fool,' Zach said when she had gone, his tone leaden. Nick turned away from him and allowed his mind to drift to the redheaded nurse and her lilac smell.

WESTMEATH, IRELAND

Kate saw Willie Fitz on his bicycle as he came around the turn in the drive. The last time he had come at this time of day he had brought the telegram, the one that had told them that Nick was missing. She thought for a moment that she might run down to the lake and take the boat out to the middle and stay there so that she could hold the world still. But instead she stood rooted to the spot and waited for Willie to puff towards her. He swung his leg over the saddle and handed her the envelope, biting his lip. It was such an insignificant thing, brown and thin, as if it held nothing more than a bill from the butcher, and maybe she could ignore it like she did most bills. It was addressed to her mother but she was in England and Kate wondered for a moment if she could send it back with a forwarding address. She looked up at the old man and taking courage from his kind face, slowly opened the envelope. Her hand shook as she scanned the page: *Your son Pte Nicholas Tottenham has been released as a prisoner of war. He is recuperating in El Katani field hospital and is expected to make a full recovery from his ordeal.*

The breath Kate had been holding onto since Willie handed her the telegram escaped from her. 'They've found him, Willie! Oh Willie, they've found him! I thought he was dead ... they've found Nick!' She was bawling now, pulling in gulps of air and letting them out in unsteady gusts. She pointed at the words on the page but Willie could not read, so he dropped his bicycle, which clanged to the ground, and awkwardly, unsure whether it was fitting, put his arm across Kate's shoulder.

'There now, miss, don't be crying.'

When Nick's letter reached her a month later, the beech trees on the drive were already turning to amber and gold and the grass underneath them was dusty and yellow. The harvest was in and the fields on either side of the drive were a close-cropped stubble dotted with stooks of straw. There was a light frost most mornings and Willie's bicycle left a wobbly wet line as he made his slow passage up the drive.

'One for you, miss,' Willie called through the old kitchen door. Kate dropped the bread she was kneading and wiped the flour on her hands on her apron. 'It's from out foreign,' he added. He stood in the doorway, clearly going to stay there until he could share the contents of the letter. Maggie and George were eating their boiled eggs, dipping soldiers of toast into them with intense concentration.

'Is England foreign?' Maggie squealed, jumping up from the table.

'Finish your breakfast, both of you.'

'Who is it, who is it?'

'In these parts England is generally considered to be foreign,' George said without looking up from the egg.

'Oh my gosh it's from Nick,' Kate said, tearing it open.

'Read, read it!' Maggie said.

11 September 1941

My dearest Kate,

I hope you are well and managing everything at home as I know you can. I quite expect the whole place to be in shipshape condition when I get home! It's a big job for you looking after Maggie and George, though I'm sure Martha and Jim are a great help. The post takes a long time to reach me but I had a letter from Mother this week so I know she is in England doing her bit. As for Poppa, isn't he the limit joining up again?! I suppose he'll be at a desk job in England somewhere and at least that will be nice for Mother.

I've had a bit of a rough time but I'm absolutely fine now. I am feeling a lot stronger. I was lucky to get through and I had some friends who were not so lucky. I wouldn't have made it without my friend Zach who I have told you about. Thank God he is fine too and we are both here with some of the lads from 'A' Company, being fed like prize pigs.

There is a very nice Australian nurse here called Jeannie who plays tennis like you do (though I'm sure she isn't as good as you are!). She has been looking after me here in Katani since I had my spleen taken out. I have asked her out on a date. Can you imagine that! Mind you a date here is going for a walk as far as the mosque and a cup of mint tea in the hotel in the old town. You will meet her one day and I know you will get on like a house on fire.

Anyway, I think our mob will be here for another few months but our job here is really done with the Vichy French surrendering. I think they are going to send us back to Oz until there is a bit more going on in Europe so I hope to catch up with Tony then. He will be eighteen today so I imagine he will be badgering the Air Force to let him in.

Take care of yourself Little Un and don't worry. We are all very good at taking care of ourselves, aren't we? Give Maggie and George a kiss from me.

With love from Nick

'Nick's got a girlfriend, Nick's got a girlfriend,' Maggie chanted, skipping around the kitchen table.

'Oh do shut up, Maggie. He just had a date, that's all,' Kate snapped. The news disturbed her. *I know you will like her,* the letter said. He has made a decision without any of us even meeting her, she thought. How could he do that? How much he must have changed. A feeling close to the one that had swept over her two years ago when she felt her brothers were excluding her swelled to an overwhelming sense of abandonment. Her family was scattered all over the place: Mummy, Poppa and Rose were in England, Nick was in Egypt and Tony in Australia. When her parents went to England at the beginning of the summer there had been no discussion about how Kate would manage, no argument that everyone would join up when they could. 'It's what we do,' her mother had said firmly.

She didn't mind, Kate told herself, that she and Maggie and George had to live in the kitchen, traipsing up through the cold dark house only to go to bed. Or did she? She wondered did any of them who had gone away ever think about the ones left at home. Their lives had moved on so much. It wasn't just that she missed them all, she was afraid she might not know them when they got home. Perhaps they wouldn't want to come home. Her mother said that she thought it might be another two years before there would be an invasion of France, and by that time Tony would also be involved and Kate would have to worry about him too. She would probably have to join the WAAF herself – well, at least she would be a part of it then. The thought cheered her and she flopped into her father's armchair, which had been brought down from the morning room to sit beside the range, and pulled the letter out of the pocket of her apron to read it again.

LINCOLNSHIRE, ENGLAND

Eleanor was always one of the first to be told the target for that evening so that she could set about calculating the effect of wind direction and other meteorological factors on flying hours and fuel consumption. She took pleasure in the purity of the numbers and equations in front of her. At last she could apply her girlhood studies after years of traipsing around the world after Gerald with his madcap schemes to Malaya and South Africa, having baby after baby. It took a war to put her back doing what she loved to do, losing herself in arithmetic where she felt completely at home.

She would have to brief the squadron leader, a mild man of the old school, within the hour. He had seemed surprised when she had reported to him that first morning. He had not expected a woman and certainly not one with a grown family. She smiled at the memory and of the pleasure she had felt at his smugness unmasked. She remembered that feeling back in university when she had been the only girl.

'I don't know how you work all that stuff out,' Felicity said from the desk beside her. 'It's double Dutch to me, all those air speeds, distances, wind factors and God knows what else.'

'I studied maths,' Eleanor said simply. 'I find it easy.' Her eye caught the poster on the wall: *Serve with the WAAF with the men who fly,* it said. With the boys who fly, she thought. 'I couldn't do what you do, talking those poor boys down to land when they limp home in damaged aircraft ... and then sending them off again the next day,' she added quietly.

'Yeah,' Felicity said and sighed.

Eleanor supposed Felicity was about thirty. There had been a husband once but Eleanor did not like to pry; these days such questions were ill advised, as there was always a tragedy or a betrayal in the answer. She was a good-looking girl with her blonde hair rolled in a halo about her head as was the fashion these days and her lips permanently a scarlet sheen. Her skirts swished with the sway of her walk. With a sense of something now lost to her Eleanor recognized that Felicity was in the early years of her womanhood, in full bloom and not yet 'gone over'. She spoke with flat A's and dropped her aitches but Eleanor had stopped noticing that long ago. She was in awe of the way Felicity could calm the panicky boys coming home in crippled aircraft, giving hope to the injured and courage to the terrified. She was the voice of the control tower and the airmen loved her.

Since she had arrived here in April, Eleanor had listened to Felicity sending out the bombing crews most evenings throughout the summer and was still struck by the cheery way her friend wished them luck, as if they were heading out to a football game. Eleanor often stood on the runway in the early evenings, waving and smiling confidently at the departing bombers – Blenheims, Sterlings and Wellingtons – heading for the German or Danish coast, or to attack the U-boats at Lorient and Bordeaux, while she tried not to think about the ones who would not come back. But it was Felicity who had to coax the survivors home the following morning. She never asked the leader how many he had with him. He could not have told her anyway as some would have to limp home on their own, bumping off the waves in the channel. Or perhaps one had ditched and its crew was hiding in a farmhouse in the

French countryside. Or worse. It was another part of the unwritten code – no one did the count until they had to.

And then at some black point during the cold hours of the early morning after a long, silent and tense night, Felicity had to accept that an aircraft she had sent off six or seven hours earlier was not coming back, that a young pilot, flight engineer, navigator, two gunners, a wireless operator and a bomb aimer were probably dead. And then everyone on the base set about patching up the damaged aircraft that had made it home, selecting and briefing more crews who might face a similar fate, identifying a new target, mapping the route and doing the calculations for the next raid. It had come from the top that this was the way to win the war, whatever the cost to young lives. Lincolnshire was being covered in tarmacadam runways as fast as the weather would allow and throughout the summer Eleanor watched the bombers heave themselves into the skies every night and go further and further over the Nazi homeland. That very morning, after another long night, Felicity sat, as the skies brightened, waiting for the radio to crackle to announce the first pilot approaching home.

'My port side's crippled, I have no landing gear,' a painfully young and tight voice had said through the static. 'Have I permission to land immediately? I can see T for Tommy ahead of me. I have wounded.'

'Come on in Henry, T for Tommy has gone round to let you in. We're waiting for you. The ambulance will meet you,' she said with the quiet assurance of an old nurse. He landed, and there was a collective release of breath in the tower.

'Well done son, welcome home,' Felicity said. 'His first trip.' Eleanor had felt a lump rise in her throat.

But both women knew about the many who did not make it home. There were no funerals or memorial services for them. A replacement nineteen-year-old pilot with three months' flying experience took over the bed of the missing man the next day.

Eleanor could not bear to see a dead boy's belongings, which had been left neatly at the foot of the bed the previous evening in the Nissen hut where he slept, being packed up to be sent to his parents. And no one talked about the sweet boy from Taunton or Macclesfield or Dublin who had been a hoot in the mess the night before. Eleanor, like everyone else, could not grieve for him. There were too many and more would follow every night.

'Have a lovely time, darlin',' Felicity called after her as Eleanor left the control tower. 'Don't do anything I wouldn't do.'

Eleanor closed the window of the room that had been assigned to her in a small cottage on the edge of the airfield. A pale pink rose still bloomed against the outside wall and Eleanor was sorry that in closing the window she was shutting out its sweet smell. But she was exhausted and needed to dull the incessant roar of aircraft. She had carried the worry about Nick for so many weeks that even now, over a month after she had learnt that he was alive, she had difficulty letting go of the dread locked up inside her. The experience had cracked the ground on which she walked and she wondered if she would ever feel safe again. She told herself firmly, and out loud, that Nick was in Egypt, recovering from his ruptured spleen, and that he would be sent back to Australia in due course. His war was over, thank God.

That evening she would celebrate her birthday with Gerald. He was coming up from London and would spend the night with her. She would not let the sadness that in a few days' time her husband would be on a ship to the Far East spoil that. Gerald had booked a table in a restaurant in Grantham – a rare treat, and something she put down to the strange effect war was having on all of them. She didn't think he had ever bought her dinner on her birthday at home. A drink in the Greville Arms perhaps, if he remembered. She looked at herself in the long mirror that stood in the corner of her room. Forty-two today. Not too bad, she thought, turning her back to the glass and admiring her reflection over her shoulder.

She had new silk stockings especially for tonight and she liked the way they caught the late September sun from the window. Even though her hair was now streaked with silver, her new perm was pretty, short but with soft curls. The colour picked up the blue-grey of her uniform, which she smoothed over her hips. But she could see that more than the colour of her hair had changed. She placed her cap squarely on her head and, pulling the peak forward, adjusted it slightly to make sure that the wings of the RAF were in the middle of her forehead. That way she could hide the haunted look that remained in her eyes. She lifted her handbag from the candlewick bedspread, took out her lipstick and, pouting at the mirror, smoothed it on with three swift strokes.

Tonight she wouldn't think about what might be in store for them all. Nick was safe; Gerald had been spared Dunkirk and was too old to be sent into the thick of it, wherever that would be. Nothing much would happen in Malaya. He had badgered his way back to a posting where an old man like him could be useful. In fact, she thought, it was rather typical of Gerald to get himself a passage on a grand old ship to a cushy post in a part of the world that he knew very well and where he could throw his weight about a bit.

She had forgotten how splendid Gerald looked in uniform. He cut quite a dash, that was for sure – so different from the shabby fellow he had become in the years since the last war, trundling past the drawing-room window on his tractor. He was a different man away from the farm. She did not think that the service dress he wore this evening was as smart as the uniform of the Royal Flying Corps he had been wearing that day all those years ago when she had met him first in Mrs Henshaw's village shop, but the sight of him tonight did make her feel like her nineteen-year-old self. She allowed herself a smile when she thought what bossy Mrs Henshaw would think of her now. She remembered how shocked the old lady had been when Eleanor, the nice doctor's daughter, sat down to tea with the glamorous Irish soldier. Her father had been disapproving too when they married three weeks later. She also remembered all the promises Gerald had made to her that day about the great house and its gardens sweeping down to the lake. She should have seen the signs back then. Gerald had told her about his own father who slept all day and drank all night, about the terrifying maiden aunts who lived in the garden house. Perhaps it was just as well that her new father-in-law had been so scandalized by their unorthodox engagement and her lack of pedigree that he would not allow them to come home. But there was no point in thinking back over all that. It had been the end of a war then and now they were in the middle of another one with her family scattered across the globe.

Gerald stood up to pull the chair back for her and Eleanor saw the other diners look up from their plates to admire him. She had forgotten how strangers could stare at them. She imagined sometimes that they looked a little like a music hall act, he so tall and she coming just up to his elbows.

'Happy birthday darling,' he said. 'You look wonderful. I love the new hairdo.'

She pecked his cheek and lifted his service cap from the table to examine it. 'I like your new cap badge. Have you ever even been to Norfolk?'

He smiled as he sat down and covered her tiny hand with his. 'It's just a staff job darling. You know, in the background, organizing supplies and that sort of thing. I shan't have much to do with the regular soldiers. The need me because I speak Malay.'

'You shout Malay, you mean,' she said, smiling. She picked up the menu.

The waiter hovered. 'We have some lovely mallard, sir, if you and the lady would fancy that? I don't offer it to everyone,' he said in a whisper, bowing low over the table. He whipped the napkin off the table with a flourish and laid it on Gerald's lap. Eleanor felt her husband's gaze on her as she examined the menu and thought about the rude waiter in the Hibernian the last time she had been taken out to eat. Perhaps Gerald was also recognizing how much they had changed since the boys left. Now there was a job to be done and it gave them back their dignity.

'Any news from home?' Gerald asked.

'I had a note from Kate. Martha's grumbling and George is being naughty. He's taken up with some local boys and they play a lot of cards. Kate thinks there might be money involved.'

'At least he has been well taught! He has your head for numbers. He will be fine. And Maggie?'

'Oh you know. The usual. Not doing her homework. It's not ideal, I know, but what can we do? There is a war on. We are lucky that they are out of the way in Ireland.'

'I'm going to miss you so much, darling. Being in Malaya without you will be very strange.'

'Oh you'll be just fine with all those codgers. Lots of pink gin and bridge. It's just the ticket to keep you out of harm's way.'

Gerald grinned sheepishly. 'And you will be here doing such an important job. I am so proud of my little bluestocking.'

It was Eleanor's turn to reach across the table and squeeze his hand. She recognized a quickening of her pulse and was amazed how it still did that after all these years.

Eleven

AT SEA

Nick stood on the deck of the Orcades and waved at Jeannie's tiny figure until she turned her back on the crowded troop ship as it sailed away from the dock. Only that morning she had told him that her orders had changed and that she was to stay with some of the boys who were not fit to travel. She would follow in a month, she told him, her hand on his arm. The disappointment that she was not travelling with them back to Australia sat like a rock in his chest. He had got ahead of himself, as Martha might have said, and allowed himself to look forward to bringing her to Twin Oaks. He had imagined her in a nursing job in Vasey, close to him, whilst he returned to the cattle he loved. It didn't seem likely either of them could be sent away again. It was all going to happen in Europe now and by the time they got home there might be an end to it. He sighed and comforted himself with the thought that he would see her again in Melbourne very shortly and they could make plans for the future then.

The Pioneers were joined on the ship by two other regiments, the 2/3 Machine Gunners and the 2/6 Field Company, all veterans of the Syrian campaign. Nick rolled the word 'veteran' around his head and thought about how different his life looked now. On the outward journey fear had lurked like black ice on the blind bends of his consciousness. Now he was comforted by the HMS *Dorsetshire* carving its way through the waves beside them like a sleek sea monster, and by knowing that the war was over for him.

Nick and Zach and the other Aleppo boys slept on hammocks slung close together on a lower deck. It was hot and the air was stale, the smell of unwashed men the same as it had been on the outward journey, but this time they could spend every daylight hour on the open deck.

'You writing another love letter?' Zach asked him.

'Yes I'm writing to Jeannie,' Nick snapped. He had tried to tell Zach what Jeannie meant to him, about the extraordinary rush of tenderness that had sneaked up on him in the hospital bed in Katani, but he sensed Zach had no interest. He wasn't sure whether this was the sort of thing that grown men talked about and anyway, he wanted to be by himself and to remember Jeannie's green eyes, the feel of her palm on his brow, the taste and impossible softness of her mouth and to the way her body arched when they kissed.

Nick thought back to that holiest of nights when she had placed his hand on the curve of her hip under her dress. She lay on the bed on her side looking up at him. He had never felt skin so smooth but then he had never touched a woman like this before. He traced his finger across the dip of her buttock. Lifting his hand, he concentrated on the tips of his fingers, unable to look her in the eye.

'You can if you want to. It's all right,' she said.

'I'm not sure I know what ...'

'I'll help you,' she smiled sleepily, 'I am a nurse after all.'

She rolled over and with her back to him pulled the dress over her head. He turned away, reluctant to watch her undress, and when he looked around again she was lying on her back with one knee bent and one arm behind her head. There was nothing shy about the way she was looking at him.

Her arms were brown and so were her legs but only up to the line of her tennis dress. The rest of her body was as pale as the moon. He understood that she meant him to look at all of her, to remember her body, and to map it for when the light was out. He had done such things in his dreams and always feared that when the time came he would be overcome with embarrassment, but the pink bruises of her nipples and the dark fuzz above the white tops of her legs were simply beautiful to him. He told her that, and it didn't sound stupid or corny. He sat on the bed beside her and drew his fingers slowly down the inside of her arm, over the swell of her breast and in a circle across her stomach.

'Come lie beside me.'

Nick hesitated.

'Take your clothes off, silly.'

He took a long time to undress and folded his clothes neatly in a way he never normally did. He didn't want her to think that he was too eager. She laughed at him then and pulled him on to the bed where he fell on top of her.

'I'm sorry ... that wasn't very elegant,' he said. She tilted her chin up towards him and kissed him.

'There,' she said, 'that wasn't so difficult, was it? And see, this is yours too.' She took his hand and placed it in that mysterious dark place between her legs. He felt for the parting in the nest of hair and then his hand stopped.

'I'm not sure I know what to do.'

'I do,' she said, and dropped her own hand to touch him where no one had before. 'You see ... you are doing it all by yourself,' she said, laughing gently.

The room filled with the noise of their whispers and sighs and the soft slap of their bodies. When finally he let out his breath in a low shudder the blissful peace was shattered by a harsh cry from the minaret outside.

'*Allah Akbar, Allah Akbar.*' The imam's voice boomed through the window of the room.

'Praise be to God indeed,' Nick said as they both broke into helpless giggles. But when he rolled away from her he knew that his life would never be the same again.

He had thought that his heart would burst. He didn't have the words then to tell her how he felt just as now he could not think what to say in his letter. He wanted to tell her about the swampy feeling he got when he thought about her, but that didn't sound romantic. Back then he had been able to pull her head on to his chest and stroke her cheek.

'God almighty, Nick, what have you got to tell her today that you didn't tell her yesterday?'

Nick took a deep breath. 'I am trying to tell her how much I miss her.'

'This is crazy. What are the chances of the two of you meeting again anyway?'

'Just leave me alone, will you?'

My dearest Jeannie,

I do hope you are well and will soon be on a ship following me out of Katani. We are continuing to get better. Billy is even a bit fat like he was before the war. My arm is coming on grand with just a bumpy bit where the bones joined. I can't wait to get back to Oz and for you to be there too. I have so many ideas about the things we might do together or perhaps you might like to visit Ireland and meet my family?

Nick lifted his pen and looked at the words he had written with surprise. Yes. He would like to take Jeannie back to Westmeath and introduce her to his father. He could also imagine telling him about Syria and the friends he had lost. The old man would understand the confusing mixture of grief, relief and guilt that he felt about surviving when some of his friends had not. He would like Gerald to meet his 'cobbers', his mates who now snoozed on the deck in the still heat of the afternoon, their shirts off, enjoying the motion of the old ship and the lullaby of the engine. And to meet Zach, the boy who now lay beside him and who had curled his body into a tight ball so that his back was arched against Nick.

'Look, mate, I'll finish the letter later. Sorry I snapped. You wanna play chess?' he said as he tried to keep hold of the feeling of contentment that his memories had fed.

'It's OK. I understand that your friends now take second place to your new girlfriend.'

'Steady on young man,' the sergeant said. 'That was uncalled for. Sure, isn't it Valentine's day? Let the lad write his letter.'

Zach got up and wandered over to the ship's rail where, with one foot on the lower rung, he smoked and stared at the horizon.

For the next fortnight, as they sailed towards Singapore, the men reluctantly complied with the military drills, turning up on deck to reveille at 7 am for morning prayers and a hymn, accompanied by the Gunners band. Colonel Dunlop, a benign doctor and no lover of military red tape, encouraged a relaxed shipboard life. Deck football and a silly game where a large balloon was passed between the legs of each team were played as the sun went down. This time Nick enjoyed them, and wondered why he had found the very idea of such things so abhorrent on the *Jervis Bay*. Zach did not join in. Nick told himself that it was because he had had such a tough time in Syria shouldering everyone's pain in Aleppo. It was no wonder that Zach might have come to resent Jeannie and the other nurses with their cheerful efficiency. Zach had done the hardest part of keeping them alive after all.

The ship's sirens screamed and the loudspeaker cracked to life: 'Battle stations; enemy aircraft and subs; all troops to make ready; gunners to gun positions.'

'What the fuck,' Shorty said, tucking his bony legs underneath him. He rubbed his eyes, and stared stupidly at soldiers rushing past him in the commotion. 'What fucking enemy?'

Mindlessly the Aleppo boys followed the lead of Sergeant Maloney, rushed below and pushed their limbs into scratchy uniforms. Minutes later, it seemed, they were all back on deck, fully battle dressed and armed. The decks seethed with soldiers and Nick concentrated on staying beside Zach, Billy, Piper and Shorty. Hundreds of men now stood on the deck in absolute silence. The men who were by the rails stared over the gunwales, scanning the endless sea. A tense silence fell over the ship and all that could be heard was the sound of the waves swishing past the bow. Occasionally a soldier pointed excitedly, imagining that he had seen something, but no aircraft or ship approached them. As dusk fell they were stood down and the men descended to their bunks for an uneasy night.

'It's probably nothing,' Shorty said. 'Just the bloody navy being windy.'

'Do you think he's right, Piper?' Billy asked. 'I told me mam I'd be home in a fortnight. It's her birthday, see.'

Piper looked nervously at the sergeant. 'You'll be home in no time, Bill.'

The Aleppo boys shuffled into line the next morning and stood neatly to the right of the sergeant. 'Ship's company! *Attenshuuun*,' roared the sergeant major, glowering at Shorty who was still complaining that his cruise home had been interrupted. Colonel Dunlop raised his hand in a lazy salute. He shot a mildly exasperated look at the bellowing sergeant major but maintained a deep frown in place of his habitual smile.

'At ease,' he said as his arm lowered. 'Good morning men,' he hesitated. 'I have today received orders that we are to divert to

Sumatra. We are ... uh ... expected to engage the Japanese and defend the island. Medical officers will report to me immediately. Otherwise you will get instructions from your own COs. We will reach Oosthaven in Sumatra tomorrow at 1600 hours.' He paused and looked at the paper in his hand. 'American artillery and the Third King's Own Hussars will join us there. We shall be under the command of Brigadier Blackburn.'

'I thought we were going home,' Nick said. This can't be happening, he thought and looked wildly at the sergeant for reassurance.

'This will be over in a jiffy,' Sergeant Maloney said. 'Everyone knows the Japs haven't got an army that could get this far. They've been tied up in China for years. They'll never get around Singapore.'

'Remember, they didn't think much of the Vichy either,' Nick said. A sensation he remembered from when they moved across the Litani shifted in his stomach. He had plans now. He had to get back to Jeannie. A tiny bright glimpse of what the future might hold had opened for him: a farm, with sheep and cattle and children, and it was being snatched away. He had seen the blood of his friends seep into the earth, and heard them cry in terror, afraid to die. He didn't think he could go through any of that again. He didn't think he would be able to walk into the enemy and fire his rifle, expecting every second, with every fibre of his body, that a bullet would hit him. Fear gripped him tighter and harder than anything he had felt in Syria.

'Shit Zach. I don't know if I can do this again.'

Zach put his hand on Nick's arm. 'Stick together. Like the last time,' he said.

'You'll be fine, lads. You're old hands now,' Sergeant Maloney said. 'Nothing will be as bad as the fort. This is just a sideshow. We'll soon be on our way home.'

The next morning, Nick and Zach stood beside each other stamping their boots and shifting the weight of their backpacks. The *Orcades* dropped its anchor a couple of miles from the shore, a wide bay with searing white sand, fringed with palms. On the quiet command of Sergeant Maloney the men moved towards the edge of the deck. Nick stepped over the void and lowered himself down the ladder on the side of the ship. Facing the black hull of the *Orcades* he felt an urge to cling on to it, to embrace its shiny bulk like a limpet. This ship was supposed to bring him home, not deliver him to some new terror, and he did not want to leave it. A smaller ship drew alongside to ferry them into the harbour and the guttural voices of its Dutch crew sounded strange, belonging to a colder place. Nick's stomach heaved although the sea was calm and his armpits prickled. He prayed silently that he would not be sick. He could hear the distant sound of the roar of aircraft and looking over the bow of the skiff to the horizon beyond the beach he saw parachutes gliding and rocking to the ground like dropping seed heads against the violet sky. Half an hour later, their boat tied up on a wharf that thronged with soldiers and coolies in batik sarongs. As he and the men from the *Orcades* disembarked and shuffled into untidy lines a fat man in a crumpled linen suit, waving a cane, shouted orders at the local men. Nick recognized a few words of the Malay that his mother had taught him in the nursery.

'*Cepat bodah*! Hurry up fool,' the man said, taking a swing with his heavy leg at the back of a retreating coolie. Boxes of tinned food, tins of milk powder and sacks of rice were being loaded into baskets, wheelbarrows, vans and lorries, as if time were running out. Native eyes stared sullenly at the men coming off the boat.

An aircraft flew low over them and the tiger's roar from its engine blotted out the noise of the bustle on the pier. It rose into the sky, banked to the right and came around for another look before maintaining a course for the east of the island.

'It's a fucking bomber,' Shorty said. 'Don't think the sarge is right about the Japs not getting this far – they seem to be here already.'

A thundering boom brought everything to a stop and tangerine and crimson rent the sky to the east. The explosion set off a series of dull thuds. It seemed to Nick that no one knew what to do and they waited for an order, any order.

'We're going back to the ship – we can't hold the island,' the sergeant said eventually. 'The Japs have bombed our positions on the far side of the island and taken the oil terminals and the airfield. We have to destroy the port so they can't use it. We're going on to Java.' Back on the Dutch boat, they bounced their way to the *Orcades* and the rip in the sky from the explosions the far side of the island folded back into the velvet of the encroaching evening sky behind them.

'Doesn't look good,' Nick muttered, 'or that we'll be out of here in a jiffy.'

'What about me mam's birthday?' Billy muttered into his lap. Even Piper had no words of comfort for him.

They reached Batavia the next morning. Purple volcanoes wrapped around the port, smouldering and reeking, their lower sides carpeted with soft green jungle. This time the *Orcades* was able to tie up alongside but the men were kept on board for two days. Again, nobody seemed to know what was happening and a glimmer of hope ignited in Nick that this had all been a huge mistake and that they could now go on to Fremantle and Melbourne. On the second morning they stood again in neat rows, as if for a royal inspection, as thick warm rain plinked off the metal funnels and the rails of the ship.

'It is my painful duty to inform you that yesterday Singapore was surrendered to the Japanese Imperial Command.' The new brigadier had a stiff moustache, which he stroked occasionally when he spoke. His voice was clipped, his vowels airy and he looked down his nose as he spoke but he managed to look almost embarrassed as he delivered the news. Although supposed to be standing to attention in the presence of the new brass, the ranks crumpled as each soldier turned to his neighbour in disbelief. 'Tomorrow we shall disembark. There will be some reorganization to allow for loss of transport, stores and weapons. We *will* hold this island against the Nips, whatever the cost.'

But if Singapore has surrendered we can't hold out here, Nick thought. Singapore with its famous guns was supposed to stop the Japanese from getting this far west. The brigadier reminded him of his father with his chin in the air at the breakfast table, denying that his cattle were dying of starvation. What was it about these men? Why couldn't they see the world as it was, instead of only how they wanted it to be?

'Christ, we've only got fifty rounds of ammunition,' Piper said later as they prepared to leave the ship.

'At least it's for the right weapon this time,' Nick said with a weak attempt at a smile, but his friend didn't see the humour in it.

Ten days after they had disembarked and moved inland to make camp in the thick jungle Nick was leaning with his back against a ditch that ran along the road to the bridge at Leuwiliang. It had rained nonstop since they had left the *Orcades*. Nick took off his boots and once again squeezed the water out of his socks. His toes were white and shrivelled. The last time he had been this scared there had not been enough water – here, all was green and wet. Fat drops slid from greasy leaves and a warm trickle ran down his back and dripped between his buttocks. A sallow captain with a high-pitched voice, whom Nick vaguely remembered being on the gunner football team, had told them that they were in a defensive position, although Nick wasn't sure what that meant. Were they waiting for someone else to make the first move? Did it mean they were not going to mount a crazy assault like the one on Fort Merdjayoun? Zach lay against the ditch beside him.

'Should make you feel at home, all this rain,' Zach said getting to his feet. 'Time to patrol ... c'mon, get up.'

'Jesus, we've been up this road twenty times,' Nick grumbled. 'This is another shambles.'

'No, this is different.' Zach pulled himself out onto the road on the vines that covered the ditch. 'The Dutch are sure that there are no Japs within a hundred miles. Mind you, they're relying on the morning paper, apparently.'

'This is not a fucking joke. Why don't those colonial bastards have any intelligence? If there are no Japs here, why can't we move forward and secure the island instead of skulking in wet ditches with orders to move back into the mountains if necessary?'

'We've to hold this position. And those stupid Dutchmen have ignored Blackburn's orders and demolished the bridge so we'll have to find another way across.'

The rain stopped the following morning but the steam, which rose from sodden clothes and pixie blankets, was so hot and thick that it made it difficult to see beyond the small clearing in which they were camped. At first they heard a low growl of heavy engines from the direction of the road on the ridge behind them. As it came closer Nick could hear the squelch of wheels making their way through the mud. Then came a burst of mortar fire from further down the river. Nick and the other soldiers of 'A' Company sprang to their feet, grabbed rifles, ammunition and helmets and flung their bodies into the ditch beside the road. A few minutes later two tanks emerged out of the clammy gloom and stopped on the other side of the broken bridge like dragons hissing and groaning in frustrated fury.

'Hold your fire. They haven't seen us. Back into the jungle!' The young captain waved his arm above his head and the men crouched slowly into the mist. They regrouped about a mile from the road. 'They can't get across the river for the moment so we have the advantage. We'll ford the river downstream and come up behind them. The Dutch seem to have done us a favour – not that they meant to, useless bastards,' said the captain as if he were discussing the half-time tactics on the soccer field. 'We'll wade the river and attack their flank.' It struck Nick that the man couldn't make up his mind whether to go backwards or forwards. Nothing he said sounded like they were holding a defensive position and his commands were full of boyish enthusiasm that could get them all killed. He remembered Smelly lying against the Syrian wall, and paying the ultimate price for such pointless gallantry.

Nick couldn't see what was in front of him. He pushed his way through thick wet jungle using his bayonet to hack it away. Slimy vines crawled across his face and bromeliads wiped his legs, leaving leeches to feed on them. His boots sank through rotting compost, which seemed to move underneath him. A green snake slithered into the black undergrowth, fixing him with its eye. He could hear the boom of other Japanese tanks pummelling to the right where he assumed 'B' and 'C' Companies to be, and the pip-pip of rifle fire. Downstream of the impatient tanks, which were still growling at the forlorn bridge, he followed Zach waist deep into the swirling chocolate water, his rifle above his head. Concentrating on his friend's back, he willed himself not to think about what was ahead of him or what had happened the last time he had followed Zach across a river.

The cloak of the jungle hid them as they approached the road and they dropped into the ditch alongside it. Nick could see enemy soldiers on the far side of the road in the trees beyond. How different they looked from the last encounter! These men were all alike, with almond eyes and short bandy legs. The captain withdrew the pin of a grenade, and, as if in a slow-motion dance routine, in unison the line of soldiers beside him pulled their grenades from breast clippers, lobbed them forward and climbed out over the lip of the ditch. They crossed the road and entered the thick jungle, from which bullets were now spitting at them. As they moved forward, the flashes of cordite from their rifles illuminated the dense foliage, making the world in front of them flicker like an old cinema reel. In front of Nick one of the bandy soldiers twisted and fell, and then another. More bodies were strewn in a crater to Nick's left where a grenade had found its mark. The captain held up his hand theatrically and the men halted and listened intently.

'The guns have stopped,' Shorty whispered. 'Maybe we got them?'

But when they circled back the road was thick with armoured cars, tanks and soldiers moving like a vast grey centipede towards the river.

'Think it might be the other way round,' Nick said. The captain waved his revolver in the air and once more they backed slowly into the thickening gloom of the jungle dusk.

They did as they had been told, and moved eastwards towards the purple mountains. A full moon hung behind the fringed hills, a bowl of silver in the soft tropical sky. The light transformed the jungle greens into black and white, a colourless world where the only noise was the swish of foliage and the soft crunch of their boots in the swampy soil as the men moved through the dense vegetation.

'We've been cut off from the rest of the battalion,' the captain squeaked, all pretence at boyish heroics gone. 'I'm afraid the radio is banjaxed – the best we can do is split up and hide out in the hills until we're relieved. That'll make it easier for us to get some food.'

Sergeant Maloney led his boys farther east along a low ridge to the right of which a narrow valley twisted through volcanic rock. Nick was relieved to be back with the men he knew so well without the distraction of the foolish captain. They camped in a clearing on the valley floor that night and ate the last of the dry biscuits and chocolate from their backpacks.

'What we lookin' for now, sarge?' Billy asked, squinting against a plume of smoke from his damp cigarette. 'I'm nearly out of smokes.'

'A kampong ... a village where we can get some food,' the sergeant replied. Nick saw a look of exasperation on his face that he did well to mask. Cigarettes were hardly a priority now. They had all learnt to look after Billy, especially Piper. He was the child in their midst but there were times when the sergeant must have asked himself what Billy was doing in the army at all.

'You may have to do without smokes for a while, Billy. Finding food is the most important thing now,' the sergeant said firmly but gently. 'And it won't be like sauntering into O'Casey's on Tullow Street and ordering a dozen eggs and a pint of porter,' he muttered.

The following morning they walked for two hours before they came across a small village of five attap huts straddling a stream. Three naked children stood in the mud, their black eyes pools of distrust. A bare-breasted woman emerged from the doorway and gathered the children to her.

'Husband?' Sergeant Maloney said as though she was hard of hearing. 'Food,' he said equally loudly and mimed putting something in his mouth. 'We have money.' He clanged some coins in his pocket.

Two men in sarongs, gathered up Indian style to expose their skinny knees, appeared like ghosts from the trees behind the huts. 'No food here,' one of them said in broken English.

'Fish?' Shorty suggested helpfully, jerking his head towards the stream beside them, which bubbled joyously over mossy boulders. He swung his long arm in an extravagant arc over his head as if he had a rod and was casting a fly.

'Fish for us,' the man said.

'We need food! We're soldiers. We've come to stop the Japanese taking your country!' the sergeant said.

'Dutch men already take our country.'

They fared a little better the next day and bought some cold rice from a farmer further up the valley. Over the next days, Piper bought a few duck eggs for an enormous price and a fellow from Queensland returned to camp, grinning from ear to ear, with a fat snake speared on the end of his bayonet. Nick taught them how to catch frogs and wished again that he had some of Tony's skills. He used some of the frog flesh as bait, which he put on a hook he made from the metal clasp from the strap of his helmet and caught a pale golden trout with rose spots.

'I'm starving,' Billy said.

'We're all hungry, son,' the sergeant said.

'I found some wild tapioca,' Piper said. 'We can boil it up in a helmet to make soup.'

The strange diet was making most of them ill. It was funny at first and Nick laughed as his mates got caught short and had to waddle into the jungle with their shorts around their ankles, but within a few days they were all sick. Their clothes started to rot and leeches sucked on their legs, blood running thickly down them like glaze on a ham. Mosquitoes attacked at dusk and dawn. Poor Billy attracted them the most and came up in angry red lumps, which he scratched all night until they began to ulcerate and run with pus. Zach moaned in his sleep, muttering deliriously. *'Mamma. Entschuldigung, Mamma.'*

'What's he going on about?' Piper asked

'God knows, but he's burning up,' Nick replied with his hand on Zach's brow and looking to the sergeant for help.

'Look fellas, we can't go on like this. It's up to each of you but I say we go back towards Batavia and try to return to the battalion and see what's going on. What you think?'

No one had any doubt that the sergeant was talking about surrender again. Since they had moved into the jungle, the hope that the Allies would hold Java, drive out the Nips and they could all go home spluttered and died. Billy started to sniff and Piper put his arm around him. Some of the men turned away and walked into the wet green mass to compose themselves. Panic gripped Nick. I can't be a prisoner again, he thought wildly. He had barely survived it the last time. Might he be better to try and hold out here, eating frogs and wild tapioca leaves? He took Zach's arm.

'What do you think, mate?'

'I can't stay here, Nick. I have fever. I won't make it.'

Sergeant Maloney's group was the last of 'A' Company to walk into the camp where they found the rest of the men from the *Orcades*. The others had already been there for a fortnight, when unknown to the men in the jungle, Brigadier Blackburn had surrendered. These last free men walked through the gate with their hands above their heads. Their uniforms were in rags, sores blotched their legs, dirty beards hid their faces and they were thin and hungry. Zach had one arm hung over Nick's shoulder, and he was shivering violently. Flies buzzed around the tennis-ball-sized holes in Billy's legs. They looked about them fearfully. They had all been prisoners of the Germans in Aleppo.

Twelve

JAVA

The camp had been a school before the invasion. Wooden desks were stacked against a wall and a blackboard still bore the faint chalk marks of an algebra equation. A full-size dirt football pitch stretched along the road to the village but a barbed wire fence now surrounded the perimeter with bamboo guard towers every 150 yards. Mango trees shaded the old playground full of dishevelled and dejected soldiers. In one corner a padre read aloud to a small group of men, while others sat on upturned crates playing drafts. Nick wondered if he too was becoming delirious like Zach when he heard a gramophone playing the 'Moonlight Sonata'. Some men, stripped to the waist and in filthy shorts, were digging holes amongst the trees. Old crates had been put over some of the holes to make seats and bamboo screens pushed into the ground around them. A clearing had been ripped out of the jungle and attap longhouses stood in a line in this brash new space.

Cross-legged soldiers sat threading the long leaves like forest elves darning gigantic socks. Others tapped their finished work into bamboo frames to make walls as their mates draped palm fronds along bamboo poles for the roofs. Hundreds of bicycles were stacked haphazardly against all available wall space and trees. As Japanese soldiers pushed and prodded Sergeant Maloney and his band towards the school building, Nick looked up and saw some of the men of 'B' and 'C' Companies he recognized, who stopped what they were doing to raise their hands in a disconsolate wave. The other survivors of 'A' Company whooped and clapped when they recognized Nick and his friends.

'Good on you, we thought you were goners,' one of them shouted. They were brought to stand in front of the steps of the school. *Founded by the Dutch Lutheran Church* said the sign. A very short Japanese man in an ill-fitting uniform emerged from the door, accompanied by half a dozen guards. The hair on his square head was close-cropped, stiff and bristly, as though his yellow skin had been brushed with a thin wash of blue black. He was the colour of a bruise. He held a whip tucked under his armpit and a long curved sword hung from his belt that, given his height, almost touched the ground. He would have been a grotesque circus geek but for eyes that danced with energy and intelligence.

'Salu! You muss salu Japanese officer! You muss salu all Japanese soldiers!' he screamed. He was perched on the top step so that his eyes were level with those of Nick and the others who stood in front of him. Sergeant Maloney adopted a truculent pose, squaring back his shoulders. He made no effort to salute, keeping his hand firmly by his sides.

'Look mate ...' the sergeant said. Instantly the Japanese officer withdrew the whip from under his arm and swiped it viciously across Sergeant Maloney's face, once to each side in a brutal figure-of-eight motion. The sergeant's face bloomed slowly into two red stripes of blood bubbles. For a few seconds no one moved and then Shorty made a stride towards the sergeant, who was bent over holding his bleeding face. A guard lifted his rifle over Shorty's head and brought it down heavily against the back of it. Two more soldiers, who had been standing beside the officer on the steps, leapt on top of Shorty's falling frame, pushing him to the ground, then set to kicking his head and belly. The noise of the guards' boots against Shorty's ribs was sickening, a soft thud followed by a dull crack as leather hit bone. More guards emerged from the shadows and in seconds Nick and his companions were surrounded, looking down the barrels of rifles pointed at their heads. Then there were a number of deadly clicks from the platform as revolvers were cocked.

'You salu now!' the officer yelled. Sergeant Maloney lifted his hand in a movement that would not have passed for a salute in his own army.

'Salu ploperly!'

'Atten*shun*,' Sergeant Maloney managed to say through clenched teeth as blood moved sluggishly down his cheeks. He snapped his hand to his head, and Nick and the others followed his lead.

'An evely time, an' to evely Japanese. Unnastood?' Sergeant Maloney nodded and hung his head. 'If no hat, you muss bow. If hat, salu. You are shameful people. Japanese soldier never taken alive. This is code of honah. You have no honah.' He turned and went back through the door from which he had emerged only a few short minutes before.

Silently, Nick and the others gathered around Shorty's groaning body.

'Jesus sarge, these are even worse than the last lot,' Piper said. A tall man in a white coat approached and Nick was glad to recognize Colonel Dunlop from the *Orcades*.

'So you've met Captain Hatu,' the colonel said, squinting professionally at the bleeding stripes on the sergeant's face. 'It is not worth taking him on. Trust me, if you don't salute or bow to every one of these bastards you'll end up with a beating or worse. We're very short of medicine and food so you have to avoid unnecessary injuries.'

'What about the rules, sir?' the sergeant asked.

'They're completely deaf to any discussion about the Geneva Convention or any of that stuff.'

'But we could escape, sir,' Piper said.

'Well, a couple of Dutchmen got away a few days ago. Of course, they know the island, the language and all that. They may have a chance.' The colonel shrugged. 'But first we had better get you sorted out as best we can. Bring this lanky fellow to the hospital tent over there and we'll take a look at that face, sergeant.'

'It's just a scratch, colonel. I'm fine. I've had worse in a game of hurley. But young Billy there has bad sores on his legs and this young man,' the sergeant said, pointing to Zach, 'malaria, I think.'

'Right, and I will want to see all of you in due course,' he said, smiling cheerfully. 'And go and get those beards off, they just encourage the lice.'

Zach, Shorty, Billy and the sergeant followed the colonel.

'I'm game if you are Nick, and you speak some of the lingo don't ya?' Piper asked. 'Just as soon as we get Billy fixed up of course,' and he set off behind the sergeant towards the hospital tent.

Nick stood alone. He fantasized for a moment that this was all a dream. Hadn't he been through this shit already? Jeannie had said that the things that had happened to him in Aleppo might come back to haunt him, but she had also said that she would be there to help him. She wasn't here and he knew that this was not the ghost of a previous nightmare but that he was in the middle of another one.

'May I see my mates?' Nick asked, poking his head into the gloom of the hospital hut. The colonel looked exhausted. Sweat ran down his face in the hot and airless hut.

'Of course, son,' he said, looking up from the man he was tending. 'It's a bit rough in here if you're not used to it.' Nick stepped in and adjusted his eyes to the dark. The smell of rotting flesh was overwhelming. 'Most of the men on this side have dysentery and I have nothing to treat them but washed clay. And the fellows over here have tropical ulcers. They're the worst, I'm afraid. They smell very bad. I'm going to have to treat your friend Billy for the same thing. Would you be able to help? It's not much fun, I'm afraid.'

'But I know nothing about medicine, sir.' Nick looked nervously down the lines of sick men.

'It's just a question of holding him down.'

God, thought Nick, I have walked into hell. Zach was lying at the far end, mercifully by the other entrance where the air was fresher.

'Hello mate. How are you?' Nick asked and he recognized that his tone was the one people use when visiting the sick, a forced joviality mixed with embarrassed relief that he was not the one lying there. Zach opened his eyes but it took him a while to focus on Nick's face.

'Better thanks ... a bit better. They've given me some quinine. I could do with some more.'

No wonder the colonel looks exhausted, Nick thought. He has to play God here in this stinking death house. 'Look Zach, not everyone's going to make it here. The colonel is doing his best, poor bugger. He gave you the medicine because he must think you will make it otherwise he wouldn't have wasted it on you. It's up to you now.'

'It's my guts ... you know how it is. Could you help me to the latrine?' His mahogany eyes welled with embarrassment. 'I hate to ask, but I just can't make it on my own, and I don't know the lads in here to be wiping ... how you say ... my arse for me.' He smiled weakly.

'Course – here, put your arm round my shoulder.' Zach had never been a big man but now he weighed less than a child. They hobbled towards one of the attap screens, both of them trying to ignore the acrid stench. It was only months ago that Zach had flown into a panic when revolted by a similar stinking hole in Merdjayoun. As Zach gripped his arm, Nick grieved at how this man, who had been destined for a fine career as a heart surgeon like his father, was now dragging his feet along the red dirt and routinely squatting publicly in such places.

He settled his friend back onto his rustic bed where he soon fell asleep. The doctor appeared silently at his side. For a big man he moved very quietly in the shadows of his awful tent. 'The quinine will bring his fever down,' he said, 'but I can't give him any more and he will need food – protein and some leafy vegetables. He's very weak. Look, you need to understand that the way to survive here is to look after your friends. No man can survive without his mates. If a fellow gets sick, you share food and then he'll do the same for you if you go down.'

'We've been through something like this before, sir. He's already saved my life. I'll get the food he needs,' Nick said firmly. He scanned the tent for Billy. 'Where's Billy? What do you want me to do?' he asked the colonel.

'He's in the other hut. Come, we'll get this over for the poor chap now, shall we?' Nick followed the doctor into an adjacent hut where the smell of carrion was even stronger and made his eyes run and his stomach heave.

'We have to take away the rotting flesh,' the doctor explained as if he were giving a biology lesson. Nick swallowed. 'Otherwise it will rot right through to the bone and then we'll probably have to take the leg off. As you can imagine I really don't have the tools here to do that ... or the anaesthetic.'

They passed a skeletal man who Nick recognized from 'A' Company. There was a plate-sized ulcer on his calf, the sides of which were crusted and the inside black. The bone was visible, luminous in the middle of the ghastly hole.

'You see? The black dry tissue is dead; the yellowy brown stuff is dying. Sometimes maggots can help stop the rot.'

Christ, Nick said to himself. His gullet rose again.

'Now Billy, here's your mate,' the doctor said gently, putting his hand on Billy's shoulder. 'We have to clean the ulcers, otherwise ... OK lad, here – bite on this and grab your friend's arm.'

To Nick's horror, the doctor extracted a teaspoon from his breast pocket and held it over the flame of the hurricane lamp that hung from the bamboo pole above Billy's bed. Leaning over the festering leg, he began to scrape the pus and putrid flesh from the ulcers. Billy, writhing under Nick's body weight, spat the cloth out of his mouth, and screamed until the doctor lifted the spoon from its gruesome job to put the unlikely instrument of torture back in the flame. Billy sobbed and then screamed again when Colonel Dunlop dug the spoon back into the dirty flesh of his leg. No one in the beds alongside paid any attention to the diabolical scene. When it was over Billy lay back exhausted, tears still running down his sunburned face. Nick rushed into the daylight and threw up, retching violently. Pulling himself together, he went back to sit with Billy, whose wounds had been dressed with banana leaves bound with his puttees.

The following morning the news that more prisoners had been found in the jungle buzzed around the camp. The camp bell clanged harshly for everyone to assemble on the football pitch. 'This didn't happen when you lot came in,' a fellow from 'B' Company said. 'Something's up.'

Captain Hatu stood on a dais in the middle of one side of the pitch, the prisoners in six rows in front of him. Two men, one fair and the other dark, stumbled between four guards as they threaded their way from the gate to the platform.

'It's the two Dutch fellas who got away last week,' someone said in a hoarse whisper. The two men were badly beaten, their faces bruised and swollen and their lips split. They stumbled through the lines of prisoners as the guards behind them pushed and prodded them with the ends of their rifles. The only noise came from the flies hovering in black clouds over the latrines in the clearing beside the football pitch. Even the monkeys and the parakeets seemed to sense the occasion and were silent. The party halted in front of Captain Hatu who lifted his cane and, with the same vicious efficiency he had used with Sergeant Maloney, made a savage cut to both sides of each man's face. No sound came from his victims. The blond man fell onto his knees where his body swayed. With a nod from Captain Hatu, one of his henchmen pushed the second man to the ground to join him.

'Water,' the first to the ground croaked.

Captain Hatu drew himself up to his full stunted height and swept his eyes across the tattered men in front of him.

'These men try escape!' he shouted. 'No plisoner can escape. If plisoner try, he shall die.'

The release of breath from the rows of prisoners was simultaneous but they continued to stare spellbound at Captain Hatu as he stepped off the dais and withdrew the shining arc of his sword. Raising it in front of his face, he bowed to it and clipping his heels together, lifted it slowly with two hands above his head. Sunlight danced on its rim. With a primeval grunt he brought it down on the neck of the fair-headed Dutchman. The man's torso crumpled on the red earth as his head with its tight blond curls rolled grotesquely away before coming to a wobbly stop. A moan gurgled from his companion's mouth but it was cut short by the same blade seconds later. Hatu bowed again to the bloody sword and handed it to a smiling Korean at his side. In the front row, several of the prisoners in front of Nick were doubled over, vomiting. Two had fainted. Nick's mind jammed. There was a whirring noise in his ears. For an instant he thought that it must be a macabre piece of theatre that he was watching and then the horror hit him and his breath shortened and his knees weakened.

The air seemed to tremble with collective horror. Nick stood stock still. Blood pulsed thickly into the dust from the severed arteries of the two bodies, snakes of vivid colour in a khaki world.

Climbing back onto the platform, Hatu pulled down the front of his uniform over his stomach. 'You see I mean what I say. If any plisoner found escaping he will be executed.' With a nod to the colonel, he marched down the gap through which his victims had moments earlier been forced to walk. Colonel Dunlop was the first to recover, absently grabbing at the stethoscope around his neck as if it might save him.

'Bring those poor fellows inside. Padre, please come with me,' the colonel said at last, his face ashen. 'Good God, the man's a madman,' he muttered.

Later, the shock of the earlier bloody scene still visible on his face, the colonel addressed the Australians who stood in untidy rows in front of him. 'There is no question of any escape attempt. The risk is too high. You've all seen for yourself what they'll do if you get caught. If you did get away from the camp, there's no way of getting off the island. Some of you already know that survival is not possible in the jungle. The local people are disaffected against the Dutch and cannot be relied upon for help.'

Nick looked up at Piper, wondering whether he would consider disobeying the colonel, and saw only his own despair reflected in his friend's face. The colonel had seen the exchange. 'It looks tempting because the guard duty on the perimeter of the camp is lax,' he continued firmly. 'There are no locked gates here, but don't let that fool you. It's lax because they know you won't get far. Any questions?'

'Don't we have a duty to try, sir?' Piper asked.

'You have a duty to try to survive. That is all. Is that clear, soldier?'

'Yes sir.'

As Nick sat reading to Zach later that day, the colonel approached and led him away by the arm. 'I can't ask you or even authorize you to leave the camp after what happened this morning, but, as I have said, this boy needs proper food. He simply won't recover on the grey rice that the Japanese give us.'

Nick had eaten the slimy ball of rice husks that morning because there was nothing else but had retched at the sulphur smell and the rats' droppings in it. The men who had been here from the start told him to eat the maggots and weevils – protein, they said – or donate them to the hospital hut.

'He'll develop pellagra, and that's not a comfortable end, I'm afraid. We call it the four Ds: dermatitis, diarrhoea, dementia and death.' The colonel sighed. 'So do what you can, son, will you?'

It was easy to get out of the camp at night. The Japanese and Korean sentries had no love of the jungle in the dark and there were few guards on the towers. The fence had a number of holes and Nick found one in the shadow of the mango tree where he could slip out without being noticed. He suffered none of the terror he had experienced at the fort or at the bridge. He had imagined back when he was training that it would be the other way around, that he would be brave when his blood was up, when in the heat of battle, and that courage would fail him when he had to act alone, in stealth, with the prospect of a sure death if he was caught.

He was not the only one leaving the camp at night, when the wispy clouds drifted away from the volcanoes to dull the moon. On the night of his first excursion he recognized two Dutchmen, civilians who had surrendered immediately when the Japanese landed. One was small and dark with black eyes like currants and the other a huge man with stiff blond hair. They were clearly surprised to see Nick out there on the jungle path and his own body jolted with fear when he saw them until he realized that they were not the Japanese. They all laughed nervously and backed into the black jungle on their separate ways. The following morning the two men approached Nick. He raised his hand in a friendly wave to them, a salute to fellow thieves, but they did not return the gesture.

'You'd want to watch yourself out there at night,' the dark one said.

'I can look after myself, thanks,' Nick replied.

'You are not getting the point. We don't need amateurs out there fucking it up for the rest of us.'

Nick was rattled. It was enough to avoid being caught without these men threatening him. He had no option but to go out there and get food for Zach, so he practised the few words of Malay that his mother had taught him in that other world of the nursery in Westmeath, and made friends with a fat Indonesian man who showed none of the reluctance to trade that they had witnessed before with the people in the jungle. With some of his last pay packet from Katani he bought a tin of salmon, some fruit and *gula malacca* fudge and carried the spoils back to camp. He propped Zach's head in the crook of his elbow and spooned the vital nourishment into him. The next night he bought some condensed milk and the following one some eggs.

A week later he could see an improvement in Zach: there was a bit more flesh on his bones, and he could get to the latrine on his own.

'I'm better now. You'll get yourself killed out there, you dumb klutz. Enough already.'

'I really don't think the Japs give a damn about us trading with the locals. I'm sure they know we do it. It's trying to escape that is forbidden. So as long as I don't stray too far from camp it will be fine. My fat friend in the village, Adi, is a decent scout and doesn't overcharge as he might. I think our money will last a while.'

Some nights later he took the now familiar path towards the village wondering what he might be able to find for Zach this time – some spinach or limes, perhaps. Adi stood, as usual, in the clearing in front of his plain wooden house, which was built on stilts in the local way with ducks and pigs rootling underneath.

'*Petang yang baik,*' Nick said as he did every night. This time Adi had no greeting for him but jerked his head to one side towards the edge of the clearing.

'I have nothing more to sell to you,' he said, avoiding Nick's eye. Nick tried to gauge his expression through the gloom but Adi continued to look nervously towards the trees at the jungle's edge. Nick's stomach lurched. Christ, the Japs are here. It's a trap, he thought. He followed Adi's jumpy glances. The two Dutchmen stood under a papaya tree, smoking. No Japs, he thought, and his pulse slowed.

'What's the problem, Adi? We are friends, *rakan-rakan,* are we not?'

'Must streamline supply,' Adi said as if he had rehearsed the words. 'I sell only to these men now,' he said pointing towards the men under the tree. 'You can then buy from them.'

'What the hell?'

'Hello Tottenham,' the small dark one said, 'let's introduce ourselves properly, shall we?' The two men drew close. In the watery moonlight the mouthful of even white teeth belonging to the tall one glowed. 'I am Hendriks and this is Meyer. We don't want any trouble here. And we have told you already how it is. We know these people, you see. We have lived here all our lives and speak the language, so it makes sense that we be the ones to make sure this fat fellow here doesn't rob us all blind, see?'

'No I don't see. This man has been very fair in his dealings with me.' There was an unpleasant curl on the man's lips. His partner stepped into the space between him and Nick, squaring back his shoulders.

'Look, you're only a kid. You don't know anything about the real world,' Meyer said.

'And what's to stop *you* putting the prices up and making a killing?'

'You ought to be more careful what you say, boy,' Meyer replied and took another step closer to Nick. Nick wondered if he was going to have to put his fists up and fight the brute. He thought fleetingly about what Adi would do if it came to that but Hendriks had put his arm out to restrain him and Meyer stepped back. 'Of course we're all in this together,' Hendriks said while Meyer shook himself down, trying to disguise the aggression of a moment earlier.

'And how can I be sure that when we need food or medicine that it's not going to cost an arm and a leg?'

The two men exchanged a quick look. 'Well, we can give no assurance on any prices. The fact is that Adi here is not going to do business with you any more. Understood?'

Nick looked at the Indonesian, who shrugged and splayed his fat fingers.

'You seem to have sewn him up all right,' Nick said. He walked back to the camp empty-handed and angrier than he had ever been.

And the prices did go up. The Aleppo boys' pay ran out after a month. Nick's watch was the first of their scant possessions to go, then Zach's and also his mouth organ. Nick twisted the signet ring angrily off his finger. His mother had given it to him on his fifteenth birthday, the family motto, *Ad Astra Sequor* – follow the stars – engraved on its surface. It seemed ridiculous now, following the stars in this miserable hole. Thinking about his family was like opening a book with no words. He couldn't see their faces clearly or remember their voices. Occasionally he jolted awake at that holy time of the night when even the lizards were asleep and he was sure that it had been Kate's laughter, like the faint tinkle of bells across water, that had woken him, but it was gone in a moment and he could not recapture it. He hoped his mother would forgive him for selling the ring. None of his cobbers wore signet rings and so it was a thing that embarrassed him. It was therefore with a churning mixture of remorse and relief that he handed it over to a Korean guard and used the money to buy four hens, which they kept in a pen beside their hut. He saw other fellows selling the gold out of their teeth for a couple of pats of peanut butter and a plug of tobacco. Hunger gnawed at them every day and they talked about food with a relentless self-persecution. What were they going to eat when they got home?

'Me mam's steak and kidney pud and a big apple pie with custard,' Shorty said, 'and then the same again and four pints of beer for afters.'

'One of me Dad's T-bone steaks,' Piper said.

'Pot roast, *latkes* and *Hamantaschen*,' Zach added.

'What the bloody hell is that?' Shorty asked.

'Potato cakes and cake filled with poppy seeds and honey. It's a special cake for Purim.' Nick had heard some of this before but laughed at the look of blank incomprehension on Piper and Shorty's faces.

'It's when we celebrate the defeat of Haman,' Zach continued, as if that explained everything. 'Haman was going to kill all the Jews in Persia. Also we celebrate the deeds of Queen Esther and her cousin Mordechai who saved the Jews.'

'Pity she's not hereabouts to get us all out of this mess then, isn't it?' Shorty said. 'And bring some of her cake with her.'

'I'd like to feed those fucking Dutchmen to the pigs when we get out of here,' Piper said. 'I saw that big bastard wearin' me dad's watch today. Thieving bastards!'

Zach recovered slowly but after two months in camp all of them were skeletal and their vertebrae jutted out like steps on a ladder. Their shoulders looked like coat hangers, and their eyes sank into deep shadowy sockets. But while they still had something to barter the Aleppo boys kept each other alive by supplementing the glutinous grey rice and few beans their captors provided with a tin of condensed milk now and then or some Chinese spinach, a few wild limes or some coconut oil with which to make rice rissoles. Nick caught frogs and they hunted for snails. A cobra furnished a one-off feast.

Thirteen

WESTMEATH

Eleanor was coming home on leave and Kate went to Dun Laoghaire to meet the boat. She did not immediately recognize her mother as she stepped out of the terminal and when she realized that the tiny woman who looked like a dormouse in her big brown overcoat was Eleanor, she blinked in shock. Her mother's eyes, normally so deep and steady, were fluttering nervously. Her face was strained, her cheeks as colourless as the white of her hair. Kate searched it, but Eleanor would not hold her gaze and looked away, fidgeting with the buttons on her coat.

First had come the news that Gerald had been swept up after the fall of Singapore and was now a prisoner in Changi. Poor Poppa. He had only just arrived in Malaya when the Japanese invaded and it was all over. Kate wondered why her father had gone to war at all. She supposed that he felt that he could not stay at home when the RAF had been so keen to recruit Mummy. His pride would not have let him do nothing when his wife and two sons had already joined up. And now Nick was missing again. His unit had last been heard of in Java months ago and there had been no news of him since. Kate told herself firmly every day that life was fair and that the God she knew would not allow anything else to harm Nick because he had already been through enough. He was lost before and had been found and he would be found again, she said to herself, and to heaven, just in case God had forgotten the rules.

She could see that her mother had not managed to convince herself of this. Everything about her appearance told her that Eleanor now thought the worst. Fear howled through her like a banshee. Kate had not seen her mother since the news came and each of them had faced their worries for Nick alone: Kate in the big house by the lake and her mother in a cold RAF station in Lincolnshire, where young men were lost every day. Kate had ached for her mother to help her stay strong and wished she would come home to be with her and the Little Ones. But now as Kate took in her mother's wretchedness she felt her own resolve crumbling. She had clung to the belief that no news was good news, telling herself firmly that Nick was still alive, scolding herself when her faith faltered. Her poor mother was in a place where death was commonplace and Kate understood with mounting dread that Eleanor had worked out the odds of Nick being found alive after all these months. She could fall into that black hole herself. Every day was a battle to keep the flame alight for herself and for the Little Ones and it would be harder when her mother had so clearly snuffed it out. Early mornings were the worst: for a few blissful seconds before she pushed off the fog of sleep she forgot that Nick was missing, and then it hit her as if someone had punched her in the chest.

One postcard from Gerald arrived months after it had been written. Parts of what he had said had been crossed out and it was clear that he had not been allowed to write what he wanted. Eleanor and Kate had seen the reports in the newspaper last year when an American escaped from a Japanese camp in the Philippines. He had told the world that prisoners were being starved and beaten to death and that none of the rules of the Geneva Convention were being honoured. Eleanor had cut the article out of the paper and read it again and again.

'Put that horrible thing away, Mummy. You are only distressing yourself by reading it. Poppa is safe. Didn't his card say he was fine and was being well treated?'

'He is not a young man any more, Kate, and he can be so argumentative. He is bound to get himself into trouble.'

'They will respect him for his age and his rank, Mummy. You have to think positively.'

'And what if the Allies bomb Singapore?'

There was little Kate could do to comfort her mother. She simply wasn't listening. She had used up all her strength when Nick had been missing in Syria and this time she could find no place for hope.

'And why haven't we heard anything about Nick ... one way or the other?' Her mother seemed to be talking to herself. She was rocking her body slowly back and forth in her chair and staring out the window across the lake.

'Now come on, Mummy. We'll have no talk like that. You thought the worst before and you were wrong. Nick is a survivor. The Japs have camps all over Indonesia and he is bound to be in one of them. The Red Cross say they simply have no idea of how many prisoners may be there.' Kate ran through all the reasons why Nick was alive that she rehearsed every morning as she lurched awake. They didn't seem so convincing now when she voiced them out loud for her mother. 'And now we have Tony's visit to look forward to,' she said firmly.

Tony was also coming home for a few days' leave. He was taking a detour – probably without permission – from his journey to

Canada, where he was to be posted. He had become a pilot officer and was being sent there for advanced training. Kate thought that sounded very grown up for the boy she had known four years ago. Surely the visit would cheer her mother and drive away the anxious pain of the all the months of waiting for news?

Despite her mother's misery Kate found it difficult to hide her excitement about seeing Tony and busily set about preparing for her brother's return. She brought Firefly in from the field and brushed her coat to a silky shine, even though the mare was old and fat now, and she polished the dirty tack in the barn so that it would be just as Tony had left it. She wanted to have the house the same as it was when the boys went away so she brought her father's chair back up to the morning room and tried to cut the lawn but the grass had grown too long and was indistinguishable from the field beyond it. There was nothing she could do about the new holes in the roof or the broken walls around the fields. Gutters had fallen from the buildings in the yard and lay on the weed-choked cobbles. The garden was overgrown with brambles shrouding the shrubs. The shutters on the top floor of the house were closed all the time now because crows, flying blind against sun, had broken the windows and there was nobody to fix them. They didn't need the top floor any more, Kate told herself firmly, and besides, Tony probably wouldn't notice.

But her mother did not share any of Kate's enthusiasm for Tony's homecoming. Kate had thought that Eleanor would be proud of her son for earning his wings but the news had distressed her further. 'Oh God, please … please let him be sent somewhere safe. Let the war be over before he finishes training,' was all she had said to the windowpane, quietly twisting her handkerchief in her hand.

Over the next two days as Kate prepared for Tony's arrival her concern about her mother grew. Eleanor sat motionless in the window seat of the disused drawing room for hours every day, oblivious to the cold and damp, staring at the far shore until it got dark. She no longer did the *Times* crossword and showed little interest in the younger children. Maggie and George, already well used to their mother's physical absence, gave up trying to persuade her to tell them stories or help them with their homework.

The morning Tony was due to arrive Eleanor went to town to get her hair done. Kate had thought that this was a good sign but when she returned and Kate pushed open the door to her bedroom to see how she was, Eleanor was rigid in the chair, staring at her reflection in the looking glass on the dressing table.

'What is it, Mummy?'

'I have got so old Kate,' she smiled weakly. 'I have marks like duck's feet around my eyes.'

'Don't be silly. You look lovely. I love your hair.'

'I'm sorry, darling. I'm not doing very well am I? I just feel paralyzed sometimes by not knowing where Nick is ... whether he is ... and I worry about Poppa. Where is it all going to end?' Eleanor took a deep breath. 'I will pull myself together. You are right. Poppa will be kept out of the worst of it where he is. And Nick is not on any KIA list. I must hold on to that thought. And as for Tony, hopefully they will use him to shuttle Americans across the Atlantic. Go on down. I'll be there in a while.'

Kate took her mother's position on the window seat. The room was as cold as always and there was a smell of dead mouse but Buster, the old terrier, his muzzle now grey and a ring of white framing his eyes, was unconcerned by it. He snored at Kate's feet, exhausted from ratting in the barn earlier when Kate had been brushing out the dried droppings stuck between the cobbles. Jim had only just left for the station in the old Riley and she knew she would have a long wait, as the train would not be in Kildare yet. But she was determined to be the first on the steps when Tony arrived so that she could get a good look at him before he saw her. They might be strangers now and he so changed that she would need a few moments to prepare. Would she know what to say to him? They had been children when they last spoke and so much had happened since then. Peering again out of the dusty window, she willed the car to come, not sure if she was nervous or excited.

The train's brakes screeched and startled Tony, who had been soaking up the lush softness of the Midlands fields. He had missed Ireland so much that he felt almost drunk at the thought of being home and seeing his mother, Kate and the Little Ones. He grabbed Aunt Virginia's battered suitcase and jumped onto the familiar platform. The station looked smaller than he remembered but otherwise nothing had changed and he was comforted by the sameness of it. And there was Martha's Jim standing at the door, flat cap in his hand and pressed to his chest. His back was more curved than Tony recalled and the bend in his short legs more pronounced but his eyes still shone with merriment.

'Master Tony! Jesus, it's good to see ya. You growed up, sir!' he said, and stooped to wrench the suitcase from his hand. Tony threw his arms out to embrace the older man.

'It's good to see you too, Jim. None of that "master" business, do you hear? That's all done with these days. And I'm big enough to carry my own bag,' he said, punching Jim playfully on the arm.

The old man led the way through the station to the car.

'When did you learn to drive, Jim?'

'After the master – I mean your father – left for the Emergency, the children had to get to school and we had to get to the shops and that … it seemed a waste to leave her in the shed,' Jim said, puffing up his chest. 'Petrol's hard come by though.' He pulled out the throttle, put his index finger to his nose, and winked. 'Unless you know a man, of course.'

Tony imagined that his father would be horrified if he knew Jim was driving his precious motor. But he was also sure that neither the old man nor indeed any of them had given a thought as to how Kate, Jim and Martha and the Little Ones would manage to carry on with ordinary life: how they would get to school or keep themselves warm and fed. They had all rushed into uniform without a backward glance or concern about those who had been left behind. What on earth would they have done without Jim and Martha? Kate and the Little Ones were very young to have been abandoned. Kate was just fifteen when their parents left, the same age he had been when he and Nick had set off for Australia. But he had Nick to look after him.

The engine spluttered into life with a sound that brought him straight back to that day when he had been squashed into the back of the car nearly four years ago.

'I was sorry to hear about Master Nick. It's a worry. He'll turn up. You wait and see. The mistress is very vexed about him.' He paused and shot a nervous look at Tony. 'It might be best not to mention him.'

'Yes ...' Tony was taken aback. 'It must be hard for her with Poppa away as well.' He had not imagined what it must have been like for his mother either. 'How're things here, Jim?' he asked eventually. 'Is it hard to get news of what's happening? Many of the lads have joined up, I suppose?'

Jim gave Tony another sharp look. 'Not that many – it's not talked about much in these parts, you know.'

They bumped along the old road towards Dalystown in silence. How could there be no talk of the war? Tony thought. In Australia there had been talk of nothing else. Jim's silence seemed to be a reprimand that he had raised the subject at all. He took the turn through the gates too quickly and the left wheel bounced into the big pothole that Tony remembered had always been there.

'Stop for a bit, Jim, would you? I just want to look at the old place for a moment.'

Jim pulled up the handbrake at the curve where the house came into view. Behind it, the skin of the lake was taut and shone yellow and blue. The horse chestnuts stood to attention along the drive, their candle flowers stiff in salute, and the fields were a carpet of buttercups. The Virginia creeper was still green and draped down the walls on two sides of the house like the flaps of a child's cap. The paint on the front door was peeling, as it had been when he left, but the mossy granite steps in front of it now lay crooked, squeezed up by the frost.

'It'll be good to get some help,' Jim said, following Tony's gaze to the holes in the garden walls. 'It's hard on my own, though Miss Kate's a topper to work of course. Last couple of days she's been cleaning out the barn and working in the kitchen with Martha. There's no end of bread and cakes being got ready for ye.'

'We'd better not keep them waiting then, had we?'

The grit on the stone slab beneath the front door screeched and the old door stuck on it. Tony could see Kate losing patience as she attempted to lever herself around the edge of it. 'Tony!' she squealed, rushing towards the car before it had stopped. Then, half running, half skipping, she was beside him, hanging on to the handle. She pulled open the door.

'I can't believe you're really here! Was the train late? I've been waiting and waiting.' She flung her arms around her brother.

'Wow. You're nearly as tall as me now,' he laughed, amazed.

'That's not saying much,' she said, 'you've hardly grown at all.' She stepped back and examined him as if she were buying a horse.

'Your ears still stick out the same, I see,' she said, and leant towards him for another hug. It wasn't just that Kate had grown taller. She was no longer a gangly tomboy and he was momentarily shy with this unfamiliar russet-haired beauty. He didn't know what to say but Kate's small talk flowed. She was gabbling about what she wanted to show him, how she had cleaned out the barn and brought Firefly in from the fields for him to ride, the cakes she had made for him from the rationed sugar, the tennis match she wanted him to play. Maybe she is nervous too, he thought. As the chatter washed over him he dropped his shoulders. She was still the same Kate.

The small dog he remembered so well burst out from around the corner of the house barking bossily, clearly outraged that he had missed the car coming up the drive. Tony swallowed hard. 'My God it's Buster. Hello boy. Don't you know me? What age is he now, Kate?'

Maggie and George followed the dog. They were arguing about whose turn it was to feed the hens. When they saw the car where they did not expect it to be, they stopped abruptly and stood staring silently at Tony and then looked to Kate for help. A soft blush bloomed on Maggie's face.

'Hello Tony,' Maggie said, looking at him through thick lashes, her big brown eyes like pansies, 'welcome home.'

'Come here. Aren't you going to give your big brother a hug? I don't think I can call myself that any more. You've grown so much!'

'Yes I am going to be the big one in the family, worst luck,' Maggie said as she stepped awkwardly towards Tony and shyly proffered her cheek.

'You too George?' Tony said but George seemed disinclined to come any closer to him and remained rooted to the spot.

'Go on George, don't be silly,' Kate said.

Words started to tumble out of the boy. 'You have to come to the garden. Mummy's there with tea and cake. It's walnut. She said it is your favourite. It's mine too. She's waiting for you. You're to come now,' Tony did not think he had ever heard George say so much at the one time. He still made no move to embrace him or make any sign that he knew him at all. 'This way,' he said in an imperious tone that suggested that Tony would not know the way, and he disappeared back around the corner of the house.

Tony followed his sisters and brother and as the lake came into view he saw his mother sitting in a wicker chair with her back to him, looking out over the water. A teapot and cups were placed on the table beside her, which was covered with a fresh tablecloth with rosebuds on it that Tony knew was the one that was kept 'for best'. He was overcome with the sweetness of belonging in this place. But when his mother stood to greet him, he felt his smile freeze. Her chestnut hair was now white and she was so much thinner than he remembered, her tweed skirt hanging loosely on her hips. Her pretty shoulders had rounded with age and her face was pinched. He felt another stab of guilt that he had been so caught up in his own worries about Nick and his father and his determination to become a pilot that he hadn't thought about what his mother was going through with her family splintered. He should have come home earlier. He forced a smile and bounced up to her.

'Darling boy,' she said, her voice breaking. 'How *are* you?' Eleanor stood to hug him. 'How I've missed you.'

'Mummy,' Tony said, forgetting that he had resolved to call her 'Mother'. He held on to her, feeling awkward as she shook with big silent sobs.

'Dear me, I mustn't be so silly,' she said, and pulled her handkerchief from the sleeve of her cardigan to dab at her eyes.

'Cake, cake,' George demanded, watching Tony and his mother in a curiously detached way. 'Can we have it now? We've been waiting all day.' It occurred to Tony that George had probably looked forward more to the rare treat of cake, made with the precious rations of sugar, than to him coming home. He could hardly blame him – after all George was only ten when he and Nick had left for Australia.

The cake did not disappoint. It had sunk in the middle as Martha's cakes always did and had a delicious undercooked wetness to it. Walnut cake, Tony thought, always produced for our comings and goings. Second helpings were devoured and in minutes it was gone, whereupon Maggie and George immediately got up to leave.

'Hey, I'll show you how to catch frogs later if you like,' Tony called after them, feeling that he needed to make a connection with these children he no longer knew. Maggie shrugged. 'If you like,' she said. George ignored him.

'You know, I'm not sure if they remember me,' Tony said to his mother. Eleanor said nothing and drew deeply on her cigarette.

'They remember you all right, they just don't know you any more. I'm afraid the two of them have got very used to doing their own thing. Their manners are not what they should be,' Kate said, looking at their mother who was gazing at the swans on the lake and not listening.

'Did you hear anything more from Singapore, Mother?' Tony asked.

A shadow scudded across Eleanor's face as if a crow had flown over her. 'Yes, there's a postcard from Poppa but it doesn't tell us anything. It's only a filled-in form, really, and he wrote it a long time ago. He has ticked the boxes to say that he is well and that he is being properly treated. I imagine he had to do that. It's obvious that he's not allowed to say anything else but at least it means that he is still alive, or he was when it was written.'

'Dad's an old soldier and he's a tough old bugger, Mother. You have to remember that. He'll be fine,' Tony recognized the tone Uncle Herbert had used to tell him Nick was missing the first time. He remembered what Jim had told him in the car about how distressed she was about Nick and decided not to mention his brother just yet.

Eleanor squinted at Tony as the blue smoke drifted into her eye. 'I've never heard you call him "Dad" before. I suppose Australia taught you that,' she said absently. 'I hope you're right. I don't trust myself to think about any of you in danger. I mean, how is your father coping with being a prisoner, especially if things are as bad as they say they are? He can be so ...' she searched for the word, '... difficult. He's sure not to obey the rules.' A ghost of a smile softened her face. 'How long will you be in Canada, dear?'

'About three months, I think. I need to get some more hours on a new aircraft.'

'Which aircraft is that?' Her eyes were following a line of geese over the far shore.

'It's called a Lancaster. It's a heavy bomber.'

Eleanor's head snapped around to face him. 'Oh no, Tony. No. No. Not that.' Her voice had risen almost to a wail. A long silence followed. 'I know it's a bomber,' she said eventually, almost in a whisper. 'Where do you think I've been spending the war? You never said you were joining Bomber Command. I had so hoped you might fly despatches or something like that. That would be enough, you know? Nobody can say that we are not doing our bit already.'

'You mustn't worry, Mother. These are great kites. They are very fast and can do all sorts of things in the air, like corkscrew. They're very easy to manoeuvre, not like the Blenheims or the Sterlings. This bird can cruise at over 200 miles an hour, so the old Luftwaffe won't be able to catch us. And it is well armoured, so the ack-ack won't stop us either. We're going to win the war with it.'

Eleanor was scratching hard at the back of her hand. She appeared to be forcing herself to breathe deeply and slowly.

'I know, so the boys tell me, the ones who ...'

'Have you been in one already?' Kate asked, glancing nervously at her mother.

'Yes, though I wasn't flying it. I was in the dickey seat.'

'What's it like? Tell us about all the things it can do.' Kate added. Tony understood that this was his cue to reassure their mother that this airplane was different from the ones she waved off the airfield in Lincolnshire every night and counted as lost the next morning.

'It is unlike anything we have had in the air before. Fast and handles really well. You can't really move around, so on long flights they say we have to pee in a bottle.'

'Tony, really!' Eleanor smiled weakly, at last.

'Sorry Mother, forgot where I was for a moment,' he said. He grinned widely and winked at Kate. 'Flying is the best feeling in the world. The roar of the engine is like a thousand tractors. It's a bit like being squashed in the back of Poppa's car but you can see all around you because the cockpit is a glass dome. It can get bloody cold but they have come up with a heated flying suit for us. Then, all the instruments are in front of you, compasses and altimeters and things like that so that you can see if you're level in the clouds when you can't see the ground. There's a gunner on the top behind me. He's called the mid upper and there's another in the tail. They are really the lookouts.' He stopped abruptly, realizing that they would want to know what these men were looking out for. He hurried on. 'Then there's a wireless operator, a navigator, a flight engineer and a bomb aimer. That's the crew.' He registered the look on his mother's face. 'But then you know all that don't you Mummy?'

'And there's no co-pilot?' Kate asked.

'No, but the wizard thing is that there's armour plating behind my head to make sure I don't cop it.'

'And that's the only plating the aircraft has,' Eleanor muttered.

'And you'll be in charge of all of them?' Kate's face was incredulous. 'It seems only yesterday that you were running up and down the passages of the basement waving your arms up and down, pretending to be von Richthofen.' She picked up the teapot and poured tea into her mother's cup. 'Aren't there a lot of people who have nothing to do with the war who could get hurt with all this bombing? Somehow I'm not sure it's very chivalrous,' she said, biting her lip.

Eleanor rose abruptly from her chair, her tea untouched. 'I'm going to take Buster for a walk.'

'We'll come too, shall we Tony?' Kate said, jumping to her feet.

'I'd rather go alone,' Eleanor said coldly.

'Of course,' Kate stammered. 'I'll take the tea things in later,' she added quietly.

Kate and Tony watched their mother disappear into the runty trees by the shore with Buster darting around her heels.

'I wish I hadn't said that. She's not herself. It seems that the shock of everything has finally caught up with her. It's strange, but the first time we didn't know where Nick was she made more of an effort ... for us, I mean.'

Tony looked at his younger sister and his face grew serious.

'I have to do this, Kate. I think Mummy knows that.'

He comforted himself with that thought. It was too late to change the settings of his life. After Nick went missing in Syria all he had thought about was how to get into the air, into the war. Now that his father was a prisoner and Nick was missing again it was even more important to him. He had to make up for the fact that Nick and his father could play no further part in it. He was sorry that he didn't know Maggie and George any more but that was something he could put right when it was all over.

'She's clearly not happy about you joining Bomber Command. You have to understand that she sees at first hand every day what it's like. I don't suppose you could fly something else, could you?'

'Look, you're not to worry about me. This airplane is almost invulnerable. I'm really excited about flying it. We can beat the Germans by getting rid of their armament factories and oil terminals and the like and if a few civilians have to take to the roads and stop the military moving about so much the better. At this rate we'll be in good shape for an invasion next year. It's very important. Old Winston is pinning his hopes on us apparently. Besides, it's the only war we have at the minute.'

'And what about those ordinary people asleep in their houses? Are you sure they won't suffer?'

'The Jerries didn't worry too much about ordinary people in the Blitz, did they? We're only bombing military targets. We've got pretty accurate now,' he said, his voice clear with conviction. 'Look, Kate, I can't sit by and do nothing, especially with Dad and Nick unable to do their bit.'

'You realize that this family can't win the war by itself, don't you? Sometimes I think we believe that we Tottenhams are the key to beating Hitler,' Kate said, smiling. 'Actually I have some news for you too. When Mummy goes back to England at the end of this month, I'm going with her. I'm going to be a radar mechanic with the WAAF. See, I have to do my bit too.'

Tony's mouth dropped open.

'What? You? Join up?'

'I don't know why you find that so extraordinary. I'm eighteen next week. You're not the only one to have grown up, you know. This is what we do in this family, isn't it?'

'What about Maggie and George?'

'Jim and Martha have already been more like parents to them than Mummy and Poppa have.' She forced a smile. 'I'll be fixing the radar masts, so that you will always know the way home. I was specially selected. Not many girls get chosen for this job. Just as well I have a head for heights.'

'You were always good at climbing trees.' He was unable to contemplate Kate not being a child any more.

Fourteen

LINCOLNSHIRE

Tony rolled over in the narrow bed and looked up at the ridges of the tin roof above him. The coke-burning stove was cold and the hut was freezing. He pulled the rough grey blanket under his chin and adjusted his greatcoat on top of it. His dreams had been full of flying, twisting his aircraft away from German night fighters, banking the Lancaster steeply and falling away to starboard to evade the enemy. But he had no actual experience of this because they had not yet been on an operational flight. Since returning from Winnipeg in September, it had been endless exercises back and forth over the Lincolnshire Wolds and he was sick of the sight of the cratered fields around Wainfleet. They had consistent bull's-eye hits in target practice now and other crews who didn't have their strike record had been sent out over Germany already. Tony and his boys were getting tetchy and wanted their first blooding. It was March and the weather was finally beginning to pick up so there had to be more operations shortly and then they would get their chance to drop a few real bombs. The waiting was excruciating and Tony knew that he and the crew needed to get into the thick of it to settle them down.

He looked down the line of beds at the sleeping mounds of his crew. Beside him Jimmy Bradley was on his back, his long thin body rigid but his jaw slack. He looked even more like a bird in his sleep, his skin taut over the hook of his bony nose. The crew had nick-named him Toucan on their first day together, which had become Touc for short. Touc was the navigator. Everyone on the crew knew that this disappointed him, as he had wanted to be a pilot. He was older than Tony, a taciturn man who was a lab technician back in Melbourne with a good degree, whereas Tony was acutely aware that he had left school at fifteen. But Touc showed no hint of begrudg-ery towards Tony as his skipper and it never occurred to Tony that he might lose face if he turned to the older man for support, and so he frequently did. Perhaps Tony had been lucky to get his wings. Everyone at home had always said that he was steeped in it but he suspected that Aunt Virginia's tuition in old-school manners had helped. It seemed that these things still mattered.

Tony got up and went over to the chipped enamel bowl in the corner and stabbed his toothbrush through the thin layer of ice that had formed across the top of the water. In the bed beside the basin, Jan Wikovski – Wiki, a wiry Pole from Krakow – lay, in contrast to Touc, in a tight ball. He was so accustomed to being wedged in his cold garret at the tail of the aircraft that he stayed in that position in his sleep. He was muttering to himself. Tony smiled. When on the ground Wiki chattered incessantly, awake or asleep, to make up for the lack of contact he had with the crew when flying; he had to sit on his own over the raging fire of the aircraft's exhaust, a beacon for any night fighter. His partner, the mid-upper gunner and Wiki's friend Jonesy, a Welshman from Sydney, slept on his other side. Both men had joined the air force as ground crew or 'erks' and had not expected to end up as aircrew. He couldn't imagine what it might be like to think that you were going to spend the war safely on the ground in a hangar and then be 'volunteered' for the most terrifying job in the air force. For Tony it had been different: he had always known that he would fly and as he had tried to explain to his mother and Kate, he could never have sat on the sidelines of this war.

Steve Matthews, the bomb aimer from Broome, held his hand up to the metal pipe that jutted into the tin roof from the cold stove, putting each bandy leg gingerly on the cold floor. They were bent from his younger years as a jackaroo on a cattle station where he lived on his own 300 miles from anywhere.

'Christ, it's bleeding freezing,' Steve said. He was a tough sandy-haired man who shared little of his lonely life with any of them. Tony had felt foolish when he tried to tell Steve that he too had been a jackaroo. His life at Twin Oaks was nothing like the hard and isolated one that Steve had lived. Sharing a billet with these strangers must be difficult for Steve, Tony thought. He was a tricky man to get to know but had a sharp eye and a cool head, which was all that was needed for a good marksman.

'Well light the fuckin' stove then and do something useful for a change. Bull's-eye, me balls,' said a man with a genial, lilting voice from the end bed. Paddy Foley, originally from Dublin, was the wireless operator. At twenty-nine, he was the eldest by a distance and so they called him Daddy. He had a photograph by his bed of his pretty wife Sile and their baby son, who were now on the other side of the world in Orange, New South Wales. Tony wondered what had made a Dubliner volunteer for the Australian air force. For Tony, Nick and his parents had already joined up and he felt left behind in Australia. There was no question but that he would follow Nick.

There was a groan and a hiss from the far side of the hut. Charlie Roberts was the only Englishman on the crew and had joined them when they arrived in England last September from Canada. He was quiet and reserved and spoke with a polished accent acquired from a public school in the Home Counties. A few years older than Tony, and like Touc, he had also hoped to be a pilot but had been turned down. Tony wondered if Charlie had applied to fly because that was what his father wanted him to do. The reserved Englishman had told him in an unguarded moment that his father had not spoken to him for months after he failed. He seemed to be afraid of his old man, a veteran of the last war, and yet desperate to please him at the same time. He reminded Tony of Nick. He wore a permanently unsettled look and Tony knew that he was prone to being airsick, which, for the most part, he had been able to hide from the rest of the crew. As a flight engineer, he could stand behind the pilot and on the other side of the spar from the navigator and so out of sight. He told Tony that he loved the Lancaster, and talked at length about the ingenuity of the Avro design to a point where the other crew members raised their eyes to heaven. Tony hoped that this was the only reason that Charlie seemed nervous about what the aircraft could do and not some real fear that would emerge when the going got tough.

'She'll not take that,' he said time after time in training when Tony dropped the nose or started to weave to show the gunners how they might get a better view of a fighter slinking along below.

'Of course she will,' Tony would answer, 'sure, didn't you say this was the best flying machine in the world?' Charlie could get a sweet tune out of any aircraft and they might well have need of those skills to nurse home a damaged kite. These days, being airsick was no reason to ground a good man.

Tony was happy to fly with these men and each of them appeared to be as anxious as he was to get their first real job. Last week, on another training exercise a couple of miles out to sea from Wainfleet, they had attracted the attention of a lone Messerschmitt. Wiki got a round off at him. Tony plunged the Lanc into a dive, down port, change, up port, roll, up starboard, roll, down port. It was a perfect corkscrew and they had lost him. They were ready.

He dressed and sauntered over to the mess for breakfast. It was early and there were few pilots about as the previous night's sortie had been Munich and so the boys were not yet home and those flying that night had no need to make a tense day longer by getting up early. He pushed two sausages and three eggs around the plate. The aircrews were fed like fighting cocks here. He stirred three lumps of sugar into his tea, which made him think of George and Maggie and George's excitement that there had been cake for tea. He would have liked to send some of the sugar home to them and they could make as many cakes as they wanted and perhaps think of him when they were eating them. A dark-haired Englishman with a flamboyant moustache sat down opposite him. An overweight brown labrador flopped at his feet.

'I say, aren't you one of those Aussie fellows who bunks with their crew? All a bit convivial, isn't it?'

'Actually, I'm an Irishman,' Tony said genially.

'Oh well, that explains it.' The man grinned. 'You can never tell what an Irishman will do. You're all so unpredictable. Different set of rules, really.' Tony smiled. He was used to this sort of thing and it was easier to assume that his breakfast companion meant no harm by it.

'I've been with most of my lads for over nine months. We trained together in Oz and in Canada,' he said. 'We haven't had a chance to do anything yet. We're pretty fed up with target practice, I can tell you.'

'There's a big op tonight. I'd say the whole station will be out.' He pushed a piece of toast heavily laden with marmalade into the hole under the moustache. 'You sprogs will get the oldest kites, you know. If I were you, I'd try and find out early which one you are to fly and go and check it out. If it's your first op McNab will go with you.'

'Thanks mate, I really appreciate that.' Tony pushed away his plate and ran back to Hut Three, hardly able to contain himself until he could tell his crew.

He sat on the grass at the edge of the airfield beside the hangars, watching the erks loading the bombs into the gaping belly of a Lancaster, two Merlin engines on each of her tremendous wings. The early morning sun glinted off the glass of the Perspex canopy at the front of the fuselage, where Tony and the senior pilot would sit that night. The .303 guns extruded like twin proboscises. A tractor approached the aircraft pulling trailers, most of them loaded with 500 pounders and one with a bomb the size of a large sofa. Here was the cookie. Four thousand pounds of destruction with three delicate fuses on its nose. Dropping it was the real purpose of their mission. Tony wanted to see how much fuel they would load so that he might guess where the target for tonight might be. Fully loaded, the Lancaster could fly over 1500 miles, enough to get to Berlin – Munich even – and back, but it was clear they were not going there that night when the order was given to stop the pumps. He sauntered up to the aircraft.

'You flying with McNab tonight?' a sergeant with grease smears on his face asked him.

'Yes, I'm flying dickey.'

'First op?'

'Yes.'

'You want to have a look around?' He handed a clean cloth to Tony. 'You'll want to polish the hood, I expect – that's what McNab will do so you might as well do it for him and get some brownie points. He's flown two tours, and he's a stickler for making sure the kite is shipshape. Helps to even up the odds.'

'You know where we're going?' Tony asked.

'Nope, but judging by the amount of fuel you're for the Ruhr valley.'

The briefing room was in another tin hut the far side of the hangars. The crews sat together on the bench seats facing the central stage, a strange collection of well over a hundred or so men from all over the globe: Brits, Paddies, Kiwis, Aussies and Canadians but Tony knew that they all desperately wanted to know the same thing. Where were they going that night? Everyone hoped that it would not be Berlin, which was protected by a wall of searchlights, but anywhere on the Ruhr would give the airmen a similar reception. Tony's crew fidgeted on the bench beside him, lighting one cigarette off another. He supposed they might be afraid and who could blame them? He was excited and looking forward to getting the job done: to crossing the Kammhuber Line, busting through that network of interlocking night fighter and searchlight zones. They had practised flying in the box formation again and again so that they might stream through the German defences and he couldn't wait. The station commander stood up and the low rumble of male voices stopped abruptly.

'Good afternoon gentlemen,' he said, pulling back the curtain. The board read: *15 March, Stuttgart*. Some groaned. Tony scanned down the information:

> *H hour 23.15. Illuminating flares in target area at H6. Aiming point will be indicated with large salvos of more red and green TIs and kept marked by Pathfinder Force. If cloud obscures the target release point will be marked with flares red with green stars.*
> > *Bombing instructions*
> > *As ordered by Master Bomber*

Beside the blackboard was a map with a red line showing the dogleg route they were to take. Tony breathed deeply. This is it, he thought. He was barely listening to the WAAF officer who gave them a met report or to the intelligence officer who told them why Stuttgart had been chosen for tonight's operation. He heard the station commander wish them luck and the briefing room started to empty. Tony's eye caught a poster on the wall: it was a cartoon of a German soldier with his trousers down revealing a large bottom in undershorts covered in swastikas. *Let's catch him with his Panzers down*, it said.

'Look,' said Tony nudging Charlie, 'that's good, isn't it?' The Englishman shrugged and looked miserable.

As the shadows lengthened and the sky darkened in the mid-March afternoon, Tony and his crew in Hut Three clambered into their mustard yellow flying suits and pulled on their boots. Wiki slopped around the hut half dressed, his helmet flapping about his chin and the zips of his boots undone, trying to emulate the studied untidiness and devil-may-care swagger of the British airmen.

'Zip 'em up Wiki, so they stay on if we have to ditch.' Tony was conscious that this was not what his rookie crew wanted to hear as they pushed on their fur-lined boots, each pair stamped with a number one to seven. They all knew why the boots had to stay on and why the primitive method of telling one body from another might become necessary. 'Right chaps, let's have a run-through the ditching drill before the transport comes, shall we?' In for a penny in for a pound, Tony thought. 'We all know where I'll be ... at the controls,' he said with a silly pull of his face.

'Should bloody well hope so,' Daddy said and the others laughed politely.

'Yes,' Tony said patiently. It was hard for them all to understand that this was for real. 'Sutton harness secured. On intercom to Charlie and Wiki. You, Charlie?'

'On my back in the rest bed, hands on fuselage, feet to bulkhead. Knees well flexed. On intercom to you skipper. Sounds like a bloody dance.'

'Touc?' Tony asked.

'Seated on the floor in the middle. Back to spar, hands behind my head.'

'Daddy?'

'Sitting on floor to starboard in rest bed compartment. Back against bulkhead door. Hands at the back of my head at my ears. God knows why they think I can save my ears.'

Tony shot him a faintly exasperated look.

'Steve?'

'On the floor to starboard back to rear spar.'

'Wiki?'

'Lying on the floor with my *right* arm around Jonesy's neck ... buttocks to flapjack and legs over it – that is, skip, if I can get my arse out of the tin can I'm wedged into for my jaunt over Heligoland, freezing my bollocks off.'

'All right, all right, enough of the comedy act – look, we've flown together for months. If we stick to the rules we'll be fine. Right, we have about an hour I think.' Tony knew he should try and keep them busy but couldn't think of any way to distract them. Perhaps it was better that way, to give each man some time. Daddy wrote a letter, the picture of Sile and the baby in front of him on his bed. Charlie read his Bible. Touc sat outside smoking. Wiki and Jonesy goofed around the hut in a clumsy attempt at a slow waltz. Tony checked his parachute and his escape kit: Horlicks tablets, a map, compass, water carrier, soap, a razor and mirror, and a fishing line. He wondered what madman had decided that these were the things they would need to keep them alive. Then he reached into the drawer of the locker beside his bed, pulled out a twist of newspaper and opened it on the bed in front of him. The black horsehair was still shiny. Firefly's tail for luck. He rewound the newspaper and tucked it into his breast pocket.

At last the transport arrived to take them to the dispersals and they rumbled past the hangars to the line of waiting aircraft. Like the other crews, the seven of them sat smoking in the grass beside their aircraft. McNab was, as predicted, giving the Perspex another polish. When he had finished, he jumped down and came over to them.

'Right, boys, I've flown plenty with all of you and you are all fine airmen. It's my job to teach you the ropes on your first op. This is a longish trip. The toughest thing will be staying alert. It's very easy to lose concentration. I don't have to remind you that if any of you fall asleep that will be the end of your career and probably the end of all of us. You two gunners are our eyes and ears. If we see a night fighter before he sees us we have some chance of getting away from him. So I don't want any heroics with the pea-shooters all right? The intercom is our lifeline and not,' McNab paused to glance at Wiki, 'for chit-chat. We must be able to react immediately to anything the gunners see and they have to be able to tell us how to get away from trouble. Understood?'

'Yes skipper,' they said in unison.

'Right, let's go.' They buttoned their suits, zipped their boots and strapped up their helmets. Slinging the parachutes over their shoulders, they trudged over to the hulking shape of the Lancaster and swung one by one into the fuselage, while twenty other crews did likewise. It was as though the airfield was swarming with yellow ants crawling into giant horsefly carcasses. Wiki wedged himself into his capsule in the tail and Jonesy into his at the top of the aircraft. Both popped caffeine pills into their mouths, stuffed the rest of the packet into their breast pockets and pulled on three pairs of gloves. Tony felt a moment of intense affection for the small Pole who would be behind him gazing backwards for the rest of the night in the freezing cold, isolated from the rest of the crew up forward in the cockpit and fuselage. Tony had caught his eye as, with a rueful shrug, he stowed his parachute; there was simply not enough room for any of them to wear one inside the aircraft and each of them would have to scramble for it if they were going down. Tony saw him tuck a hatchet at his feet. Poor Wiki – did he really think he could hack his way out? Out of the corner of his eye he saw Charlie dart behind the hangar to be sick, but he was not alone. He knew that it took some fellows that way and that the build-up to the op and the waiting all day for the dispersal truck to take them down to the aircraft were intolerable.

McNab slid back the cockpit window and gave a thumbs up to the weary ground crew by the battery cart. Tony settled into the seat beside him. McNab lifted the starter button, pressed it down and a belch of grey smoke and fire coughed from the starboard inner engine, which blasted into life. When all four engines were running their great throaty roar masked all other sound and the aircraft throbbed with their power. Adrenaline pulsed through Tony's body. A memory of his father starting up the old black Riley and trying to get the heater to work suddenly washed over him. There was even less room here in the cockpit of the Lancaster than there had been in the back of his father's car. McNab checked the oil pressure, tested the throttles and checked the revolutions and the magneto drop. A sergeant on the ground handed the paperwork to Tony.

'Go on, you sign it son – put your name on the pages of history.' Tony scribbled his initials. He could hardly believe that he was finally going to fly a bomber over Germany.

'Engineer to pilot,' Charlie said uncertainly over the intercom. 'Rear hatch closed and secure. OK to taxi.'

'Speak up, man!' McNab said. He waved to the ground crew to clear the chocks and closed the window. Daddy's voice broke through the roar.

'Receiving you loud and clear. Strength nine.'

The three aircraft in front of them pulled their tails behind them like dull-witted dragons and each of them took its place in the queue at the end of the runway. As the lead Lancaster turned it stopped, as if deciding whether to go or stay, and then lumbered forward to face the runway. McNab and their Lancaster crept behind them, fourth in a line of twenty-one, bumping around the perimeter of the airfield. As McNab edged the nose around Tony could see the small crowd of ground crew and WAAF girls waving at the three aircraft already airborne with forced smiles on their upturned faces. He fixed his eyes on the instruments in front of him. The engines roared and the Lancaster lurched forward. The ground rushed past Tony's peripheral vision and at the very end of the runway twenty tons of clumsy aircraft, five tons of fuel and another five of bombs lifted, surprisingly gracefully, into the air.

They now joined hundreds of bombers over the patchwork fields of Lincolnshire, where the seagulls swirled behind the ploughs working to catch the last of the spring evening. Tony watched, mesmerized, as the swarm of aircraft grew magically from airfields all over the east of England. McNab and his crew of sprogs were flying as one of the lead crews and as they peeled off others stepped in behind them. A total of 863 bombers were flying that night in tight formation and they were so close that sometimes Tony could read the instrument panel of the aircraft beside him. It was like a swarm of angry bees, designed to drown the German radar system. And there was huge comfort in it. When Tony looked to his left and his right and the sky seemed black with bombers, it was easy to believe that they were invincible.

'Enemy coast ahead,' Touc said deadpan from the darkness behind them. His maps were laid out on the table behind Tony and McNab where Touc would spend the next seven hours trying to work in the enforced blackout with a pencil torch as his only light.

Exploding anti-aircraft shells dotted the sky around them like clenched fists. Tony waited for the shocks to hit the Lancaster. As the black puffs got closer, the aircraft bumped violently and shuddered. So this is flak, Tony thought. Another pretty mushroom bloomed in the sky beside him. It looked harmless, but he knew that if it got any closer it would punch a hole through the Lancaster and bring them tumbling out of the sky. As the light faded he allowed himself to drag his eyes away from the instruments and gaze at the star-studded purple canopy above him.

Two cold black hours later they climbed to bombing height for the long run into the target. Now they would have to fly straight and level and there could be no corkscrewing or clever acrobatics to avoid a night fighter until the bombs were gone. They were a sitting duck. In front of them was a dazzling web of lights, flickering with flak. The pathfinders had dropped their green and red tracers and they curled around each other like gypsy ribbons. Tony looked out of the cockpit at the show below with his heart thudding and eyes shining. A stream of incendiary shells came up towards them in a lazy red arc that increased in speed as it approached. It flashed past a few inches above the port wing so close to the hood that Tony winced. The shells seemed to be deflected by the airflow over the wing and curved away behind them, backlighting the rim of the wing with a fiery orange glow. Bizarrely, Tony was reminded of one of Kate's wildflower paintings.

'That was close, sir,' Tony said.

'Not really,' McNab said through gritted teeth.

Below them burned a pulsating, glowing carpet and a gorgeous display of soundless fireworks as the great roar of the engines blocked all noise. The blue lances of the searchlights stabbed the sky, split, came together again, stopped, reversed and splayed out, mercilessly searching the sky for these nocturnal predators.

'We've got to stay out of the cones,' McNab said, unnecessarily. They all knew that if a searchlight fastened on them the anti-aircraft fire would immediately follow. It was a deadly dance with the Lancaster in the middle. A Sterling exploded in a white and magenta flash 200 feet below them. Tony tried not to think of the men being incinerated and reminded himself that he was, as he had told his mother, lucky to be in a Lancaster.

'Bomb doors open, skipper.' Steve's voice was tense with concentration as he lay on his belly underneath them with a grandstand view of the ground below. McNab was throttling back and then accelerating as he tried to read the cones. Tony watched him intensely. It would be his job the next time.

'Bombs away, skipper.' Steve's relief was clear this time. The nose of the aircraft lifted steeply as five tons of bombs dropped from her belly.

'Flight engineer, re-trim please,' McNab said firmly into the intercom while he struggled with the stick, but there was no answer from behind the pilots' seats. Tony turned to see Charlie standing rigidly facing the wall of the fuselage, gripping one of its ribs. He was frozen, unable to move, his body shivering uncontrollably, mesmerized by the shuddering blue and yellow dials in front of him.

'I'll do it. Flight engineer is just a bit sick, sir,' Tony said, as he unclipped his harness to go back to the stricken man. As the aircraft levelled out, Tony put his hand on Charlie's shoulder and bade him silently to sit down.

'It's OK, Charlie,' he mouthed at him. 'Happens to lots of people the first time out.'

'Heading back. Let's get out of this shit.' McNab's voice was cheery over the intercom. 'We'll stay low. The Jerries will reset their radar to catch us on the way home. Set us a course please, navigator.'

Fifteen

JAVA

Weeks passed with every day dragging like the one before. Nick had been bored at home but it was nothing compared to this. The numbness of it sapped his energy and only hunger forced him off his bed. He planted tapioca and bought tomato and onion seeds and potatoes to plant alongside the hut he shared with the Aleppo boys. Soon all the other huts followed his example and small gardens sprang up everywhere. But gardening was not enough to fill the long days; the tedium was made worse by the fact that their guards applied 'Tokyo time' and forced them to get up in the middle of the night for Tenko, or roll call, which meant that much of their 'day' was in the pitch dark.

'That's the end of that Bible,' Piper said, ripping the last page from the disintegrating cover. He placed the thin paper on the crate in front of him and carefully laid a line of dried cherry and papaya leaves along the middle of it. His square chin was set rigid and he held his tongue between his teeth in concentration.

'I don't know how you smoke that shit,' Shorty said.

'It gives me something to fucking do, doesn't it,' Piper replied. The normally placid butcher had grown very tetchy as the weeks passed. It was hard for any of them to cope with the torpid boredom of their daily lives but Piper was distraught about Billy, whose leg still festered in the hospital hut.

'The padre said you had to read them first, it being the Holy Book and all. He was rightly vexed about you smokers using them pages as cigarette paper. Never seen the man so upset. S'pose he's at the end of his tether, with all the fellas dyin' and the like,' Shorty said. He seemed to realize what he had just said and looked apologetically at Piper.

'Fuck it Shorty,' Piper said. 'I don't feel like a smoke now.'

'I'll read the bleedin' page for ye's and give ye's all a laugh,' Shorty said, gently moving Piper's stash of dried leaves to one side. He lifted the page to his nose so he could read the tiny print. 'Habb ... a ... kuk,' he said, stumbling over the name. 'Zeph ... an ... iah. What kind of names are those for Christ's sake? I never learned any of them in Sunday school.'

'Here give it to me, I'll read it for you,' Zach said. 'I'll tell you the story and make Jews of you all.'

Zach read and Piper, Shorty, Nick and the sergeant listened. No books and no paper, no food parcels and no medicine either. Just like the last time, Nick thought. They were forgotten again.

As he had done in Aleppo, Nick pictured his family grieving for him: a dejected little group gathered at the church at the end of the drive in their moth-eaten Sunday clothes. He imagined them traipsing back up to the house, perhaps with the few neighbours who might come to support them. They would pull the dust sheets off the furniture in the drawing room, even light a fire, and bring the decanters in from the morning room. They would try to give the impression that they used this room all the time but the smell of damp and mothballs would still clog the air. He imagined his father standing with his back to the Italian fireplace, his arm stretched across the shelf, his chiselled features like a matinee idol catching the light from the bay window overlooking the lake. As the drink drove away his hangover and fuelled his vain boasts, Nick pictured him waving his hand expansively and speaking of the improvements he had made to the front meadow and the great beasts he had bred from a new bull. It gave Nick little comfort to know that from now on his family might begin the process of recovering from his death whilst he still had to face it. So many had died already: dysentery, beriberi, pellagra, tropical ulcers and starvation fought a daily battle to win the war for souls and every day he saw men give up the will to live.

Billy died three days after Colonel Dunlop took off his leg. There were not many volunteers for cemetery duty but Nick and Zach had promised Billy that they would bury him. Piper was inconsolable and lay on his bed staring at the fronds of the roof above him, refusing to accept that his friend was gone. 'I can't see him put away like that, fellas. You understand, don't you? You'll do it for me, won't you? Do it proper,' he said.

There was only one coffin, which was used to carry every man who died to his final resting place and then brought back to camp for the next one.

'At least we can put him in the ground in his blanket,' Zach said as they lifted Billy's emaciated body into the box. Nick thought of the dogs, cats and little birds he and his brother and sisters had solemnly buried at home. They were not much lighter than poor Billy and there had been shoeboxes for them.

'I'm sorry, boys I'm afraid we must have the blanket back. We'll have none left if we bury everyone like that ... please bring it back,' the colonel said firmly.

As they dug into the thick red clay the ground was so wet that water poured into the hole with each shovel of dirt they lifted. They laid Billy into his seeping grave, no more than a parcel of bones, the yellow parchment of his skin stretched across them, his mouth and nose plugged with khaki. His hair was still flaming red. The brown water gurgled as it closed over his face.

'Oh Christ,' said Nick. Zach rushed into a panicked prayer in his own guttural tongue, into which he retreated more and more these days, as feverishly they heaped the loose dirt on top of their friend to obliterate the gruesome scene.

When they laid the next man into his damp grave beside Billy it didn't seem so horrific, and the third less so. And as time went by neither did scraping rotting flesh from the crusted sides of gaping ulcers, nor the awful smell in the hospital hut, nor holding down a man as the colonel sawed his leg off. The dying clutched at Nick or Zach's arm as the boys gently encouraged them to take one more pointless spoon of soup.

'You'll take me out of here, won't you boys? Make sure the padre says somethin' nice?' the dying wretches entreated. And so the two boys regularly tramped down the jungle path towards the docks to the cemetery to honour a promise made in the death hut. Digging watery graves for men with no shrouds was just another thing Nick now did routinely that would have been unthinkable only months ago. That was the worst of it, he thought. Nothing appalled him any more. In the darkest moments of the night he fought blind terror that he had lost his links to the person he used to be. His memories were disappearing over the horizon and when he tried to clutch at them, they grew pale and ghostlike. What could the rest of his life be like after all this? The landscape of his childhood, with all of the blots he thought it had, his life in Australia where he had broken free of it, and the life he wanted to have with Jeannie – it would be a wilderness for him, with all the familiar signposts smashed into smithereens.

There was little food to be found to supplement their rancid rice diet and the Dutchmen cornered the black market in anything that could be bought or stolen, helping themselves before they released anything to the rest of the camp. Most could not afford to buy from them anyway. The colonials kept the medicines for themselves and the paltry supply that Colonel Dunlop had tried to dispense with godlike wisdom dried up entirely. The coffin now made the trip down the jungle path at least once a day to lay another man into the sticky red earth, another soldier or airman who had died after an amputation, or wasted to his death with dysentery, or who had simply lost the will to live.

When supplies did come to the island that were to feed Hatu and his men, the prisoners were sent to unload the ships on the wharves in Batavia, out beyond the cemetery. To Nick's astonishment, he was paid for this work – twenty-five cents a day in Japanese banana money. It was enough to buy three duck eggs and some tobacco, so every prisoner who was physically able volunteered. Better still, working on the docks provided an opportunity to steal food. Nick became a good thief and most days when there was work on the docks he could pocket a tin of fish or a packet of sugar from the crates. He watched carefully when the guards took their smoke breaks. There was always one who was so contemptuous of the prisoners that he didn't bother to watch them as they worked. These extra rations kept the worst of the misery at bay but hunger gnawed at their bellies every day. Most of the stolen food went to the hospital hut. The colonel now relied on Nick and the work parties to feed the sick but he was fighting a losing battle to keep men alive. Nick became used to seeing his friends die of starvation or as a result of an unprovoked beating. It was hard to keep hope alive but what killed any remaining spirit was that no one had any information as to what was going on beyond the prison camp. Adi and his people in the kampong didn't seem interested in the war. It was all the same to them, one colonizer much like the next and so they had no news to pass on. Prisoners working on the dockside eavesdropped on the quayside and although they told themselves that anything they heard was unreliable, and polluted by the Japanese view of things, it was hard to ignore the fact that Japanese military successes were mounting. One morning as Nick and Shorty were hefting crates on the dock the guards erupted into raucous cheers, slapping each other on the back in what was clearly a celebration.

'What happened?' Nick asked, risking a beating but bowing low.

'Japanese freighter *Lisbon Maru* sink,' one of them said with a delighted grin. 'But it full of plisoners and we kill them in the water.'

The men were in sombre mood when they got back to camp that night. The rules of war had been flouted again. 'Like shooting fish in a fucking barrel,' the sergeant said. With each new savagery, Nick lost another piece of the smidgeon of hope that one day the war would be over and they could all go home.

'Why are they paying us, sarge?' Nick asked, walking back from the docks that evening. 'I mean, that's an odd rule to keep when they break all the others. All the beatings for not saluting properly or not bowing, starving us and giving us no medicine. For Christ's sake, they killed that fellow from Sydney the other day for keeping a diary. And yet they pay us. I mean I know it's a pittance but even so surely they wouldn't do that unless they think that we might live to tell the tale and that one day someone will judge them?'

'I hope you're right son, we have to keep believing that. But it's hard to think they give a tuppenny damn,' the sergeant replied.

'Maybe the fellas on the *Lisbon Maru* were the lucky ones. At least it is over for them and they don't have to spend every waking moment wondering what these bastards will do next,' Piper said. 'And they didn't have to die like Billy did.'

One morning a freckle-faced man with a wide smile, soft green eyes and a lieutenant's pip on what was left of the shoulder of his shirt approached Nick as he prepared to go to the docks.

'Hello, I'm Mick Kelly, Royal Corps of Signals.' He stuck out his hand and gave Nick's a firm shake. 'I need you to do something for me out there this morning – this is a job for a good thief from Mullingar.' Nick's face must have registered his surprise because

Mick Kelly smiled wider. 'I mean, it'll take a fellow Irishman to sort this out.' The ends of his words lifted as if he were singing. It was a Cork accent and Nick felt a giddy flip of pleasure because this man clearly considered him to be one of his own tribe. He fought back nostalgia for something he wasn't sure he had ever known, but he knew that he had always wanted.

'We need batteries – the Nip trucks have six-volt ones. Do you think you could get me a couple? Liberate them, so to speak.' He winked. 'Once we have them we'll be able to get the news from Delhi, perhaps even the BBC. It'll do the fellas no end of good to hear what's going on.'

Nick didn't know how he would get the batteries back into camp under the noses of the Japs but he did know what would happen to him if he were caught. He shuddered at the thought of the red water of the cemetery filling his eye sockets. He looked at the man in front of him. What had brought him here from the rolling fields of his home in a country where there was no conscription? And if he were to get back there after the war, his neighbours would doubtless consider joining the British Army an act of betrayal. What gave him the courage to risk certain death if he were caught with a radio? Nick wanted to be more like this Irishman. It struck him very clearly that he was more afraid of disappointing Mick Kelly and his Aleppo mates than he was of being caught and executed by Captain Hatu's sword.

At dusk three days later Nick shuffled towards the gate of the camp carrying the head of the battered coffin with Zach behind him at the other end as usual. Nick was concentrating hard, trying to look the same as he did every other night when he and Zach returned from the graveyard, saddened by another inadequate funeral and relieved of the emaciated body now buried in the Javanese mud. Tonight the coffin was heavy, weighted down with the two batteries taken out of idle Japanese trucks on the wharf and hidden in the cemetery the previous evening. The camp was quiet with only the background thrum of the cicadas taking up their nightly metallic song. There was a whirr of flying foxes overhead and they landed in the trees at the edge of the camp, cracking the branches. The noise seemed deafening to Nick but the guards in the tower paid no attention to the foxes or to him and Zach. They were an all too familiar sight coming back from the cemetery with the empty coffin but there was always the risk that the guards might need the fix of dishing out a beating for no reason and challenge them. All he and Zach had to do now was get past the schoolhouse and to the hospital hut with its awful smell and groaning men. The Japs stayed well away from there.

Nick was exhausted and what was left of his muscles were cramped with the weight of the load. He feigned a limp in the hope that it would disguise his creaking body. His heart was thudding and sweat dripped off his brow into his eyes. Just a few more steps and we will be out of sight of the schoolhouse, he thought. As they passed Hatu's office a hinge screeched and Nick glanced nervously towards the door of the schoolhouse. To his horror it opened and Hatu emerged. It was the nightmare that he had willed himself not to think about. Hatu stopped abruptly and fixed his eyes on the spectacle of the coffin bearers in front of him. To Nick's astonishment, Zach started to whistle. Hatu's gaze moved away from them as he lifted his stunted arms in a bored stretch to the sky, yawned and went back through the door. The relief that flooded through Nick was so intense that he feared he would drop his precious load. Zach was still whistling and Nick now smiled at the audacity of it. They shuffled back to the hospital hut as they always did as though they were laying up the empty coffin for the next man. This time Mick Kelly was waiting in the shadows. Without a word the Cork man jerked his thumb up and cocked his head to one side, his eyebrows raised. Nick nodded. He thought his chest would burst, whether with pride or relief he couldn't tell, and he didn't think he had ever felt so good.

After that, they smuggled in coconuts, sweet potatoes, oil and any food they could get as well as books, nails, bits of Japanese aircraft, scrap and rubbish foraged from the docks that might be bent and twisted into something useful. There was invariably some food in the coffin and every soldier knew it. For a starving man it was an act of supreme self-control not to stare at it, but the Australians knew to avert their eyes when they saw the sad box coming back in the falling dusk. A hungry gaze following it through the camp might make a guard suspicious, but the Japs continued to ignore it.

'They'll never look in it,' Zach said, 'they're scared of disease from the dirty blanket.'

'Yeah, and maybe somewhere in their black souls, they know that the poor devil we just buried was a human being,' Nick said.

Nick and Zach's scavenging damaged the trade that the Dutchmen had wrenched for themselves and, even after they had given the lion's share to the colonel for the sick, the rest of them were now protected from the worst of the price gouging by the Dutch. The Dutch stayed within their own part of the camp and there was no fraternizing and no love lost between them and the Allied soldiers. They were forced to meet only when camp dispersed after Tenko and this they did as quickly as possible. So it was with some surprise one morning that Nick saw Hendriks approaching him at a smart pace.

'Don't think you are going to get away with this, Tottenham,' the Dutchman said, taking him firmly by the elbow and wheeling him away from the other Australians. 'We will stop you, one way or the other.'

Nick looked over his shoulder for support from his mates but they had walked on.

'Look, I knew you bastards would hike the price of everything and you still have an iron grip on medicines. We will starve if we don't look after ourselves. You look after your colonial friends and we will look after the soldiers.' His words sounded brave but he was shaken.

'Don't say I didn't warn you,' Hendriks said, turning on his heel.

Later Nick told Zach about the encounter. 'It's hard to believe that we came to this bloody island to save those shysters.'

'They frighten me Nick. They will stop at nothing. No *mitzvoth* in those people. They won't give us any medicine and I am afraid they will try and stop the coffin food.'

'What can they do Zach? There are more of us than them. It's not like those villains in Vienna where they had strength in numbers. And sure, here we can all look out for each other.'

The following morning, the big man, Meyer, who usually shadowed his *baas* Hendriks, but this time was on his own, sauntered up to the hut nonchalantly picking his large teeth. 'By the way,' he drawled, 'the gramophone is only for the Dutch now. Also,' he paused with an unpleasant smirk on his wide face, 'the price of quinine has just doubled.' He made an elaborate play of his shrug but his face was slit in a satisfied leer.

'Fucking bastards,' Sergeant Maloney said. 'They think they can bully us into buying from them? No fucking way. We'll start a choir. That'll show them we don't need their bloody gramophone.' He busily set about auditioning for places, more to fill the empty hours than to make any meaningful selection. Anyone could join and very quickly a group of thirty men were clearing their throats and trilling through the scales. The first sing-along was to be outside the hut shared by the Aleppo boys, and they lit a fire and gathered cans and sticks for some percussion back-up.

The concert started predictably, with an enthusiastic bellowing of 'Waltzing Matilda' by the Australians with Sergeant Maloney's lusty voice leading them. Some Poms drifted in towards the fire and answered 'Matilda' with a fervent rendition of 'Land of Hope and Glory'. A haunting crescendo bloomed slowly as more and more voices joined. Nick had never heard anything like it. The fellows all around him had no strength left and yet the harmony was deep and powerful, a hundred male voices, swollen with emotion, drifting out across the jungle in the tropical night. The silence after the last verse closed out was absolute and even the jungle seemed to have turned itself off. Everyone sat staring into the crackling fire, the light from the flames dancing on their gaunt faces.

For Nick, it had touched a long-dormant memory of why he had thought he should be a part of the war. He was surprised by a ghostly remnant of the childish pride he used to have in his old man and what he had done in the Great War. Perhaps Nick had joined up to be like him after all? He snuffed out the unwelcome thought but as he stared into the red embers he continued to dwell on the memory he had of going into town as a small boy with his father when the old soldiers living in the tenements in Mullingar doffed their caps to him. It had embarrassed Nick back then but now he thought he understood it. His father had gone to Flanders with them, suffered with them, lost friends and come home to a place where they could no longer talk of it. He looked over at the sergeant staring silently at the fire in front of him and wondered was he too thinking about his father coming back to Dublin from Gallipoli in 1916. And there beside him was Mick Kelly lost in his thoughts perhaps of how he would be remembered amongst the green hills around Midleton. Would they be all shunned at home for joining up for this war? Home? Where was that for the likes of them?

'Plisoners, no singing,' the guard screamed, shattering the heavy silence.

'They don't want us doing anything that makes us feel ...' the sergeant said, searching for a word, '... together. Singing hymns and the like will lift us and then they might not be able to control us.'

'They might be right,' Shorty said.

'Come with me to Hanukkah,' Zach said to Nick a few days later. 'I need to talk to my God too.' He smiled his rueful smile. 'I got some coconut oil for the rabbi – we celebrate the miracle of one day's oil lasting eight days at the siege of Jerusalem. We Jews were outlawed back then too. It is the miracle of our own survival. The triumph of the pure over the impure.' Nick had to look twice at him.

The menorah sat on a table in the dark room, light from the cup in the middle of its branches dancing on the wall behind it. Nick was unsure how to conduct himself, recalling a similar feeling of embarrassment back in Jerusalem when he had left Zach to pray at the Temple Wall. The strange ritual beginning in front of him triggered nothing that reminded him of his own childhood devotions, where no one even knew the words to the prayers. Not for the first time he asked himself why he and Zach had become the friends that they were. But then they were both displaced, he supposed, young men who felt they didn't belong anywhere.

Nine other Jewish boys stood with Zach at the table. Each of them had fastened a piece of cloth over their heads and sang together with a sweet melancholy, swaying back and forth slowly as Zach had done at the Wall.

'*Maoz Tzur, Maoz Tzur*,' they chanted softly, recalling perfectly each lilting cadence of the ancient language.

'It means Rock of Ages,' Zach told him. 'You have a song like it, I think.' Nick nodded numbly, having no idea what he was talking about, but he was moved by the emotion on Zach's rapt face. It *was* a miracle that here were ten Jewish boys who had escaped from the Nazis and were somehow surviving this hell. Every man in the stuffy hut, Jew and Christian, stared at the tiny blue flame in the middle of the menorah. These ancient people had survived before. Perhaps they would live through this as well.

Something caught Nick's eye at the side of the room, something out of kilter with the devotion all around him. Hendriks was leaning against the far wall with his chin in his hand, his sidekick

Meyer brooding beside him. They were an unusual addition to this gathering as they never attended anything involving the other nationalities, especially since the tension had tightened over the coffin food and this ceremony was against prison rules just as singing 'Land of Hope and Glory' was. There was something aggressive in the arrangement of their bodies, each of them leaning with studied disrespect against the wall, one leg crossed over the other, a foot tapping crossly against the floor.

'I thought we had picked up all that Jewish stuff before the invasion,' Hendriks said sourly. 'I don't know how that fellow got hold of that candlestick. It would make a good price.'

These people still think that they own this island, Nick thought. Sometimes they are more frightening than the Nips. An unpleasant thought crossed Nick's mind that these men might be here to spy for the Japs and that they would now go and tell them about this forbidden ceremony before the rest of them could disperse. He was relieved when it was over and he could still see Hendriks and Meyer. He waited outside to make sure Zach would not tarry there lest the colonials still intended to shop them. He should also warn the rabbi about the candlestick. Others emerged from the hut, quiet and thoughtful, clearly moved, as Nick had been by the service and by the hope that the Jewish people kept alive over centuries. When the rabbi closed the door of the stuffy room behind him, a lanky, hawk-nosed squadron leader in a remarkably pristine RAF uniform approached him.

'I say, you fellows have a lot at stake in this war, don't you,' he said in a pleasant tone, trying, in that stiff and incompetent English way, to convey his support.

'I think we all do' replied the rabbi quietly.

It was Zach's idea to put on a musical.

'I don't know how you got away with it,' Shorty said when Zach announced with childish glee that Hatu had agreed to it.

'He's bored, like the rest of us. Anyway, it's not rousing stuff. Not like those songs that got you all teary-eyed. We're going to do *Anything Goes* and I, my friends, shall play Sally.' He lifted his arms above his head as if he were a ballerina and pirouetted on his toes. The boys were happy to help and they set to work digging out a theatre from the earth at the butt of the hill at the back of the camp. Piper and Shorty wheeled a wormy piano out of the old school and a fellow who had played in a band at the South Sydney Rugby League club before the war helped to tune it. He also made a banjo mandolin from a mess tin, nuts from the handles of old toothbrushes and frets from copper wire that Nick pilfered for him from the docks. Another put strings across a coconut shell and used it to strum in folksy harmony along with the banjo.

'This is coming on great,' the sergeant said, 'and you'll never believe it – Hatu has given us some paint. We can use those old tent flaps to make the scenes.' Nick's job was to hammer the boards for the stage.

'I'm no good at painting or anything like that,' he said.

'Come on Nick. You should have a part in the play.'

'Christ, no. No thanks. I can't sing a note and I'm not one for standing up and making an eejit of myself. It'll be great craic seeing you dressed up as a woman.'

But he did feel left out and Zach's increasing giddy enthusiasm was beginning to irritate him. Only the cast was allowed to see the rehearsals although everyone could hear the piano plinking away merrily every day and the chorus competing with the chattering of the monkeys and the crowing of the green jungle fowl. He saw much less of Zach now than before and stifled a childish feeling of abandonment that he recalled from his schooldays when a new friend changed his mind or an old one found another more interesting. When Zach did come back to the hut after rehearsals he seemed different. The sadness that could haunt his face when he thought about his family lifted but there was something else that Nick could not put his finger on. Maybe Zach had always been a frustrated song-and-dance artist.

'I need a brassiere, Nick. What about old Adi? His big fat wife must have a spare one I could have.'

'That might test my Malay.'

'I can stuff it with kapok,' Zach beamed.

'You'll never wear that. You'll be scratching yourself all night like a dog with fleas,' Piper said, laughing for the first time since Billy's death.

'Look,' he said, 'I can make a dress from a mosquito net and a lovely curly wig from this coconut fibre. I shall have big hair like the ladies in the films. And best of all ...' He reached under his bed and pulled out his tin mug, stuck his index finger into it and smeared it across his lips. They were now crimson. 'Betel juice,' he said clearly delighted with himself. 'Aren't I gorgeous?'

Nick tried to ignore his unease as he continued to forage for tiny bits of metal and coloured pebbles that Zach wanted to stitch onto his costume.

'Oh, this will add so much *chic* to the dress,' he said holding up the string of polished papaya seeds. 'Do you think they would look best as a necklace or a bracelet?'

'Come on Zach, let's see the finished thing – put it on for us,' Shorty demanded.

'Yeah Zach, give the lads a preview,' Nick said quietly.

'Now, now, boys, you'll have to wait,' Zach said with a flounce.

'That fellow is really staying in character, isn't he?' Piper said.

As Zach waltzed off to rehearsal with his mosquito net dress over his arm, Nick sat with Piper and Shorty outside the hut and watched him go. Hendriks and Meyer were leaning against the mango tree with some of their cronies. They too were looking at Zach. One of them lifted his thumb and index finger and put them between his lips, and gave a long and slow wolf whistle.

Zach looked back at them and grinned as if it had been a genuine compliment.

'Your friend is sissy, *ja?*' Hendriks shouted at Nick.

The camp jostled into the space in front of the stage, mates keeping places for mates, the Australians, British and especially the Dutch maintaining the usual invisible apartheid. 'What makes those toffee-nosed Poms think they can have the best seats? This is an Aussie show,' Shorty said as the squadron leader with the patrician nose walked airily past the Aleppo boys sitting cross-legged in the front row.

'Jesus, look at your man, he has a bloody tie on,' the sergeant said. A surprisingly portly corporal from 'B' Company parted the canvas drop doing duty as the curtain to announce the show, amidst much good-natured heckling.

'Good man, Slim!' they shouted. 'Show us your leg, corporal!'

The men sang along with the opening song. The Japs were unconcerned and chattered to each other, wide-eyed and pointing excitedly to the men dressed up on the stage. Their rifles lay on the ground beside them, the war suspended. The audience shouted encouragement and abuse in equal measure at every member of the cast on his first entrance. Then it was time for Sally to come on, for her to sing 'Take it on the Chin'. Nick's palms sweated with anxiety. He had heard Zach practise the song and he had a good voice, but, putting himself in his shoes, he imagined that he would get stage fright or forget his lines.

She made her entrance. There was no heckling for Sally. Nick froze, and like every man there, he stared at the stage in stunned silence. Sally was beautiful and, from the plucked arch of her eyebrows to the tip of her toes in shoes of parachute silk, she was a woman. Nick watched, horrified, as she swayed her hips and pouted her betel-nut lips. Her long fingers twirled the curl of her coconut hair.

Nick shifted uncomfortably on his seat bones. His mouth was dry. He could not look at the beauty on the stage who was clearly enjoying every minute of her limelight, and he dropped his head and stared into his lap. After what seemed to him like an eternity, the fellows behind him recovered and mercifully the heckling started again, hesitantly at first, then building up raucously. But Nick's throat was too tight and he could not make a sound. When he tried to join in his voice cracked and he laughed nervously instead.

'Cor, Sally, you're a smasher – can I see you later darlin'?' And there were more bursts of bawdy laughter. Appalled, Nick thought he saw an English corporal wink at him. His face and neck were hot and there was nothing to do but endure it and pretend he too was enjoying it. The applause seemed endless. It was clear that they loved Zach. They made calls for more and then more again. But Nick could not forget the silent shock that had met Sally's entrance.

'Bring back Sally!' they called. When he could face looking up again Nick saw with dismay bordering on disgust that the guards were staring open-mouthed at Zach swishing in time to the music, his face whitened with tapioca flour like a geisha. Captain Hatu was cheering and licking his lips, his black eyes shining with manic lust.

Nick was glad that the show was to be performed for three nights: that would keep Zach busy. Nick was not going to watch him again. Only the day before he had been feeling sore that Zach seemed to have no time for his old friends, so obsessed was he with his damn play. Now he didn't want to see Zach at all. He also knew he didn't want to be seen *with* Zach. He couldn't take any more lewd suggestions like the ones he thought he had heard and the gestures he had seen when Sally first came on stage. He couldn't blame them as, after all, he and Zach had always been inseparable. Without knowing precisely why, he instinctively understood that their friends and others might think differently about that now. Perhaps he thought differently about it too. It alarmed him that he could not think about Zach now without calling up the image of Sally blowing kisses.

'What did you think of your man?' Shorty asked when they returned to the hut. Nick wondered if he and Piper were as embarrassed as he was.

'A bit over the top maybe,' Sergeant Maloney said, 'might be wise to tone it down a bit for the next performance.'

'Did you see the guards and Hatu? Thought they might jump on him,' Shorty went on.

Nick felt the muscles at the side of his face twitch. He did not know what to say or where to look so he got up abruptly and left them. He wondered miserably whether the boys would go on talking about what Zach had been like; he might have been wiser to stay and to be part of that conversation. Had he known Zach was like that? Pictures of all the things they had been through together flashed through his mind. He felt sick.

Over the next couple of days Zach chased him like a puppy but Nick found a reason to be helping in the hospital hut during the day and then sneaked back to the hut when the next performance was on. He made sure he was asleep when Zach came in. But he couldn't hide from Zach at Tenko.

'Well, what did you think of the show?' Zach asked him

'What the hell did you think you were doing?' He knew that he was drawing up the drawbridge on a chasm but he wanted Zach to stay away from him. And then when he was alone again, when his anger and revulsion had cooled a little he remembered the *Jervis Bay* and how lonely he had been before Tony had introduced Zach to him and he felt overwhelmingly sad. Did it matter so much to him what other people thought that he had to behave like a prick? He was lonely.

Nick was watering the tapioca plants at the side of the hut when he heard a groan behind him. Looking around he saw Zach leaning against the pole at the opening to the hut doubled over, grabbing his belly. His right eye was yellow and swollen up, and his lip was split. A thick trickle of black blood oozed from his ear.

'Christ, what happened to you?'

'You don't want to know.'

'Jesus, was it that Korean bastard?'

'No it wasn't,' Zach muttered. He stumbled inside the hut and lowered himself slowly onto the bed. He turned his back on Nick.

'Who did this to you?' Nick persisted. He had to bend over Zach's curled body to hear what he was saying.

'It doesn't matter. Forget it.'

'You need to get that eye seen to. Where else are you hurt?'

'My ribs are broken,' Zach said quietly.

'Please Zach, tell me what happened,' Nick said gently.

'I'll tell you if you swear you will do nothing, absolutely nothing about it.'

Nick was alarmed. He had no strength left for another thing to fear. 'All right,' he said hesitantly.

Zach stared out through the door of the hut at the ferns and the tangled web of vines slung over the mossy trees as if hypnotized by the dappled light flickering on the knotty floor of the jungle. 'They don't like the coffin food,' Zach continued mechanically. 'They called me Yiddish Nancy. Who is Nancy, Nicky?' He was barely conscious.

'Who called you that? For Chrissakes, who?'

'The big one with the teeth,' he said and passed out. Nick turned him gently onto his back to that he could look at his ribs. A bruise was darkening on the right side of his friend's bony frame.

Shorty helped Nick carry Zach to the hospital hut where the colonel looked him over. When he had finished he shook his head grimly. 'He's had a bad beating. I'm afraid there may be damage to his organs. Bound to be, when he's so thin.'

Nick sat with him for the next two days as Zach lapsed in and out of consciousness. When he eventually woke his eyes were slow to focus, but when he saw Nick he smiled faintly. It felt like absolution, but it was not enough to dissipate the fear that had sneaked into his brain and lodged there and strengthened as the hours passed. Zach was not going to live through this. The picture of the colonel's face pressing his lips and shaking his head loomed into his head and Nick fancied that the gentle officer's finger was pointing at him like a revolver. This would not have happened if he had been a more loyal friend.

'You must eat. Look, I have some chicken for you – old Adi gave it to me. Please Zach, try and eat. You got through the last time and you can make it this time. Come on now.' Desperation was making his voice crack, and a sob broke through. He held the spoon with the chicken soup to Zach's lips, cradling his head in his lap, but Zach did not open his mouth.

'It's all right, Nicky. Thank you, but I have had enough.'

'I'll keep it for later then,' Nick said and he laid Zach's head back on the kapok pillow.

'That's not what I mean,' Zach said. His hand trembled with the effort of raising it to put it on Nick's arm. 'What have I got to look forward to even if we get out of here? This is going to happen to me wherever I go.'

Nick had seen the look of giving up before. Billy had looked like that too, when he had stopped screaming. He smelled the same terrible sweetness of cinnamon and almond on Zach's breath. 'Please Zach, don't talk like that ... we've been through so much. You can't give up now.' He searched desperately for some words that would remind Zach of their friendship. He wanted to tell him what it had meant to him, terrified that he had left it too late. 'We'll keep the doors open,' he said.

'Ask the rabbi to say *Shemah* for me, you black Protestant *nebbuch*.' He smiled and drifted off to sleep.

Zach did not wake again. His breathing slowed to a rattle and each rib loomed white against his yellowed skin as his lungs grabbed at the stale air. While he waited for Zach to die, Nick sat beside his bed and twisted some twigs he had collected from the jungle to fashion two triangles. He placed one on top of the other to make a crooked Star of David. He wasn't going to let anyone carelessly put a Christian cross on his friend's grave.

Sixteen

'For if ever your engine should stall
You're in for one heck of a fall
No lilies or violets for dead bomber pilots
So cheer up lads
Fuck 'em all'

LINCOLNSHIRE

Wiki was a line of the song behind everyone else as Daddy ran his fingers up and down the keyboard with a flourish after the last bar. The men around the piano cheered, none too soberly.

'Another round, skipper?' Wiki called. Tony squinted in an effort to bring him into focus. No light came through the diamond panes of the window and the low ceiling of the pub, stained brown with years of tobacco smoke, made him feel claustrophobic. This is absurd, he thought. I must have had too much to drink. How could I feel hemmed in here when my life is now spent flying in a space the size of a dog basket? The crew from the hut beside them was grounded because they had pranged their aircraft on landing the previous day so they ambushed these new boys, flying without

McNab for the first time, for a piss up in the Horse and Jockey. They weren't going to take no for an answer.

That was hours ago and Tony was not handling his jar too well. He supposed he was still a bit tense even though his first trip as skipper had gone well. They had avoided a Messerschmitt. Jonesy had spotted the German aircraft early and directed Tony away from it calmly and expertly. The gunners had not been tempted to take a pot shot at him for sport as they had done when they encountered that one in training. They knew better than that now. On Jonesy's instruction Tony pushed the stick violently forward, which had made everyone sick. The portable loo had upturned and Touc and Daddy had been thrown hard against the fuselage but they had lost the fighter. They went on to hit the target outside Frankfurt. All his boys had been great, especially Charlie, who showed none of the signs of freezing up as he had done on the first trip to Stuttgart with McNab. Tony had been right to stand by him.

The empty green bottles were lined up along the bar in two rows, one for them and the other for their hosts from Hut Two. The challenge was to drink the longest line but Tony could drink no more because he was seeing double.

'Another time, lads,' Tony said, raising his hand sloppily to concede defeat, which resulted in a victorious cheer erupting from the Hut Two crew. An odd feeling nagged at the edges of his fuzzy consciousness that there was something just a bit aggressive about the way these chaps were forcing drink on him and his crew.

They never got the chance to return the challenge. The boys from Hut Two did not come home the following night, blown out of the sky by bombs falling from another Lancaster above them over Frankfurt. After that Tony and his boys preferred to drink alone. Knowing they might never meet again made it difficult enough to mix with other crews and make friends but there was something else that made them reluctant to socialize and which was never discussed. It was what Tony had sensed in the bar with the crew from

Hut Two. They all knew that, given the attrition rate, some of them there would not return from their next operation. By sticking with their own they could hide the guilty hope that it would be someone else's turn to die. They also understood that everyone else having a pint and forcing drink on them must feel the same.

With each trip Tony felt his crew knitting tighter together. He knew these lads better than he had known anyone before. Daddy's wife liked a port and lime and sneezed when she made love. Touc was bad-tempered if he drank whiskey. It wasn't wise to tease Wiki about his height and Charlie's father seemed to be a merciless bully. Jonesy was in love with a raven-haired Welsh beauty who worked in the control tower, but he hadn't had the courage to ask her out. Tony also knew that they shared his instinct for danger and understood exactly what they had to do when the going got rough. Wiki and Jonesy were their eyes, their lookouts in long dark hours over enemy territory; desperately staying awake in their freezing turrets to scan the sky for German fighters. Steve, on his stomach in the belly of the aircraft, guided Tony on to the marker fires with pinpoint accuracy. He also had to keep a sharp eye out for what they all feared most, an enemy aircraft slinking up underneath them like a great white shark from the murky blackness and blowing them to oblivion with deadly Schräge Musik canons. Each man had fine-tuned his antennae to listen to warnings from the others and understood that his life depended on every other man in the aircraft.

Tony's hangover did not improve with coffee and he couldn't face breakfast. He nipped down to the hangars and asked the erks to give him a suck of oxygen.

'Overdo it last night, did ya?' the sergeant asked. After their first sprog run to Stuttgart the sergeant had adopted Tony. He was old enough to be his father but Tony liked the squat Yorkshireman with his ruddy smiling face and gruff humour. It was ten days since he had flown his first trip as skipper to Frankfurt. Tony thought himself to be an old-timer now and by some standards, God knows, he was.

'Bottle challenge with a pathfinder crew. Felt we had to keep up. You know how it is when they think they are the bees' knees and everything,' Tony said, rubbing his temple with his thumb. 'And now I'm late for the briefing and the squadron leader will have me on report. Thanks mate,' he added, handing back the tube.

He ran from the hangars to the briefing Nissen, stepped quietly into the back row and sat down. The curtain had already been pulled back. *Berlin. Maximum Effort.* Flying time seven and a half hours. Thirty-three Lancasters were to go that night from this base alone. His head still throbbed and his mouth was dry. He waited for the met information, massaging the bridge of his nose.

'Three-tenths cloud expected, moderate westerly wind,' the lady was saying. Her voice was firm but light and sweet, Irish softening the consonants. Was he dreaming? He lifted his head and swallowed hard. His mother stood on the stage pointing at the map with a bamboo cane. Tony lifted his hand tentatively to wave at her, and her face broke into a smile that lit up the whole room.

'What a surprise, Mother! Not your usual stamping ground is it?' As he kissed her on both cheeks he was overwhelmed by nostalgia, the smell of lavender and the softness of her cheek.

'Not really. But I generally hear before anyone else where the op is to be, so when I realized ...' she checked herself. 'I mean ...'

'You mean Berlin, the big one,' he said. He could see that she was trying to make light of it but the corners of her mouth trembled. She laughed to hide it.

'Well, I just thought it would be a good excuse to come and see you so I volunteered to do the met brief today. You look as though you could do with some food.'

They sat opposite one another in the corner of the mess. Tony's plate was piled high with Spam and fried bread. Eleanor nursed a mug of black coffee, folding her small hands around the mug.

'You don't mind if I give you some advice, do you?' she asked, staring into the black liquid. 'God, I hate this chicory muck.'

'I suspect that you'll give it to me whether I want it or not.' He raised his eyebrows.

'Don't look at me like that,' she said with mock crossness. She flicked open her lighter and lit a cigarette. 'You see, I've been watching the bombers go off for many months now and I've listened to what works and what doesn't. It's more than just luck, you know.' Tony recoiled. He didn't want to talk about luck – no pilot did.

'To begin with there's a foolish belief that the IFF, you know, the Identification Friend or Foe ...' She faltered at the look of mild disgust on Tony's face.

'The squawk, Mother.'

'Of course you know what it is. Sorry darling,'

'What about it?' he said evenly.

'Well, some of the boys think it jams the German searchlight control so they put it on before they've left the enemy coast. It doesn't, and you'll only tell them where you are so don't put it on until you're going to show up as a blip on one of Kate's radar screens.' She had his attention now. 'You know I like to think of that,' she hurried on, 'I mean, that Kate is making sure the radar works to get you home safely ... and Rose is looking at the screens and interpreting what she sees there as well and me too, I suppose, working out the weather, fuel consumption, air speeds and all that stuff. We're all involved in the same operation. It's a sort of family business, isn't it? That is, if that weren't such a vulgar term.' She drew deeply on her cigarette. 'Nevertheless, it gives me comfort.'

Tony knew fellows who turned the IFF on over Germany. Daddy had talked about doing it only the other day.

'I've worked out some patterns – statistical ones I mean. I know you'll laugh at me.' His mother saw arithmetic in everything. But what she had said about the IFF might save their lives, so he sat back.

'Go on Mumm ...' He cut himself short. It was time to stop calling his mother by nursery names. 'I'm listening.'

'Well, it seems that the best thing you can do is to try and operate at 4000 feet. Just beyond the maximum height when German light flak is effective and is too low for the heavier 88 mm flak.'

Tony was stunned. How did his mother know any of this stuff?

'Of course you have to climb to bomb – I understand that – but try to slip back to deck level for the run home. The pilots doing that seem to be surviving.'

He couldn't think of anything to say to this extraordinary woman sitting in front of him who was so achingly familiar and yet seemed to know more than the squadron leader. She leant forward.

'I know I can't fly the airplane for you,' she said. 'Actually I'm told you are a very good pilot.'

'Oh, checking up on me, are you?'

'Of course.'

It had been a long night. The wall of searchlights around Berlin had looked impenetrable with decoy fires everywhere, making it difficult to find the TIs and the aiming point. There had been a lot of flak, which had pitched them violently about the sky. One shell had found its mark and there was a gaping hole in the fuselage but they had made it home. They had survived Berlin and that would count for something on the base. They were well blooded now. It put a lift into Tony's tired steps as he dragged his parachute from the cockpit and the sun brightened the sky to the east.

'Good work, Charlie. She was very stiff on the rudder there for a while,' Tony said, and gently punched his flight engineer's arm as they trudged back to the briefing hut, their faces grey in the half-light of the dawn.

'It's a big enough hole. I'm not surprised the stick was stiff. Good piece of flying, skip.' Tony felt a warm glow of affection for this quiet Englishman.

'We're all in this together. All for one and one for all, eh?' Tony said and then felt a blush creep across his face. What a silly, childish thing to say.

The Englishman leant back on his heels and held out his hand, bidding Tony to hold up but he was not laughing at him.

'I just want to say, skipper – thanks for standing up for me on the Stuttgart run.' He hesitated. 'I don't know what happened but I felt I was drowning, like a dam had burst over me.'

'Look Charlie, it's okay. I'm lucky; it just doesn't affect me that way. You're a braver man than me, fighting your way through it, I mean.'

'Yeah, I was very frightened I suppose, but thank God, I seem to have found a way to deal with it – for now anyway. You could have reported me to LMF, had me sent to Matlock and all that, but you didn't. You gave me a second chance. My father would never have forgiven me. It would be better to have been blown out of the sky.'

Tony winced. 'You're a damn fine engineer, Charlie, and I wouldn't want to fly without you. If it weren't for you, losing the port outer tonight with the fucking wind whistling through the hole in the kite's belly, we might be traipsing through the French countryside right now, or worse. Anyway "moral fibre" or the lack of it is not something the brass, sitting safely at home, can measure, is it?'

After Berlin, they flew almost every other night, over Essen, Aachen, Munich, Schweinfurt. Then attention moved to France: Aulnoye-Aymeries, Juvisy, La Chapelle, Saumur, Cherbourg. Tony had faith in his crew but knew that he had to be strict with them. They spent every waking hour together and many a night in the Horse and Jockey, which in another world might have affected his authority, but even during the ten black hours in the cold on the run back from Munich when he insisted that there was to be no smoking, no unnecessary talking on the intercom, no lights over the continent, no one argued. He checked on each man every few minutes to make sure no one had fallen asleep, or was suffering from frostbite, or had been hit by a pot shot from a night fighter before it skulked off into the black sky. A crew from Waddington had miraculously made it home to discover the unfortunate mid upper with a hole in his forehead. They had unknowingly been flying blind and were a sitting duck for a Messerschmitt. The boys had to stay awake to watch out for other Lancasters too, especially as they came in to land. Too many mid uppers had fallen asleep on that last sweet sweep home when the sky was black with returning bombers. He was acutely aware that without Jonesy searching the arc of the heavens above them and Wiki, sitting on his own over the furnace of the exhaust and scanning the skies behind them, they would not survive.

'France again. Fuck it.' Jonesy threw his cap on the ground. 'And in bloody daylight! There's just as much chance of copping it on these hops across the channel as there is going to Berlin when we are fucking heroes. Why do they only count as a third of an op? We'll never finish the tour at this rate.'

Tony shared his crew's frustration. The boys were right. It was going to take a very long time to finish the thirty-four ops they needed to complete the tour when they had to fly three French trips for every German one. Once the tour was over they would be given desk jobs or instructing posts and then the terror would be over. They had been bombing France for over a month now, attacking marshalling yards, airfields, radar and wireless installations. They seemed peripheral targets to the crew compared with the targets in Germany, the armament factories and the industrial giants, Germany's pulsing heart. Bomber Command obviously thought so too, given the skewed arithmetic, which didn't count the French sorties as a full op, although the risk was just as great.

And now *Sugar* had been given to another crew. *S for Sugar*, the Lancaster considered by everyone in Bomber Command – when they allowed themselves to think of such things – as blessed. Flying her had made up for the unfair maths. *Sugar* had now flown almost a hundred missions and the boys believed that she was indestructible. Tony had been wrong when he told his mother and Kate that the Lancasters were invincible. He knew the statistics now, and his mother certainly did. The truth was that few of these great hopes of the war flew more than ten or eleven operations before they were blown out of the sky and it was not surprising that *Sugar* was now a legend in Bomber Command and beyond it. She was the old lady of the sky. Everyone on the base looked out for *Sugar* and the control tower waited anxiously to hear her call sign in the early hours of the morning. The fellows on the ground said that Touc could go to sleep because *Sugar* knew her way home. She had acquired a personality, and was treated like a family pet. Fellows returning from leave would check on her, airmen and erks patted her wheels when they walked past her at dispersals and called her 'old girl' as they did so.

The crew who flew her became special too. It gave Tony, Touc and the boys a sense of invincibility, but one imbued with the heavy responsibility of making sure that she came home for all of them. The Lancaster represented something constant and permanent in a world where life could be so very short. They became celebrities both on the base and off it. Some women in a sugar factory in America adopted *Sugar* and the boys received letters and photographs from pretty girls with red nails, pouty lips and blonde hair piled high on their heads, which were pinned up on the notice board beside the briefing hut with messages of undying love for her crew. Tony and his crew loved the attention but they also understood that *Sugar* bucked the odds.

But then one morning in the first days of June, when they returned from a few days' leave, they learned that the famous

Lancaster had been assigned to another crew. Tony and his boys had flown her for months, including her ninety-eighth mission and now they wouldn't fly her hundredth. It was hard to stand on the sidelines sipping bottles of warm beer as the crew for that centenary flight, new boys really, posed for the photographs. Tony did his best to smile as he lifted his drink to the old girl. He looked over to Wiki and Jonesy, who looked downright sour. Tony's boys were disgruntled and, worse, they were rattled. It took so little for any of them to feel that their luck might be changing.

'There's something odd about today's briefing, don't you think?' Tony was trying to distract the sulking Jonesy. 'I mean, we're not to jettison bombs in the channel, not to use the squawk even on the way home. What's so special about Saint-Pierre-du-Mont, I wonder?'

'Gun batteries, apparently,' Daddy snapped.

Twenty-eight aircraft left the base together the next morning. The nose of their Lancaster lifted off the runway just before 3 am as the tangerine dawn brightened the sky on their port side. Half an hour later Steve's normally calm voice broke the silence on the intercom, bright with excitement.

'Jesus, look at this. It's on. It's fucking on. The invasion. Oh, it's brilliant. Look, skip!'

Tony looked down through the break in the clouds. Below him on the choppy grey waters of the channel were hundreds of gunships steaming slowly towards France, grey slugs leaving silver lines of surf behind them. From those closest to the French coast landing craft were spilling onto the water like a hatch of fly.

'Right boys, we have to get those gun batteries before the fellows down there reach the beaches,' Tony said quietly. He felt a warm rush, like strong drink – finally it didn't seem as though Bomber Command was fighting this war alone.

'My vision panel has iced up, skipper.' Steve was focused on his job again.

'We're right over the TIs now, Steve. Let them go.'

With a now familiar twang, the bombs dropped and the nose of the Lancaster lurched upwards.

'Bombs away, skipper.' Tony watched the 500 pounders fall like pellets being tipped from a sack, clustering right between the markers.

'Good job, Steve. Right, we're for home. Our job's done today.' It was not yet 5 am. What would the day bring for the thousands of men in the landing crafts?

'Look, skip.' Now it was Jonesy's turn to be excited. 'There must be every bomber in England out this morning – the sky is thick with them.'

'Keep a close eye, Jonesy.'

'Will do, skip. Ah Jesus, here come the Yanks. Christ, they're like a swarm of locusts.'

Flying low, their path took them directly over the black belching hulk of an old ship carving its way sedately through the steely waves towards the coast of France. Tony dipped the wings of the Lancaster over the ship's decks, jammed tight with soldiers, boys who had never been to war before. From above, their tin hats made the deck look like a black honeycomb. And then, as the Lancaster left its shadow over their heads, the deck turned pale as hundreds of faces turned towards the sky and the men of the first wave of the D-Day invasion force saluted the Lancaster heading for home.

By mid August the end of the tour was in sight – they were all tired and needed a rest. The night of the run to Brest on the 14th was moonless and Tony could hide the Lancaster in the clouds but there was a lot of flak about and the aircraft bumped and rattled through it.

'TIs to port side one degree, one minute to target.'

Tony adjusted the stick, as instructed by Steve, and waited for the nose to lift to signal that the bombs were gone. Balls of shell-fire were bursting all around him. Behind them the formation of fellow Lancasters had lengthened, those in the rear now mere dots in the distance. At last he saw the string of winged shells falling, black against the scarlet and orange fires below them and then the bulk of the monstrous 12,000-pound tallboy, the biggest bomb of them all. The aircraft bucked upwards.

'Good man Steve.'

'I'm hit, skip ... my leg.'

'Shit! Daddy, go and bring him up. Charlie, more power please. More. I can't move the stick.'

'Bandits on port side,' screamed Wiki from the tail.

'Right, watch them closely now, chaps,' said Tony calmly. He started to weave as he had practised so many times over the Wolds as a pack of Messerschmitts tore in amongst the leading bombers, picking out its victims like wild dogs. To the port side a Lancaster started to corkscrew, but it was too late and flames sprouted from its wing. The fighter wanted to make sure and continued firing; a shroud of smoke swirled around the stricken aircraft and it twirled slowly out of the sky like a sycamore seed in the wind. Tony forced himself to concentrate on the information the crew was yelling at him.

'On the starboard wing, skip.' Tony dived to port.

'He's gone, skip, but ...' Jonesy's words were obliterated by the ear-splitting crash of an explosion, then of metal tearing and the roar of rushing air through the fuselage.

'Fire on the starboard outer,' Charlie said. 'We're trailing smoke.'

'Feather it, Charlie – I can hold her,' Tony said through gritted teeth as the Lancaster jumped and shuddered. 'I'm going to dive to try and put the fire out.' The port wing rose steeply and Tony pulsed the throttle back and forward. As the ground came closer he wrenched the stick back and the Lancaster swooped sickeningly upwards. The three functioning engines screamed and metal crunched. The Elsen rattled down the torn fuselage, the smell of shit now joining that of sick and cordite. Then the engines seemed to suck on air as the propellers windmilled, but the fire died out and the cockpit was again thrown into darkness without the light from the flames. There was a terrifying silence before an engine spluttered into life again.

'Everyone all right? How's Steve?'

'Unconscious. I've given him morphine,' said Daddy.

'Here's another Jerry on the port wing, skip.'

Before Tony could bank there was a series of dull thuds and a spray of holes popped open along the cockpit. Tony felt a thump to his left arm and the air rushed out of his lungs. He had often wondered how it would feel to be hit by a bullet. There was no pain, only wetness. His arm hung uselessly at his side.

'Charlie! Give me a hand until I get her level again.'

'You all right skip?'

'Right as rain,' Tony said. 'Wiki, you all right?'

'Thought you were trying to throw me out, skipper.'

'Jonesy?'

'Fine, skip.'

'Daddy?'

'It's a fucking mess back here and there's a huge hole but we seem to be still flying. Starboard fuel tanks are leaking.' Daddy's head poked through a gaping hole of bent and twisted metal.

'Touc, can we make it home on the port tanks?'

'Not to base and not if we follow the stream ... possibly if we hedgehop as far as the channel. But these gauges are never fucking right so who knows. It'll be tight.'

Tony didn't think he had ever heard Touc curse before. He sat silently staring at the instruments shuddering in front of him. Waves of pain washed through him. The only sound was the swish of the French bocage whistling past only a few hundred feet beneath them. He felt lightheaded.

'Right, fellas, you chaps want to bail? I'll carry on and hope I can get Steve home,' he said quietly. There was no point in them all going down.

'I'd rather stay with the kite if you don't mind, sir,' said Touc.

'Me too,' came a chorus from the others.

'You sure? Now's the chance if any of you want to go.'

'No thanks, sir.'

'Right Touc, plot a course for Manston please. The rest of you throw everything out to lighten her up.' He lifted his good arm to beckon Charlie forward to the cockpit. 'Charlie, I have another problem. I have good control at 105 mph but I can't hold her at anything lower so we're going to come in very quick even if we do make it to Manston. I want everyone in the ditching position as soon as we hit the channel. Get Wiki and Jonesy forward. Time to put all that dancing practice to work.'

It looked like their famed luck had finally run out. They had no fuel, he was flying with one arm, and he would have to land the stricken aircraft at an impossibly high speed. He didn't mind for himself but felt overwhelming grief that the lives of his crew, whom he now knew he loved, would be lost. He had to pull himself together because these boys were relying on him, and this time on him alone.

The Lancaster seemed to sense when a bit more was required of her, heaving herself over the treetops like a fat pony. As she bounced across the channel they could smell the salt from the waves.

'Manston coming up ahead,' said Touc. And there in front of him was the welcome red wink of the beacon. Tony felt as though he had forgotten to breathe for the last hour but he took a deep one now and shifted in his seat for what was ahead.

'Right Daddy, tell them we're coming straight in with speed problems and wounded. Have the ambulances standing by, please.'

A primeval scream erupted from the aircraft as her belly scraped the ground. She spun like a child's top, shuddering, and, with bits of metal flying off her, slewed to a stop in the middle of a field standing high with golden barley. Only two more trips and they would complete their tour.

Seventeen

Kate and Eleanor sat at a round table in the corner of the tea-shop in Coningsby. The day outside was warm and sultry with heavy clouds threatening to burst. No one moved to open the windows as the roar of aircraft was almost intolerable, though the air inside was stale and stuffy. Kate's face was flushed pink with the heat but Eleanor seemed unperturbed and sat with her uniform jacket tightly buttoned. She sighed and lifted the cup, appeared to think better of it, and replaced it on its saucer, her hand trembling. She fumbled in her bag for a cigarette and lit it, the smell of petrol escaping from the lighter. Eleanor's cheeks hollowed and the tip glowed furiously. She fixed her stare over the fret of the window. Kate looked at the two fairy cakes on the plate in front of her. The wings of sponge were wedged into some jam and cream and she remembered with a twist of sadness how Martha had taught her and Maggie how to make them. With rationing both the jam and the cream were false but the cake was still a treat.

'Aren't you going to eat it, Mummy?'

'What? Oh ...' her mother said, clearly unsure of what had been said to her. 'Not today dear. Why don't you have it?'

'Everything looks like an aircraft around here, even the fairy cakes,' Kate said, hoping to make her mother smile, and turned her plate to examine the bun from a different angle. There was no reaction from her mother. 'Have you had any news of the Little Ones?' she tried again.

Eleanor seemed reluctant to drag her gaze from the window. 'Oh they're all right I think. They don't write much and poor Martha isn't one for letters. I believe George has made some new friends in the town and they play a lot of cards ... it must be fun for him. He doesn't seem to be as keen on the tennis club as the rest of you were. You've probably heard more from Maggie than I have. You were always as thick as thieves.' She smiled weakly, then resumed her vacant watch of the airplanes through the window.

'I think Maggie is lonely, Mummy. You know, neither of them went to school much and if George has got some new friends, she will feel left out.'

'That is hardly the priority right now, is it?' Eleanor snapped.

Kate sat back on her chair, blinking with the shock of her mother's tone.

'What is the matter, Mummy? This is not like you at all.'

Eleanor said nothing and continued to draw the smoke deep into her lungs. 'I'm sorry Kate.' She hesitated. 'It's just knowing ... I mean, *always* knowing when he's flying over Germany. I wish I wasn't so close to it. Apart from planning the raids, I have to monitor them when they are out there. It's torture. We have to count them home you know, in the morning ... And I feel so bad when I hope and pray to any God that will listen to me that a missing aircraft has got somebody else's sons in it. That's awful, isn't it?' Her mother looked down at her hands where one thumb rubbed the other as if she was trying to remove a stain.

'There would be something wrong with you if you didn't feel like that,' Kate said, swallowing hard. 'Drink your tea. Try to put it out of your mind. You will drive yourself crazy.'

Kate was deeply disturbed by her mother's outburst. She had breached the unwritten and absolute code that they did not speak of the risks, or of what might happen. Their fears were too raw to have words put to them. But it was also unlike Eleanor to talk about emotions at all. Kate knew that her mother loved them all but she had never been a demonstrative parent and much of the practical mothering had been left to Martha. Kate and her brothers and sisters had always thought that the absent way her mother dealt with domestic life was endearing, that she was too clever, too much of an eccentric academic to devote herself to rearing six children. And they loved her for her crosswords, algebra and her stories of the life Poppa had promised her. The war had not come between Eleanor and her children because she had always seemed to be in a different world from them anyway. It was Kate, and not Eleanor, who brought the Little Ones into these conversations in the teahouses and pubs around the airfields of Lincolnshire when they met. Kate had never seen this maternal anxiety before. There had been none when her mother had waved goodbye to Nick and fifteen-year-old Tony as they left for the other side of the world. Hadn't she shot off to England in 1940 without a backward glance at Kate or Maggie and George in the belief that the war effort needed her mathematical skills more than they needed their mother?

But looking at her mother now Kate could see that something had changed. Perhaps now as she sat in the control tower night after night, moving the markers across the map of enemy Europe, one of which represented Tony's Lancaster, and Nick still on the missing list, she was being forced to reassess what her children meant to her.

They sat in silence. She is only concerned about Tony and Nick, Kate thought. Maybe we have to be in unspeakable peril before she can mine her feelings and know that she loves us? Kate was hurt but she was angry too and some of the resentment at being left behind four years ago bubbled to the surface. She felt nauseous and pushed the precious fairy cake with its wing tips sticking out of the fake cream into the middle of the grubby table. 'We lost a radar mechanic last week. His name was Archie. Mummy, are you listening?'

'Yes dear ... that was sad,' Eleanor replied, her tone flat and uninterested again.

'He took the shift after me ... and the winds got up when he was trying to fix the parabolic antenna on the mast. We had lost the AC and W.' Kate looked intensely at her mother who appeared confused. 'The Aircraft Control and Warning,' Kate said, as if she were speaking to a child. Eleanor's face remained passive. 'It could have been me who fell.'

Eleanor stubbed out the cigarette, savagely twisting it against the ashtray, and took a deep breath. 'Kate, we cannot think in terms of what might happen. It is just too much for all of us. I am very sorry I mentioned the control tower. I should have kept it to myself. Where is Tony anyway? Why is that boy always late?'

Her mother had made it clear that the discussion about how Kate and her mother were coping with their worst fears was now to be closed and that Kate was being instructed to rearrange her features, lift her voice and appear jolly when Tony arrived. Her mother's momentary lapse into the dark pit was over.

'Are you looking forward to your leave next month Mummy, over your birthday? It will be wonderful to be home together for a few days and see Maggie and George and Martha and Jim and everyone, won't it?' Kate said, mustering all the cheer she could.

The air in the teashop freshened when the door clattered open. Tony pushed it closed behind him, sweeping his cap from his head.

'Sorry Mum ... late night,' he said pulling a silly face. 'Hello Sis. Gosh it's good to see you.' He bent to kiss them both and flopped in the chair beside them. 'Brilliant. Fairy cakes. Are they real? How was the train, Kate?'

'Late of course and so that means we don't have a lot of time I'm afraid, because I have to be back tonight.'

'Better get some tea quickly then. We mustn't waste a second.'

Kate glanced at her mother but was afraid to hold her eye. 'I'll get it. You talk to Mummy. How is your poor arm?'

'Oh it's nothing, just a scratch. I'll be back in the air in a day or two.'

By the time Kate returned to the table her mother seemed happier.

'I've been saving this until you got here Tony ... I've got the most wonderful thing to show you.' Kate said putting the cup down in front of her brother.

'What is it, Sis? A new spanner?'

'A letter from Poppa,' she said smugly. 'It's dated months ago but he seems to be well. Look ... isn't it just wizard to see his writing again? It came yesterday. It has been all the way to Ireland and then Martha sent it on to me at Hawkshill so I suppose it had to go through all the vetting and everything. You know what the RAF is like. They don't trust anything about Ireland.' Kate remembered how shocked she had been when her friend Susan, who had been stationed up in Lancashire in '41, told her of the celebrations there when the radar teams confused the Luftwaffe into bombing Dublin instead of the docks in Liverpool. She sighed. She didn't think her mother could cope with the possibility that Maggie and George might also be in danger. Nor did she want to think about that or the fact that Susan's story had made her question where any of her misfit family belonged in this war. 'He says he has planted a vegetable garden, which is the envy of the camp.'

Eleanor had the letter in her hand now. 'I never saw your father with a spade or a trowel in his hand at home. He always left all that to Jim.' Eleanor seemed to be talking to herself. 'Oh, he was full of enthusiasm of course for the gardens he would make for me but nothing ever came of it. I wonder will we know each other at all when we get them home. If ...'

'Now, none of that mother,' Tony said gently taking the letter from her shaking hand. 'This is all going the right way. The Yanks bombed Salang a few weeks ago so the pressure is really on the Japs. Old Louis Mountbatten has been put in charge with General Slim. It's going to make a huge difference. We are weeks away from winning the air war over there. There are some chaps on the base who've just come back, Mosquito boys mostly, and it has really turned for us. They say they'll be softening up Singapore in a few weeks. And the Japs are on the run from India. It's only a matter of time before they are driven out of Burma and then Malaya.'

And as if his words had decided the matter he turned to Kate. 'And so, Kate, what high jinks have you been up to? We all know what they say about WAAF girls. Oh, sorry Mum.' But Eleanor had taken back the letter and was forensically examining the Japanese hieroglyphics stamped on the envelope. She was once again paying little attention to them.

'Don't you start! I'm fed up with that sort of talk. "Officers' groundsheets" indeed. It's so unfair and completely untrue,' Kate said, laughing and hitting her brother's shoulder with her hat. 'Actually I've been really busy. You of all people should understand how important our work is. If I can't keep the masts working or fix the electronics on the aircraft you won't know where you're going and we won't be able to see if you need help. Why, only last week we were able to direct Air Sea Rescue from Dover to pick up one of your mates in the channel. What's more, we are now able to put down a navigational beam and can guide your Pathfinders to within ninety yards of a target. So more respect please.'

Kate returned to her base in Kent that evening, consoling herself with the thought that she would see Tony again in a few weeks when she went back up to Lincolnshire for her brother's twenty-first birthday. She was getting used to life in the mess although at first she had been intimidated by the sophistication of the other WAAFs, most of whom had been to smart boarding schools and had 'done the season' in London. They primped and preened themselves for the evenings with the airmen at the bar and Kate felt like a country bumpkin. They were radar operators and filter room plotters like her new friend Susan, who had to analyse all the information on the screens as aircraft headed towards the coast at 300 miles an hour and then feed it through to people like her mother in the operations room.

To make her feel even more out of place Kate was the only WAAF officer who dressed in overalls every morning and the only woman on the mechanics team. She had to remind herself that when she was recruited she had been told that only the brightest were taken on as radar mechanics and that she should be very proud of that.

'Mares eat oats and does eat oats and little lambs eat ivy'. It was the latest number from America and everyone was dancing. She watched Susan who was with an American pilot with high cheekbones and perfect teeth. Her friend was taller than her partner and tonight her hair had a coif on the crown of her head in the new style. She had new lipstick too, a dark blood red. Kate leant against the bar and ordered an orange squash. She wasn't sure she liked parties at the best of times but she had also had a disconcerting day. She had climbed the mast in the morning and had found it difficult to force the memory of Archie's awful fall last week out of her mind. The channel was calm and the water slapped softly against the foot of the cliff below the station. It was the best view in England from the top of the mast and usually she loved to work up there on a day like today when she could see Calais easily and imagine the Germans hiding in their horrible concrete gun batteries dotted along the coast. Hawkshill was the closest radar station as the crow flies to the Ruhr valley and she told herself that her job, hundreds of feet off the ground, meant that Tony could get home. Up there she felt she was an important cog in a mighty Allied effort.

But today it had been different and her heart had thudded with anxiety. She had allowed herself to look down and felt sick. She was tentative as she moved her feet across the scaffolding and when she dropped a spanner and heard it crashing off the struts of the pylon she was light-headed and panicked. She hurried to finish, the intricate electronics failing to absorb her as they usually did. When she got back to the ground she allowed herself to question what had got into her. She was alarmed at her fumbling because if she did not keep a steady head she would fall the next time. After all, she thought with guilty detachment, Archie was not the first friend she had lost. But in her heart she knew what had changed. In trying to convince her mother that she was in danger, like Tony and Nick, she had simply frightened herself.

A tall, broad-shouldered boy in Canadian air force dress uniform placed his elbow on the bar and turned slowly towards her.

'Hello, you're the lassie who fixes the kit right? Odd job for a girl, isn't it? Especially a pretty one like you.' He had soft lips that lifted at the corners so that he seemed to be teasing as he spoke. He held her gaze and blew a smoke ring into the middle of the room. He had green eyes with dark centres and when he blinked his lids closed slowly like a cat. 'Do you like the song? A friend of mine in Bomber Command who just got here from the States gave it to me.'

'I think it is rather stupid actually. Lambs don't eat ivy.'

He laughed easily. 'Do I hear an Irish accent by any chance?' He tried to affect a stage one himself and it was now Kate's turn to laugh. 'Dance?' he asked.

It was a five-minute walk to the farmhouse tucked into the woods and set back from the cliff top where Kate and Susan shared a room.

Mrs Biddlecombe the landlady was a round, jolly widow, diminutive in height but with a bawdy chuckle that filled a room. She reminded Kate of Martha and fussed over the two girls like a Bantam hen. Every evening she left out a pitcher of warm milk for them to take to bed after partying in the mess. For Kate the farmhouse was a respite from the hothouse competition amongst the WAAF girls.

'You were having a good time tonight,' Susan said as she linked her arm though Kate's, 'with that handsome Canadian. He is a dish all right. Crash-landed at Manston a couple of weeks ago, didn't he?'

Kate kicked a stone off the path. 'Yes he did and not really. I mean, I was not having a good time.'

'What's the matter, silly?'

Kate stopped and turned towards the sea and stared at the lights of Calais blinking on the horizon. 'To be honest, Susan, I really don't understand the rules. I mean I liked him and he was charming and funny and a good dancer and everything but I'm just not that sort of person ... I mean. Oh, I don't know what I mean. I think he expected more from me.' She looked at her friend and felt the blush rise from her collarbones.

'Oh Kate, my sweet Irish ninny! Of course these boys will say anything ... including that you owe it to them because this might be their last night alive and all that, but some of them are playboys, especially the Americans and the Canadians and I think perhaps Mr Winnipeg may be one of them. Pay no attention to him darling. You just wait for Mr Right.'

'But I don't want anyone. I don't want another person to worry about. I know I'm not the only one to have a brother in Bomber Command but there's Nick and Poppa and I just couldn't cope with ... You understand that, don't you?'

Eighteen

JAVA

Day after day Nick lay in the hut, staring at the ants in the dry fronds above his head. Under Zach's bed he found a box in which his friend kept the pathetic fragment of cloth he had put on his head for Hanukkah, a toothbrush of coconut fibre and some of the polished stones from Sally's costume. Nick turned the precious things over and over in his hand. It was his fault. If he had watched out for Zach the way they had always looked after each other before Sally, those bastards would not have been able to do what they did. If he had been man enough to ignore the laddish nudging and winking, Zach would still be alive. When he could shuffle off his self-loathing for a second or two, he swung into a festering hatred of the Dutchmen and planned meticulously what he was going to do to avenge Zach.

'Come on lad, you've got to keep yourself going. You did what you could,' the sergeant said when Nick had not left his bed for three days except for Tenko in the black mornings. He was tortured. His garden started to wither and the three surviving hens poked their featherless heads into the hut, demanding food. He no longer noticed the gnawing ache in his belly or thought about food at all. Obsessively he imagined how he would expose Zach's killers and make them pay. The black dog of depression sat on the end of the bed, licking his lips, ready to devour him.

His feet began to sting, and then the soles burned as if he were standing on live coals, and within a few days his hands did the same. When he got to the football pitch for Tenko, his knees, now like tumours on his twig-like legs, gave way, and Shorty and Piper had to help him to make the bow. The little he did eat he vomited up. He no longer heard Kate's laughter on the lake in his dreams. When he awoke in the black hours of the night he did not know where he was and sometimes he did not know who he was. And then it was only the pain from his raw scrotum where the skin had split and peeled that landed him back into his miserable reality.

'You have beriberi,' the colonel said. 'Look son, you've got to stop grieving for your mate. We'll all die if we give in to that and then the Nips have won.'

'But those bastards ...' his voice trailed off. He was suddenly overwhelmed with tiredness.

'Someone other than you will take care of them when this bloody show is over, but you have to live to make sure they face the music. It's imperative. For all of them who have died. Do you understand that? And don't you think that the other boys have enough to be doing keeping themselves alive without worrying about you? You have no right to choose to be ill.' The colonel's eyes locked on Nick's. 'Most of the Dutch have already left camp. It seems the Japs have other plans for all of us. POWs are being loaded onto ships in the docks as we speak. There's a rumour we're to be used to build a railway in Siam so they can get at India, so God knows what's ahead for any of us.'

The colonel was right of course. By wallowing in his anger and grief Nick was asking too much of everyone else. He and Piper, Shorty and the sergeant were still a team, a smaller one to be sure but a team nevertheless. Nick felt a rush of warmth for this officer who had done so much to keep them alive and to stand up to the worst of the barbarity of their captors.

'I'm afraid you're going to be even more uncomfortable before there is any improvement in your condition. There will be some swelling in your neck, feet and ankles mostly, and the Java balls – the old unmentionables – will be badly aggravated,' the colonel said as if he were discussing a bus timetable. This big gentle man was exhausted. He had delivered these messages, and worse, for many months now. There were deep lines on his face and he looked twenty years older than he had when they had landed in Java, but then perhaps they all did.

At first Nick's ankles swelled up and his feet looked like loaves of batch bread. The stabbing hot pain caused him to cry out and he had to bite down on his loose teeth to prevent himself screaming. When he put them in water to relieve the heat, it was as if knives of ice were sticking into them. Then his legs, stick-thin for months now, grew to gateposts. His neck was so swollen that his head seemed to emerge straight from his shoulders.

Piper and Shorty nursed him and lifted the spoon to Nick's mouth with thin spinach soup three times a day. They sold everything they had, even Piper's tooth mug, and bought a duck's egg for him, whisking it up with palm sugar. They brought him a lime, some *blanchang*, and scrounged a chicken leg from Adi. They went out into the jungle and collected wild tapioca leaves and Nick ached with the memory of feeding Zach like that. They bartered for emetine and mag sulph pills with the few remaining Dutchmen who had inherited the black market. Shorty gave up his St Christopher medal for the medicine but the weeping sores between Nick's legs remained and the swellings hardened.

A month after Zach died, the colonel stood facing the 400 men still left in camp and urged them to move in closer so that they could hear him. The formality of military parade grounds had been abandoned long ago and, in any case, the colonel did not have the strength himself to lift his voice for them.

'Right lads, this is it. We have orders. We knew this day was coming. As you know we're the last of Blackforce here in camp. I can't tell you where we are going, I'm afraid. I believe some fellows have been sent to the Philippines and some to Japan, but the chances are we will be sent north to work on the railway. The Japs are keeping their cards very close to their chest so I can't tell you any more than that. We leave tomorrow at dawn.'

The sun was low in the sky and fine mist still swirled around the foot of the mountains as Colonel Dunlop led his bedraggled men out of the old school for the last time. Nick was very weak and the bloating in his groin made each step Herculean. Sergeant Maloney shut him up when he said he would rather stay where he was and that they should leave him behind. He and Piper, being much the same height, nudged their shoulders in under Nick's armpits and hefted his scrawny weight onto their shoulders. He dragged his swollen feet behind him, leaning heavily on his friends, down the worn path to the cemetery and the docks.

The column crawled towards the sea, past the last of the guard towers and the kampong where Adi lived. When they reached the cemetery the colonel held up his hand to bring the men to a stop. One of them raised a bugle to his lips as Nick and the others did their best to stand to attention, squaring back their jutting collarbones. The mournful notes of 'The Last Post' rolled across the luscious fringes of the jungle and up to the mountains. As the sun crept out from behind the volcano its rays fell on the graveyard and kissed the hundreds of crooked white crosses, lighting them up like stars in a red sky. The Star of David stood in the corner, heading the constellation. Salty tears ran down Nick's face and he felt no shame in failing to hold them back.

There were three holds on the rusty ship, accessed by small ladders bolted to the wall. The others helped Nick negotiate the ladder and they shuffled and groaned like cattle as more came through the narrow hatch and pushed them up against the hull of the ship.

'We need to stay near the hatch,' the sergeant hissed. Sticking out his elbows he led the other three in a determined squeeze towards the small hole of light. No matter how close they got, it still looked like a pinprick as the hold filled with men until there was no room for any of them to move or sit down. The sergeant and Piper continued to stand under Nick. With his arms over their shoulders to keep the weight off his searing feet, his neck throbbed with the pressure so that he had to alternate between standing on his bloated feet and hanging from the cross of his friends.

'Don't worry son, they can't take us far like this,' the sergeant said. They all looked longingly at the tiny patch of daylight. Nick searched the sergeant's face for reassurance but saw a shadow darken his pale blue eyes. The Japanese were going to fill the holds until no one could move an inch. The heat was insufferable. When the engines clanked into a bad-tempered growl, fumes seeped into the hold. They're going to cook us alive in here, Nick thought. He forced himself to think of the sweet cool air of Westmeath and to imagine himself pulling in a great lungful of it while the swans hauled themselves off the lake on thumping wings.

A guard lowered a bucket through the hatch, his eyes bright with malicious pleasure. 'This ... latrine,' he said, laughing. It was impossible to pass the bucket to those who called for it and in any event it soon filled and spilled and the guards refused to take it up and empty it. The ship bucked and rolled and the smell of excrement and vomit overwhelmed the fumes from the engine. It became clear all too soon that the sergeant had been right to fight for a spot close to the hatch as the men against the hull in the bow, where it was hottest and the pitch of the ship at its most violent, were the first to succumb. A single flagon of drinking water was grabbed by desperate greedy hands and emptied before it could it reach the poor beggars retching themselves dry. The sergeant tried to instil some discipline but this was a hell where no one obeyed orders. One man who had been packed against the hull tried to drink the blood of his dead companion until his horrified neighbours strangled him. The dead bodies were passed over the heads of the living and handed up to the guards on deck who threw them, unshrouded, into the sea. Then came the vicious swish and splosh of sharks. Nick could hear the guards laughing before they went back to hosing themselves down to keep cool. While the prisoners sweltered underneath they could hear the delicious water pouring over the gunwales into the sea.

As men died some space cleared for the sick to sit down. The sharks skulked around the ship all the time now, bumping off the hull, each strike a hollow boom, as if demanding their next meal. Men were moaning incoherently and Nick didn't think it would be long before he lost his own reason as his neighbours died beside him. He let his mind wander to the lake all the time now. He was in the little grey boat, rocking on the short waves. There was Kate with her sketchbook on the lakeshore beach. He forced himself to try and list the names of the wildflowers she loved to paint.

The tone of the engine changed and dropped to a deep bass.

'Sarge, we're slowing down,' Piper said.

'Let's hope so son. If God has any mercy we must get out of here soon.'

The men emerged from the hold like lab mice, squinting painfully into the white sunshine. Nick coughed as the raw air caught in his throat, icy fresh after the stagnant stench of the hold. He stood unsteadily on the wharf as the ground heaved beneath him. Piper and the sergeant again pushed their shoulders into Nick's body and gratefully he dropped his weight off his stinging feet onto his friends. A man in ragged shorts approached, followed by another dressed only in a white loincloth.

'Welcome,' the first one said and smiled lopsidedly. 'You guys look pretty beat up. We'll get you sorted in jig time. Follow us.'

As they passed under an arch Nick could make out a sign, *Selarang Barracks*. Attap huts lined the path down which they now shuffled. Rows of vegetables grew in plots beside them and poultry pens knocked together from sticks and broken crates housed skinny hens and scrawny ducks. Through the open gaps of the huts wasted men lay on their beds wearing only loincloths. They looked like starving children in nappies and stared with hollow disinterest at the new arrivals. Another prison, another country, Nick thought desolately. He was tired, so tired of it all. He wanted nothing any more but for it all to be over, to lie down and let the blackness come.

'*Kora. Bakaero,*' a Japanese guard screamed.

They all knew what it meant. 'Come here. Fool.' The two men in front of them bowed low and the new arrivals behind them did likewise. They knew what to do. A guard prodded Nick and Piper viciously with the end of his rifle. More of the same – Nick didn't think he could bear it.

'This is the bureau. This is where we will take down who you are, your unit, where you have come from and anything else you can tell us about missing men and so forth,' said a man with a plummy British voice. 'It may take a bit of time, I'm afraid ... so many Java parties are coming through. We have a bit of a backlog. We don't know how long you'll be staying with us, but most of you will be pushed through up north to the railway pretty quick. Stand in line there.'

Nick shuffled forward waiting his turn. 'Tottenham. 'A' Company 2/2 Australian Pioneers,' he said at last to a ruddy faced man behind the desk.

'Good man. We have you now.' He wrote in the ledger and then looked up at Nick and smiled. 'We'll get you to the hospital lickety split,' he said.

His accent had the same singsong quality as Mick Kelly's and Nick ached at the echo of home it dredged up. 'It'll be a minute, son, before we can get you a stretcher. Can you just sit outside?'

At last Nick could sit down. He hung his head between his knees as much as the swelling in his neck would allow and thought about what the man had said about the bureau. Now at last his family might be told where he was, and where he would die. After all the months in Java he had become used to believing that he would simply be counted as 'lost' by his family and by history, a small word, which meant the end of life for him and would give them no comfort. For a long time he had thought that he would be just a statistic with no grave, no record of valour, no date of death. The thought that they might now know what had happened to him seeped into the fringes of his mind like cool water on a burn. The hard knots of pain and disappointment that had tightened there as hope diminished began to loosen. He closed his eyes and his dry lips cracked into a painful smile.

The front of the bureau was thronging with wretched and starving men. Threading through them were filthy soldiers and airmen with clipboards and pencils behind their ears, who barked instructions while Nick sat with his mates staring dumbly at the chaos around them. A bald man in a filthy dog collar put his hand on Nick's shoulder. '*Teed apa,*' he said almost merrily, 'nothing matters, *teed apa*.' Nick thought he was wrong. It mattered that someone would tell his family what had happened to him. That was all he had wanted for months.

'He's an odd one,' Piper said with a nod of his head towards the padre. He touched his index finger to his forehead and twisted it back and forth, raising his eyes to the sky.

'There's another,' Shorty said. A lanky older man was pacing up and down on the far side of a high fence on the edge of Nick's vision. There was a stoop to his back and his head poked forward in compensation, like a tortoise from his shell. He wore homemade glasses with metal rims, over which he peered crook-edly at the faces of the new men.

'The Poms are that side of the fence. He's one of those Brit officers who wants to be saluted as if we were at Sandhurst,' said the man who had met them at the ship. 'He comes here every time there's a new Java party. He's looking for his son, poor bugger. What are the chances of that? The lad wasn't even in the same army.'

Nick allowed the conversation to drift over his head. He was so tired.

'Jaysus, look at him Nick. He's real old school,' Shorty said.

Nick had no more interest in this relic of the last war than he did in the deranged padre. All he wanted was to lie down on the hospital bed he had been promised and to obliterate forever the misery around him, but to humour Shorty he raised his head with one last effort. The man had a yellow star on his shirt, from which one sleeve had been ripped. His shorts were patched with hessian and he wore sandals made from pieces of tyre rubber. He was much older than everyone on the Australian side of the fence and had been tall once but now his bony shoulders were rounded over a sunken chest, giving his upper body a caved-in appearance. His misshapen glasses might have been made from a coat hanger and the joins were messily fixed with copper wire. He squinted as if the glasses were new to him.

He stared at the old boy's face, which was still handsome despite its decrepitude. He was afraid of the tricks his mind was playing and looked away to clear the image, then reluctantly returned his gaze. His head was spinning and he thought he might pass out. Entranced, he watched the strange old man lift his hand from the wire to push the wobbly glasses up to the bridge of his nose. Nick knew that hand. It was as familiar to him as his own. It was the hand he remembered from the morning room the day of his sixteenth birthday shaking with the china teacup. A painful lump rose in his throat and threatened to burst through his chest. He swallowed hard to cut off the wail.

'Dad?'

The older man froze. Adjusting the spectacles, his watery eyes fixed on the boy on the ground. His gaze rolled down to the lumps that were Nick's feet and then up again to his face as if he were trying to recalibrate a memory to make it fit with the misshapen body in front of him. Someone helped Nick to his feet and grabbing the wire for support, he leant his forehead against it.

'Son? Is it really you?' Gerald whispered. His skinny chest was heaving and a gasp escaped through his teeth.

'My God. Oh my God. Oh Nicky.' And he kissed Nick's brow through the fence.

Nick felt his knees buckle and the blackness came at last.

Nineteen

CHANGI, SINGAPORE

The walls and the frayed cotton sheet over Nick's bed were the same colour of toothpaste green. A sharp, artificial smell caught the back of his throat. He had no idea where he was. His eyesight had deteriorated badly but he could see and smell enough to know that he was not in the jungle. There were no attap fronds above his head, nor any ants stealing along the poles. It occurred to him that perhaps he had died but when he tried to turn his head to see better what else was around him, pain stabbed through his neck and there, in the beds beside him, packed tight head to toe in the big square room, were the same scarecrows of men he had known in the jungle. Slowly a hazy memory of Shorty, Piper and the sergeant carrying him here came back to him but he was no longer sure what was real and what a dream.

He preferred to be in his dream world but as the days passed he drifted back from those lovely places in his mind to his hospital prison bed no matter how hard he tried to stay away. At times the dream world and the real one came together. Kate appeared in a nurse's uniform beside his bed with a spray of wildflowers in her hand.

Someone was sitting on a tea crate by the bed. Nick was overwhelmed with pity, but he wasn't sure whether it was for himself or for the old man beside him, a crumpled, much older version of his father.

'Hello, son,' Gerald said, 'you're going to be fine now.' This man beside the bed had lost two of his teeth, which gave his smile a rakish air.

'Where am I?' Nick croaked. 'Who are you?' He tried to lift his head but the swelling in his neck choked him.

'It's Poppa, son. You're in the hospital in Changi, the best place to be, believe me. Here, let me help.' Gerald cupped a shaking hand behind Nick's head and lifted the water canteen to his lips. 'Do you know, I used to feed you as a baby like this, isn't that strange? You were such a bonny child – I thought I would burst with pride just looking at you.'

Nick didn't trust himself to speak. Four years had passed, during which he had turned from boy to man and the old man beside him, in his odd glasses with his missing teeth and his bizarre outfit could not be the one that he had fought with at home every day from breakfast until bedtime.

'How long have I been here?' he whispered.

'A week or so, three maybe. To be honest, I gave up counting time a long while ago.'

'Have you seen my mates?'

'They have been in a few times. Good boys those.'

'My best friend died,' Nick said, catching his breath. The words had burst out of him unbidden. What did he want to tell this man who said he was his father?

'I know son, it's hard.'

But you don't know, Nick wanted to scream at the spectre. His father had never understood Nick's loneliness, and had never had the need for a friend himself.

'Now rest. I have to go to my man in the kampong and get some more medicine for you. I'll be back later.' At the door the strange old man stopped and turned. 'Corporal. See that boy gets everything he needs,' he barked at the medical orderly.

Here was the father that Nick remembered. He might have been talking to the rogue who came to buy his cattle. Nick caught the eye of the soldier in the bed beside him, the remnants of a man he recognized from 'A' Company.

'Friends in high places, eh mate?'

'Not really,' Nick mumbled. He felt the bloated skin at the back of his neck grow hot.

'Funny, these Pommie officers. You'd think they'd drop all this them-and-us stuff in here, wouldn't you? Haven't we enough to be doing coping with the bloody Japs? Word is, they do nothing in here but play bridge and keep the best food for themselves. Geneva says they can't be asked to work, neither.'

Nick nodded miserably.

'Not like our lot, eh? Look at Colonel Dunlop. He's a beaut' isn't he?'

'Yeah, a really good fellow,' Nick said, and meant it. Relief that the man had moved away from the old-school British officer gushed through him, and then he was overwhelmed with disgust. Did he understand loyalty at all? As tears pricked against his swollen eyelids. Nick turned his back on his neighbour and stared at the antiseptic green walls.

Thanks to the food and medicines that Gerald brought in from the kampong Nick began to feel better. Within a week or two he could shuffle a few steps without having to swing his legs in exaggerated arcs to avoid his swollen and peeling scrotum. The burning sensation in his feet and hands lessened to an itchy glow. He could still not see properly and viewed his new world as though he were looking at it down a pipe. When he woke he was frightened that he had lost his sight altogether but then the pinprick of light in the middle of the blackness slowly opened wider. Nor could he turn his head because his purple neck was still hot and swollen and thick with beriberi. Like a moody elephant he swung his torso to move his head and shoulders to face in the direction he wanted to look. He was locked into a metal box and voices banged off the sides of it. He felt isolated and alone.

Gerald came every day with something for him to eat. Coconut, papaya, tapioca pudding made with lime – lime and slime his father called it.

'Where do you get all this stuff?' Nick asked. He was afraid that some other fellow was doing without because his father had pulled rank.

'Some of it is from my garden. Who would ever have thought that my green fingers would have been so useful in a war? And then I have some friends in the kampong. I can talk to them, you see. I speak the language. Your mother and I used to live amongst these people many years ago so I know their ways.' Gerald stared absently out through the rusty mosquito screen. 'It was not what she was expecting I'm afraid. Your poor mother, what I have put her through over the years! The local people are very kind. They even give me the odd cigarette or a cheese biscuit or maybe a banana. "*Ada baik Tuan?*" they ask me. It means, "Are you well, sir?" It reminds me of the old days.'

'I know what it means,' Nick said. He felt a familiar twist of irritation. His father appeared to have no understanding of how Nick had survived the war this far. His thoughts in the kampong, Gerald didn't seem to notice the bite to his son's voice.

'I always find it humbling that they are interested at all in how I am when they have nothing. Imagine calling me *Tuan* when I look like this! The Dutch and the Americans try to bully them, you see, and they don't like that. Hardly surprising really. Sometimes I barter an egg or two from my ducks for something I need, like a pineapple. Very good vitamin C. Or some emetine or quinine.'

'Quinine? Do you have malaria?'

'No, I think that my pickled liver is too much for the mosquitoes. But others do so I bring it in for them. The doctors know I can get medicine when no one else can.'

Nick was unsure that he had heard correctly. 'You mean you get stuff for all these people in here?'

'If I can,' Gerald said, looking around the ward in a grandfatherly way. The ward orderly, a pink-faced lieutenant with a heavy black moustache that sat on his face like a dead mole, approached the bed.

'Morning, Major,' he clipped. 'I wonder would you be able to get some magnesium sulphate today for the poor blighter in bed ten? I don't think he will make it otherwise.' He turned to Nick. 'We really couldn't manage without this … supply line.'

Shorty, Piper and Sergeant Maloney stood at the end of his bed. They looked better than they had done on their arrival in Changi over a month ago. Their backs were straighter and there was some colour and flesh on their faces.

'You fellas have fattened up,' Nick said.

'Still got the bloody shits,' Piper moaned, 'and I've got ulcers in my mouth and fucking Java balls, only they're now called Changi balls, but it's the same thing.'

'We was rodded yesterday,' Shorty added, his face like thunder.

'Rodded?'

'Yeah. The Japs stick a glass rod up yer arse to test for cholera. It's a sure sign that we're about to be sent up country.' The other two nodded in agreement.

'We've just been told we're off tomorrow. All the boys who came in with us from Java are going. There's 5000 of us leaving by train at 0600,' the sergeant said. He was looking intently at Nick.

'Tomorrow?' Nick asked. 'But I ...'

His father loomed into the blurred edges of his vision and the scrawny shoulders of his three friends pulled back, each of them snapping their hands to their temples.

'Sir!'

'At ease, chaps,' Gerald said crisply. Nick cringed. Only the Japs demanded this pre-war fucking shit and Colonel Dunlop had never insisted on it.

'We was just telling Tottenham here, sir, that we are going to Bam Pong tomorrow ... on the work party to the railway,' the sergeant said. 'We've been expecting it, sir. Most of the others brought over from Java have already gone. We didn't want to go without the lad here.'

'Nobody told me,' Nick said and looked furiously at his father. 'I have to go with the boys.' He raised himself onto his elbows.

'Forget it, son, you're not going anywhere. You're not fit, and that's an end of it,' Gerald said. He peered at the sergeant over the top of his wobbly glasses as if daring him to disagree.

'But there are others going who have been sick, right sarge?' Nick asked.

The sergeant hesitated before he replied, exchanging quick glances with Shorty and Piper. 'No mate, the major's right – there's no one as bad as you coming with us,' he said eventually. 'They'll send you on when you're better and then we can all be together again like we've always been.'

Nick numbly shook each of his friends' hands. There was nothing else to say. 'See ya,' they managed and left the ward.

'You had no right to stop me going,' Nick said to his father. 'Those fellas are more important to me than you can know. We've kept each other alive from the beginning. They were coming to get me to go with them. I want to go. You can't speak for me any more. It's just like it's always been, isn't it?'

'You wouldn't survive up there in your condition. You probably wouldn't survive anyway. Half of the boys have died already and they were fit when they left. Count yourself lucky, Nicholas, that I was here to look out for you.'

Gerald turned as smartly as he could on his thick rubber sandals.

He was back the next day, bright and cheerful and it was as if the discussion about Nick going north had never happened. He brought fish paste and a duck's egg, more protein than Nick had seen in weeks in Java. Gerald then sat down as he always did, on the tea crate, and leaned his elbows on the bed.

'It's a real struggle, you know. It's unbelievable that these Nip bastards only give us half rations for the sick in here when you're the ones who need it most. Sometimes I just can't get enough for all of these boys. Chaps are dying of bloody starvation here every day. Do you know we even cook up maggots from the rice with fish paste? It's called prawn *risque*. Clever name, isn't it?'

'We did that in Java too,' Nick said sullenly.

'Yes. I sometimes forget what you've been through. I'm sorry son. We're all inclined to think that we've had the worst cross to bear, but the local people have had it tough too,' Gerald continued. 'Just after the surrender, the Japs beheaded eight Chinese and put their heads on the railings outside the camp. We were told that if we tried to escape or disobeyed the Japanese Imperial army in any way we would lose our heads too. We had to watch as the maggots crawled through the eye sockets and ears. I'm afraid I've never been able to contemplate eating prawn *risque* and never will.'

'Captain Hatu was keen on beheading too,' Nick said quietly. He was still nursing his fury from the day before and had been rehearsing all night how he would tell his father to go to hell and that he intended to get up to Bam Pong as soon as he could. To his embarrassment he saw the old man's bottom lip start to tremble.

'You've had it rougher than I thought son.'

Nick's anger evaporated. 'Thanks for the stuff, Dad,' he said instead.

Although Nick was not an officer, Gerald wangled it so that Nick was allowed to bunk in his hut when he finally got out of hospital. Nick still found it difficult to walk and had no peripheral vision. He was listless and bored and spent his days lying on his bed imagining what Shorty, Piper and the sergeant were doing. To his irritation Gerald fussed endlessly over him, making him drink *lalang* juice that he prepared diligently every day by pulverizing the tall grasses he gathered from outside the prison wall with the same enthusiasm with which he used to fix a gin and tonic for his mother before the war. And then Nick felt guilty about being irritated and short-tempered with the old man, and the long hours lying on the rope-slung bed were studded with remorse and self-contempt.

Three weeks later Nick could make it to roll call by himself. An Australian corporal poked his head gingerly through the gap in front of the officers' hut. He looked uncomfortable and embarrassed and Nick could see that the man was struggling with the fact that an enlisted Australian was bunking in a hut with British officers. He looked around him in awe.

'I'm sorry mate ... I mean sir. I'm afraid you are deemed fit for work now,' the corporal said, eyeing him narrowly. 'The Japs expect you to turn out tomorrow. Is that okay?'

Nick's neck flushed hot and red. Now it was his turn to feel awkward. Here was his NCO calling him 'sir' and asking him if he *agreed* to obey an order. For Christ's sake! Being in the same hut as his British officer father meant that he was neither fish nor fowl.

'Of course,' he managed to say through gritted teeth. 'I could do with the twenty-five cents,' he added with a wry laugh. It was a futile attempt at ingratiation. He blocked out the uncomfortable thought that he was again denying connection with his old man, just as he had done in the hospital.

That evening Gerald hobbled into the hut wearing an enthusiastic grin and triumphantly holding out two tin mugs. 'It's grog,

Nick. I made it from some rotten rice ... been waiting for the right occasion.' Nick thought of the decanters on the sideboard at home – no special reason had been needed to pull the stop from their crystal mouths back there when his father needed a sharpener mid morning to chase away the demons from the night before. Nick looked blankly at his father's rosy face and a flicker of disgust curled at the edges of his mouth.

'It's your birthday, for God's sake. Had you forgotten?' He lifted the tin mug to his lips as if it were a cut-glass whiskey tumbler and took a happy slug.

Perhaps there was something to celebrate. Being fit for work meant he was not dying. Nick took the battered tin mug from his father's shaking hand and drank to his own health. It was the first time that his father had ever remembered his birthday and Nick had forgotten it.

Twenty

It was a relief to join the work party and get out of the officers' hut. Not only were the occupants considerably older than he, they were absurdly formal with each other. Everyone seemed to be 'sir' to someone else, tugging forelocks and clipping their heels. At best, he felt he was being merely tolerated because he was 'the Major's boy'. He was acutely aware that some of the officers in the hut felt he should not be there at all, no matter how extraordinary the circumstances of him meeting up with his father. He didn't hold a commission, had joined the Australian army as a Digger and knew nothing of the regimental traditions that these men seemed to hold so dear. A captain called Donaldson from Belfast was particularly malevolent.

But Nick didn't feel that he was a lesser mortal than these stiff and stilted men. He had been in action twice and, although he hadn't been a hero perhaps, he had not disgraced himself. All of these British officers on the other hand had been swept up in the surrender of Singapore without lifting their field glasses in anger. He didn't have to arse-lick to them. Although dressed in rags, some of them only in Jap nappies, they acted as if they were still in the officer's mess in Sandhurst. It was not what Nick had learnt from Colonel Dunlop about leadership and he found the British officers' behaviour ludicrous. His father was by no means the worst offender but all of them roared like tyrannical sergeant majors when they felt a junior officer was not pulling his weight on garden duty or had failed to carry out some servile task. There was constant bickering about food.

'You had an egg last week,' a bald bull of a man from Yorkshire screamed at a captain in the Norfolks.

'But the egg came from his hen,' said Gerald mildly, coming swiftly to the defence of the man in his own regiment.

Nick missed the easy companionship of the sergeant, Shorty and Piper. He didn't seem to be able to make any new mates to replace them. It was easy to blame the odd circumstances of his billeting for his loneliness and a short step of habit from there to see his father as the root cause of it all. To be fair, his father showed little of the foul temper that had marked his life at home. Nick assumed that it was the absence of the decanters to feed it, the big house to bolster his arrogance and the decaying farm, where the only thing that grew was its debts, that made Gerald seem almost benign now. He was an eccentric to be sure, a funny old chap chirping excitedly when a pepper plant produced a fruit, plodding around the kampong looking for food like a stiff old labrador. He was an expert at catapulting sparrows for the pot.

But there was also something Nick had not anticipated he would ever see in his father: he was calm now, with a quiet dignity. All Nick could remember from home was the bluster, noise and tension that had accompanied his father everywhere he went. He was reluctant to reset the dial of his relationship with him, afraid that he might be misreading the changes. He had lost his own parameters too. Without the familiarity of his friends on the one side and the wall of his father's bullying to kick against on the other, he couldn't find the boundaries that he thought defined him.

Nick trudged out of camp to the airfield to hack and hew at the white rock every morning but knew none of his companions. 'A' Company had all gone to Bam Pong. He supposed that the men alongside him had also been left behind because they had been too sick or injured to make the journey, and he imagined that they shared his guilt about not having been sent north to the railways with their friends. But as the endless days of backbreaking work passed, it became clear to him that he couldn't have been more wrong.

'Mugs' game,' said a man called Chalkey from the East End of London, a name that was too benign for this tough thug. 'For some cigs and quinine, I got our sarge to sign me sick so some other sucker had to go. All's fair in love and war, eh?'

'Yeah let's hope the bastard dies,' Nick said, his voice heavy with sarcasm. He already knew that hardship could produce both honour and treachery in all men. He had seen it with the Dutch colonials in Java.

'Listen sonny, in a world where most of us will die, it's every man for himself.'

The cockney was right of course. It was a numbers game that God was playing here where an extra ration could mean the difference between life and death, and that made everyone an enemy. When he woke up to that Nick kept a close eye on these men. These London lads would take the eye out of his head, as Martha might have said. Like Hendriks and Meyer, Chalkey and his cohort were resourceful and ruthless, running a lucrative black-market trade in things that in ordinary life would be worthless and disposable. A man had died, a delighted Chalkey told him, in a fight over a tin mug – it seemed probable that Chalkey had killed him for it.

'When people want things badly there is always a few bob to be made,' he said, rubbing his hands together as if he had just backed the winner at Kempton.

Just like in Java, being on a work party and getting out of camp provided Nick with more opportunities to forage for and steal food. It gave him respect when he could bring it back to the bad-tempered hothouse of the British officers' hut. He was a good frog catcher. He caught a cobra from time to time, and had to bury the memory of Captain Hatu's sword as he severed the spitting heads with his pickaxe. He gathered snails, fat and glutinous and full of protein. The disturbed vegetation crawled with them and he returned to camp with his pockets bulging. Curried, they were delicious. The first time Nick twisted the heads off a nest of baby rats he vowed he would stay hungry rather than eat them, but the man in the cookhouse back in camp was not so squeamish.

'I'll take the meat off the bones and make rissoles. No one will know what wee animal has donated it. We can't afford to waste the protein, can we?' he'd said with a wink.

One morning the work party was marched out of camp, but this time away from the hot dust of the airfield and towards the town instead. As they turned down Havelock Road, Nick and the posse of men with him grew silent, each staring numbly at the neat colonial buildings and manicured gardens. Frangipani trees bowed low over clipped lawns surrounded by beds of begonias and tiger lilies. Chinese coolies picked the dead leaves from the hibiscus bushes and swept the verandas. Bicycle rickshaws squeaked up and down the leafy roads delivering packages tied up neatly in brown paper.

'Christ, did I just die or somethin'?' one fellow said. Nick stared, dazed and open-mouthed, at the opulence around him. At the curve of the old boulevard there was a large crater in the middle of the road, which the work party had been sent to fill. When they reached it, a small Chinese woman emerged from the bushes at the side of the road. A tray piled high with amber biscuits was strapped around her neck. She had a large bruise on her cheekbone and a cut above her right eye and Nick wondered if she was deranged, as there could hardly be a trade for coconut biscuits amongst these grand houses that had now been commandeered by the Japanese brass. Did she not know that the prisoners had no money for this kind of thing? He could not take his eyes off the biscuits and his tongue moved painfully in his dry mouth. 'For you,' she said and her hand beckoned him to come and take her food.

'Good business if we had the money,' Nick said bitterly to the man beside him.

'That's Sung Li. She makes the biscuits to give to us. She comes every day with food to where she thinks we will be and then the Japs beat her up for it and she still keeps coming back,' he replied. 'We've told her not to come, that we're all right, you know, that we're not starving. "Soldiers good men, need food," she says. She's quite a lady.'

She surely is, thought Nick as he bowed low to her tiny frame and thanked her for the three fat biscuits she handed to him. He saved them to share with his father. He shared as well the picture of Sung Li's sad, bruised face.

'I suppose one day they'll go too far and kill her. All for a handful of biscuits,' Nick said as Gerald dunked his into his tapioca leaf tea. 'Perhaps we shouldn't take them?' He glanced at the biscuit with something closer to disgust than relish.

'Perhaps she could make walnut cake like Martha's instead – that might be worth dying for,' Gerald said with a chuckle. Nick looked up sharply.

'And what was all that guff about the local people having it hard you were telling me when I was in the hospital?'

'Christ, it was a joke, a poor one I admit. Perhaps you should give your old man a break now and again.' Gerald's face was intensely sad.

'What have you been doing all day?' Nick asked. His father was right. The comment was unnecessary. He wanted to make amends but his tone still carried the echo of his rebuke.

'Look, I've nearly finished this,' his father said pleasantly as he bent low to rootle under his bed. He pulled out a parcel wrapped in a rag, laid it on the mattress and then untied it as if it were a priceless antique. He lifted a small doll from the cloth. Its blue eyes and painted lashes gave the creature a startled look. Her elbows and knees were moveable joints and she had soft yellow hair made from coconut fibre. A scrap of batik was wound around her body in the local style and tiny sandals were painted onto her feet, two bands across five exquisite toes with painted nails on each foot.

Nick picked up the doll and turned it over in his hands. He lifted his index finger and closed the lid of the doll's eye, which shot back open when he released his finger. 'I didn't know you could do this sort of thing.'

Gerald smiled widely, clearly pleased. Taking the doll back, he laid it on the palm of his hand. 'Look – the eyes stay closed if you lie her down.' He leant forward and pushed the doll towards Nick. 'It helps pass the time,' he said. 'It was really hard to find blue paint for her eyes.' He reached again under the bed and placed a small red train with yellow wheels and two green wagons beside the doll, like a shopkeeper pushing a trade in the bazaar. A tractor and a hay rake followed, a miniature of the old Massey at home. 'See, the spokes on the rake actually turn. That was quite difficult, I must say, but I have the hang of it now.'

'What are you going to do with them?' Nick asked. He was astonished. Where did the old man learn the patience for this kind of thing? He examined each piece closely. The work was intricate and perfectly executed.

'I'm organizing a collection for the civilian children who are interned here on the island. For next Christmas. We should have enough by then.'

Gerald picked up his paintbrush to redden the lips of the doll, his tongue between his broken teeth in concentration. He looked absurdly like Kate and Nick wondered if he knew this man at all.

Nick watched as his father strained the contents of the bamboo pole that framed his bed into two tin mugs. The liquid was milky white. 'I put banana peel in this time. It should be much better.' The toddy had been fermenting since they had drunk the last brew for Nick's birthday in May. The old man was in high spirits. He had salvaged some jam pastries and was in the mood for a party. A brigadier appeared at the opening of the hut, his large frame filling its space and blocking the light.

'They've released some letters at last.' He held a number of faded blue envelopes above his head, 'and a couple of Red Cross parcels.' He smiled at the reaction this extraordinary news had on the men in front of him.

'Good God, we must be winning the war,' one of them said. 'We've never been given the parcels before – Japs put the stuff onto the black market, the bastards.'

There was a letter from Eleanor to the old man that had been written months ago and before his family knew that Nick had been found in Changi. Gerald sat down on a crate and carefully unfolded the letter. It had been opened already and read by the Japanese. When he had finished reading he looked up at Nick. The flimsy paper shook in his big hand.

'What does it say? Is Mum all right?'

'Yes she's fine, they're all fine. It was written before they found you and is in a kind of code but she is obviously under a lot of strain.' Gerald stopped to take in a deep breath. 'Tony has his wings. Imagine that! And he's in England. Rose is there and Kate too. They've all joined up.' He paused and looked into the distance. 'And the two of us here. Go on. Read it.' There were tears in his eyes that he made no effort to hide. 'Just give me some time, son,' he said apologetically. He stood up from his bed and shuffled out of the hut.

My darling Gerald

I have just had tea with Kate and Tony and Kate brought your letter for me to read. I am trying to imagine how you are and what life is like for you. I remember Singapore so well and the wonderful smell of frangipani everywhere. I imagine you can smell it now. We have heard nothing about Nick but I am trying very hard to take heart from the Red Cross when they say that there may be very good reasons for this and that I should not despair.

It has been wonderful to see Tony again. He was only a boy when he left with Nick, don't you remember? He now has his wings and is close by. There is quite a strut to his step now but then there always was, wasn't there, dear? I am not allowed to say what he is doing but I can watch his activities and knowing what I do about the risks, it is the last posting I would want for him. He thinks nothing of it of course and goes out every time as if he were racing over the hedges and walls at home after the hounds. Well, that it what it looks like to me but maybe he hides these things well, as I must. I suppose we have to just hope that the bright star that has shone over him up to now will keep him safe. Rose and Kate are both working with me though not exactly in the same place. Kate fixes things on the tops of masts and Rose works in the office looking at the blips. We are all trying to keep Tony safe.

Martha tells me that Maggie and George are well. Maggie has grown and is much taller than me and George is going to be more like Tony, which is annoying him terrifically. Martha says he spends hours hanging from the beam in the barn hoping that he will stretch.

I pray that you will be home soon and all the worry can then be over. There is hay to cut at home and things are a bit

rundown there. I so need to be a family again and have every-
one home safe and sound. I have grown old and grey with worry
and hope that you will still love me when you get home.
We all send our deepest love my darling.
Eleanor

Nick sat down to write to her.

Dear Mum,

It was lovely for Dad and I to get your letter even though
it was written months ago before I arrived here in Changi. At
least that is one less thing for you to worry about, as I am safe
now. Both Dad and I are fine. I was very sick when I got here
and he was really marvellous at helping me to get better. He is
a very different person now. He is quite the hero around here
and does good work for the sick. He is a great gardener, which is
important so that we have better food. Even the toddy he makes
is kept for proper occasions! We seem to get on much better not
just because we are in the same boat but also because I now
understand what it means to be a soldier and have obligations
to others and all that stuff.

The words he had written jumped off the page at him. Was
it really his father who had changed? Perhaps everyone in this
fractured family will be unrecognizable when this is all over. His
connection with them hung on a thread. He did not feel cheered
by the letter from home, as others around him appeared to be, but
profoundly depressed by it.

It was typical of Tony – when he put his mind to doing something he was oblivious to the obstacles in his way. He might be
over Germany right now. His mother in the ops room. Rose at
her screens. And Kate? Was his family not doing enough already?
Surely she could have stayed at home? It was dangerous work she
was doing, climbing radar masts probably somewhere on the coast

and in all weather. She could slip or be picked off by a rogue German fighter. He wondered miserably what he thought he was doing back in 1940, joining a bunch of road menders. What had he done to save the world from Hitler or the Japanese?

Like his father, he needed to escape the jollity of the men opening letters all around him and the rancid maleness of the hut. Outside, even the sight of the boys ripping open the Red Cross parcels like hyenas at a fresh kill did not put a smile on his face. He had long preferred slow walks around the camp to sitting in the hut where he felt like a frog in a fish bowl. He could then practise his Malay with the local traders who hovered by the gates hawking cigarettes and razors. As he had done at home in the boathouse and on the *Jervis Bay* behind the funnel, he had a place he liked to go to be alone, a space he had found for himself inside a hollow tamarind tree on the edge of what was once a cricket pitch. By force of habit he headed for the tree to read his mother's letter again.

His body ached from the long hours of heaving his pickaxe and, folding the letter back into the envelope, he closed his eyes. There was a commotion coming from the old playing field. It was race day, piggyback racing, and this evening they were running the 'Melbourne Cup', which brought the POWs who liked to bet out in force. Shouts from fellows calling the odds in colonial accents carried across the field to him.

'I'll lay six to one on the two boys from Sydney,' yelled a South African standing on a soapbox.

'What odds on your own pair, the African donkey with the goblin on his back?' came the Australian retort.

'Hello Nick.'

Nick opened his eyes but the man's body blocked the sun and he could not see his face.

'It's Mick Kelly from Cork. Remember me?' The sandy-haired Irishman sat down. 'Good place for a bit of shut-eye. Hard to find a bit of peace, isn't it?'

'Oh hello – I didn't know you were still here,' Nick said, and held out his hand to the freckled man. Not still looking for batteries, are you?'

'No, but there *is* something you could do for us.' He looked apologetic and smiled ruefully. Nick remembered how he had felt the first time he had been asked to help with keeping the radio alive – it lost none of its sweetness the second time.

'Of course. What do you need?'

'I hear you're bunking in a senior officers' hut.'

'Yes, but my father ...'

'No. I understand. Extraordinary story. What an amazing thing to happen. It gave us all a real boost, I can tell you. It's just that the Nips don't search that kind of hut as much as they do ours. I suppose they know it's beyond most of the brass to build a radio,' he smiled, 'and being Signals Corps they're going through us with a fine toothcomb every day, so we need somewhere to keep the spare radio. It's well hidden – in a water canteen, actually – and there's some stuff in a broom handle. We need a man we can trust until we might need it. Do you think you could keep it for us?'

It wasn't a big ask. The device was ingenious. Even if a Jap picked it up it was almost impossible to detect the radio. The hole in the broomstick, into which the copper wires had been threaded, was at the brush end so, bar taking the head off, it was also highly unlikely to be found. It wasn't necessary to tell anyone else what he was doing, indeed safer not to. Nick felt he had been thrown a lifebelt.

Twenty-one

It was 11 September, Tony's twenty-first birthday, and he was to meet Kate at the Horse and Jockey. He was looking forward to showing off his pretty sister to the crew. She was bringing a friend so they would have quite a party.

He pushed open the door of the pub and stopped to enjoy a private look at Kate who was sitting in the corner with a girl with fair hair and long legs. Two glasses of beer sat untouched in front of them and the girls' heads were bent together in intense conversation. Like everyone else in the pub they were in uniform. When they had met with Mother a few weeks ago he had not logged how Kate had grown up. Now sitting amongst a sea of airmen – some of whom were eyeing the two girls up and down in a way that made him want to take them outside – he had to concede that she was not the teenager that he liked to think she was. Her hair had lost that mad frizzy quality that had annoyed her so much as a child and now shone in bonny brown curls and she was wearing a deep red lipstick. How sad that he had missed all the time in between.

Kate's friend looked older than his sister. There was something sophisticated about her; the way she returned the roving glances of the airmen was assured and not something he could imagine Kate doing. He was relieved that she still looked relatively homespun beside her friend although he had to admit he wasn't sure that his mates would see it that way. Kate's friend looked up and scanned the room. She locked her gaze on him. Her eyes were warm and humorous. He had been discovered.

'Isn't that him?' Tony lip-read her words and he stepped hurriedly forwards, embarrassed. Kate would accuse him of ogling no doubt.

'Oh Tony,' how *are* you? How's your arm?' Kate said looking down at the sling.

'Right as rain. I'm back in the air. How are *you*? Gosh it's good to see you,' he said and hugged her.

'Happy birthday, twenty-one today! I brought you something.' Kate reached for the parcel beside her, wrapped in pink tissue paper and tied with a white ribbon. Something caught in Tony's throat and he was surprised by tears hardening like grit under his eyelids. The girls and the gift were from a world he didn't think much about these days. It was easier that way. He carefully undid the ribbon and peeled back the paper. Inside was a book on how to tie fishing flies. He blinked.

'Don't you like it?' Kate asked, searching his face for an answer.

'I love it! It'll be great when this is all over and I can get home. Those trout in the lake had better watch out,' he said, and he bent to kiss her cheek.

'Oh, how awful, I forgot to introduce Susan. This is Tony.' Tony pushed out his hand to shake Susan's and they both laughed to cover the awkward moment. It was strangely affecting and Tony found himself looking into her eyes longer than he meant to.

The door of the pub swung open and Wiki burst through it. 'Hey skipper, you got a gong! You got the fucking DFC for getting the kite home from Brest!' he said, beaming. 'Pardon me language, ladies.' Wiki was still thumping Tony on his back when the rest of the crew came crashing through the door.

'Oh Tony,' Kate whispered when she could get a word in edgeways, 'Mummy and Poppa will be so proud.'

Later that evening Kate sat beside Susan at a small table in the corner of the restaurant. She was pleased with the evening she had organized. It had been fun in the pub and dinner in the hotel had also been a success. There was all the good news about Tony's medal and now it looked to her as though Tony and Susan were getting on well – very well. She was surprised by the flutter of agitation that now ruffled her, but the truth was that the current passing between Tony and Susan made her feel left out. She had to be less childish and possessive about her brothers.

She made a plan to go and celebrate with her mother tomorrow. In her wildest dreams she could not have hoped that Nick and Poppa would be together. Everyone was saying that it would be over soon. Tony had almost finished his tour. He'd had a lucky escape over Brest for sure but he was such a good pilot that of course he had got them all home safely. Someone was looking out for them, as she had always known. She glanced towards the bar where Tony was buying more drinks.

'He's gorgeous,' Susan said. 'Has he got a girlfriend?'

'Gosh no. I don't imagine Tony has ever been kissed.'

The slightly conspiratorial smile on Susan's face evaporated. 'You mean he's been going out every night, not knowing whether ... I mean ... and he's never been with a woman?'

'He's only twenty-one, for God's sake. Anyway, he's almost finished his tour. He'll go to some nice cushy instructing job where he can be safe and have all the girls in England if he wants to.'

'One port and lemon, one brandy and ginger,' Tony said, placing the glasses down in front of the girls.

Kate pulled a cigarette from the packet, put it to her lips and leant forward so that Tony might light it. She hadn't smoked much and she felt self-conscious. Blowing away the smoke from the first puff she saw Tony catch Susan's eye and smile, and knew that she had not been meant to see it.

'Where will they send you now? Your instructing post? Will it be back in Australia or here?'

Tony appeared to be finding it difficult to drag his attention away from Susan back to her. He put down his glass and stared through the diamond panes of the window. 'The thing is, Kate, I've signed up for another tour.'

It was as though he had slapped her. She stared at him, stupefied, trying to form words, but her lips wouldn't work properly. Her breath stuck in her throat and she caught at it in snatches.

'What? Why would you do that? You've done enough,' she said, her voice rising.

'Well that's rather the point, I think. You see, they need experienced pilots like me to finish the thing off. There are still pockets of Germans holding out on the Atlantic wall. They've developed some very nasty bombs that fly by themselves and we have to get rid of them. Someone has to, well, firstly find them, and then destroy them.' He was talking very fast.

Kate was looking wildly about her. 'But ... but you can't!' she wailed. 'You know how many have died. You've been so lucky, and also,' she persisted, 'there are people saying that what you are doing is wrong. All those innocent people. The whole thing is very ...' She stood up, still trying to find the right word, 'selfish of you. We've only just found Nick. How could you do it to Mummy?' She wiped her hand across her nose in what she knew was an absurdly childlike gesture before she flounced out of the door.

'I'll go to her,' Susan said. 'Perhaps you'll wait for me?'

When Kate woke the next morning, her eyes were swollen. For the briefest of moments, she could not think why she should be distressed, and then in that awful half-light between sleep and being awake she remembered the conversation the previous evening. She felt sick. Had she really called him selfish? Nothing she would say would make any difference to what her brother would do. That was the cut of him, as they would say at home. And now her words would stand between them forever. Even if he forgave her, which he would, she could not forget what she had said. Worse than that, she knew that a pilot had to believe completely in what he was doing and have no doubts whatsoever – otherwise the terror would creep in and that was when mistakes were made. She would have to shore herself up and support her poor mother for more months of pacing the radar rooms and counting the blips on the screens.

She found him in the mess eating eggs.

'I'm sorry,' she said and sat down opposite him. 'For spoiling the evening, your birthday, and for the things I said.'

He put his hand over hers. She couldn't look at him and pushed her top teeth into her bottom lip until it hurt.

'It'll be all right, Kate. I know what I'm doing now. And you didn't spoil the night. I must say your friend Susan is great, isn't she?' He blushed, and Kate understood then why Susan had had that knowing smile at breakfast. She would never get used to the way these things went so quickly with the war. She had seen it so often in the mess at Hawkshill but she hadn't thought that Tony might be like that. An image of her brother in bed with Susan and all the gasping and moaning that she understood went on embarrassed her and so she blushed as well.

'I've never felt happier,' he rushed on, the tips of his ears now bright red, 'more set in my job, I mean. I'll miss my old crew but the show is nearly over I'm sure, just another month or two. I might as well see it through. Please understand, Kate.' She pulled at the quicks of her nails in her lap.

'Don't worry about me. Nothing will happen now, and if by any chance it does, you are to put on that lovely lipstick, get a new perm and go up to Buck House and collect my gong for me.'

It was typical of Tony to make a joke about something so unspeakably dreadful. Her anguish cracked her face and he leant across his eggs to hold her hand. For once his own face was straight and sad.

'It's something I have to do Kate. If the worst should happen, you'll mind them all, I know.'

The briefings were very different for his new tour. He was assigned to film duties, flying low and alone, fully bombed, to look for the hidden V2 sites. That meant flying in daylight. He had not told Kate or his mother about what he would be doing now. With all his mother's dire warnings about always flying in formation, a lone Lancaster being a sitting duck and all that, there was no point in having her worried sick. It was Cap Gris Nez today with two extra bods on board to take the pictures – a milk run, really, just across the Channel. After all, Cap Blanche Nez was already in the hands of the Canadians. Did these bastard Germans think they could protect the V2 sites with a handful of gun batteries, which was all that was left of the Atlantic wall? They would have to go in very low and circle to get shots from all sides, then drop the cookie. That would be the end of the wall and then they could find where the V2s were hidden and get rid of the vile and cowardly things. He would have time to send his mother a telegram for her birthday when he got back.

Twenty-two

CHANGI

It was the end of another gruelling day. Nick's dry eyes were red-rimmed and painful. Now that much of the jungle had been scraped back, the great expanses of newly exposed white rock made the glare of the sun even more vicious, with no relief afforded by the vegetation. He squinted as he entered the hut, trying to establish who might be there.

'Have you seen my father?' he asked Donaldson whilst groping to find his bed in the gloom. He didn't like the Ulsterman and found him unpleasant and snide. Just as Nick was getting used to seeing his father in a new light this man's disrespect irked him and he surprised himself by siding with his old man when Donaldson was openly insolent to Gerald. The offence would invariably cause his father to thunder at the Belfast man and threaten all kinds of retribution, which might have been effective in the last war but cut little ice in this one and certainly not in a prison of war. Nick would have been embarrassed by his father's old-school pomposity once but now he felt only pity for him.

'There's been a bit of a fracas,' Donaldson said, his vowels long and slow with the hint of a smirk dancing on his thin lips. 'I believe your old man is in the cooler.' His mouth widened to an unpleasant smile.

'What on earth ... whatever for?'

'Something about a water canteen, I believe. God knows what the old fool thought he was doing.'

Nick shot a look at the pole in the apex of the roof behind which he had tucked Mick Kelly's canteen. He knew with mounting dread that it would not be there.

'What happened?' His panic was like milk boiling over. There was a drumbeat in his chest and a pulse throbbed in his ears. 'Yeah.' Donaldson was looking closely at him. 'The Nip went straight for it, like he knew it was there. He shook it and then he opened it. You know something about it?'

'It's my canteen,' Nick hissed through clenched teeth.

'What is it about you people who think that your ancestral acres earn you respect and that you can put the rest of us at risk with your heroics?'

'Why the fuck did he say that it was his?'

'Saving his wee boy, I suspect.'

The brigadier was sitting at a tea crate playing cards with three other senior officers.

'Hello son,' he said, rising to his feet. He took Nick's elbow to steer him away from the others. 'I saw your father about an hour ago. He's fine really, considering.'

'It was my canteen, sir,' Nick said miserably.

'I thought as much. Well, it's just as well they haven't got you in solitary, I can tell you. They'd kill you. That's the odd thing about the Japs. Somewhere in their twisted minds they believe that there'll be a bigger stink if they execute an officer. He smiled.

'The one thing they respect is age – and your father has plenty of that. General Saito is a brute but these things appeal to his sense of *bushido*. Don't worry too much, son. Your father is a tough old bugger. He's been through it all before, you know, early on, when the administration here was even more brutal. Some fool soldier was up to heroics then too and Gerald took the rap for him.'

'Really? I'm sorry, sir. I didn't know that,' Nick stammered. 'What will they do to him? What did they do the last time?' He felt a mixture of horror, shock and intense curiosity.

'It's not very pleasant, I'm afraid, but it won't kill him.' The brigadier hesitated as if he were deciding whether Nick needed to hear this. 'They hold him down, fill his stomach with water through a funnel in his mouth so that he thinks he's drowning and then the brutes jump on him.'

'Oh Christ.' An image of a leering Japanese animal with his unpolished boots on his father's swollen belly floated up in front of him.

'Remember son, as I said, your father's war record impresses Saito, and of course the fact that he's well over fifty. It is far, far better he takes the beating for you. Let's hope the worst is over and that the Jap bastard doesn't intend to give him another dose of that medicine.' The senior officer smiled and put his hand on Nick's shoulder – a fatherly gesture that suggested forgiveness. It would have been easier for Nick if the brigadier had been angry.

'But if he's been through this before, Dad must have known what he could expect when he told the guards that the canteen was his.' His voice was almost a whisper. An appreciation of his father's courage was rising through the silt of his horror.

'Yes, I suppose he did.'

Nick looked wildly around him. 'I'm going to Saito now to tell him the canteen was mine,' he said.

He started for the guardhouse but the senior officer caught his arm. 'Don't be a fool, boy – your father is an old soldier. He'll be all right. If you go in there, they'll kill you. As I told you, I've seen him and he will live. Now go and see if you can find him something to eat.'

Nick contemplated ignoring the brigadier.

'That's an order, soldier,' he said firmly.

They brought Gerald back on a stretcher. Nick was waiting for him at the opening of the hut. 'You shouldn't have done that, Dad. I'm so sorry. Are you all right? Christ! They might have killed you.'

'And they would have definitely killed you. No ... no ... I'm proud of you taking a risk like that. It was my decision and mine alone to take the brunt for you. Your mother would never have forgiven me otherwise.' He held out his hand, looking for his son's.

'How bad is it?' Nick asked.

'My jaw is a bit sore but nothing broken, I think.' Gerald smiled. It was if he were talking about a mildly unpleasant tooth extraction. 'Now let me sleep.' He shifted his battered body painfully on the bed, trying to find some comfort. Then he sighed deeply and slowly closed his eyes. 'You might just make sure that my peppers have enough water, there's a good chap.'

Nick sat by the bed and watched the laboured rise and fall of his father's rib cage. The old man's mouth hung open and his lips were purple and swollen. Nick was profoundly miserable. How could he have allowed this to happen? He was an incompetent fool, caught up with some *Boys' Own* heroics. He had almost been the cause of his father's death, a fate that the old man, on the other hand, had accepted calmly and without fuss and to save *him*. 'I'm proud of you.' Had he said that?

He rose from his vigil beside the bed, sure that his father was now asleep, and went outside. The air was thick and wet. He stood in the parched lines of his father's vegetables, overcome with affection for him. Taking an unsteady breath he looked up at the bruised sky. Thunder rolled in from the sea and a white scar cracked the sky. The weather was breaking and there would be a violent storm, but everything would be fresher after that.

Twenty-three

WESTMEATH

Her birthday was Eleanor's favourite time of year, when the leaves turned and the lake was bathed in the rusty light of autumn. Fat rosehips and blackberries laced the hedges and the first morning frosts crisped the stubbly ground. She was looking forward to spending the week with Kate at home. She felt much better than she had done the last time when she thought they had lost Nick. That awful emptiness was gone now that he had been found and she could laugh again. She had plans to paint the morning room.

Kate pushed her arm through her mother's as they walked along the stony path down to the boathouse. Buster waddled stiffly in front of them.

'When we get Nick back I shan't mind a bit if he spends the whole bloody day in here.' Kate smiled and squeezed her mother's arm.

'Yes I suppose we can dare to think it will all be over soon.' Eleanor watched a line of birds unfurling and drawing a line across the pink sky the far side of the lake. 'The Canadians have almost mopped up the Pas-de-Calais and the Germans are on the run.'

'Oh Mum, won't it be wonderful to have everyone home again? I've been thinking: do you suppose that I might go to university when the war is over? I could study maths and then perhaps engineering. I have a lot of experience in what they call "electronics" now. It's a new field.'

'One step at a time, Kate. You sound just as you did as a child, always in such a rush.' But Eleanor knew well that her daughter was no longer a child. She still spent hours thrashing a tennis ball against the yard wall to get her eye in for a match and painted wildflowers as she had always done but over the war years Kate had quietly stepped into the role that she had assumed with Maggie and George when they were babies and throughout the black and empty months she had looked after them all. It was she who made sure that Martha and Jim were coping and it was to her that the Little Ones had turned when their mother had been saving Europe in the ops room. It was Kate who rescued Eleanor when she was convinced that Nick was dead. Of course Kate should further her studies, Eleanor thought with a swell of pride. One of her children might become the academic she had once supposed she herself would be. Her daughter had been selected to train for one of the most demanding positions in the air force, after all. That was unusual for a girl, just as it had been for Eleanor to study mathematics at university all those years ago. Perhaps something good would come out of this awful war.

'Come with me into town, Maggie. I have to get some things for Mummy's tea party this afternoon. We can have lunch in the Greville. It will be fun, just the two of us. Run up and put something tidy on.'

When Maggie appeared at the top of the stairs Kate could not believe her eyes. Good God, she thought. She did not recognize the woman making her way down the oak stairway. Maggie had powdered her crimson cheeks and rolled her wild hair into a neat bun at the nape of her neck. A tight skirt creased over her voluptuous hips as she moved. The skirt forced her to place one foot on the step precisely behind the other and the movement was startlingly provocative. Maggie had left the top buttons of her cardigan undone and Kate could see the promise of a bountiful bosom. Since Kate had come home she had seen Maggie only in the dungarees and the work boots she wore when she headed out every morning to help with the foals in the nearby stud at Ballinagore. She had never imagined that her younger sister could look like this.

'My goodness, Maggie. What's happened to you? You look gorgeous. Oh, I didn't mean it like that. I mean you were always gorgeous. It's just. Well ... you're all grown up.'

'What did you expect? I'm seventeen. I've had a job for six months now. Time didn't stop for George and I just because the rest of you were all away.'

Kate had missed the Little Ones terribly. She thought with something close to anguish that she would have to stop calling them that. She was hurt by Maggie's words, but then hadn't she felt like that when the boys left *her* behind? Did she know them at all? They had grown up without her just as Nick and Tony had done. She had no idea who Maggie's friends were or how she and George spent their time when they weren't at school. Nick and Tony had been away from her for these years too. Why did everyone in this family have to grow up so damn quickly? She had been left out of all of it.

'I'd better go and put a face on then. I can't be outshone by my baby sister in the Greville, can I?'

They sat down in the dining room. It had not changed since Kate was a little girl, when Poppa had parked her and the others there with a Club Orange while he had a 'quick drink' at the bar. She had had plenty of time back then to study the big golden swirls on the red carpet and the faded dinginess and now found it oddly comforting. The sandwiches were also still just as they always were, made with margarine and filled with slimy ham or processed cheese.

The door opened and a ruggedly good-looking boy in a tweed jacket and a rugby club tie approached their table. To her surprise she saw Maggie jump up to greet him. Her sister was clearly flustered.

'Hello Jim,' she said, 'this is my sister Kate. She's home on leave – I mean she's on holiday from England for a few days. Kate, this is Jim. His father is my boss.'

'How do you do Kate. I've heard a lot about you,' he said.

'Really?' Kate had heard nothing from Maggie about the boss's son. 'Why don't you join us?' But she didn't want to share her sister with this boy. She was reminded of the evening with Tony and Susan when she felt she was being left out of a secret. Maggie and Jim's eyes were locked on each other.

'I saw George on my way in,' Jim said. 'He was heading into O'Neill's with those lads he plays cards with. They looked like they'd had a few already.'

The talk was of mares and foals while they self-consciously nibbled on the sandwiches. It was not the cosy time that Kate had hoped to have with Maggie and Kate wished he would go. When Jim did finally get up to leave Maggie rose to go with him. 'I'll just see him out,' she said. Kate watched her sister leave the room, the tight skirt hugging her swinging hips. Jim's hand dropped to pat her sister on her bottom. She was sure Maggie hadn't walked like that a year ago.

Martha had made her famous walnut cake and Kate found some sparkling wine in the cellar. It was such a warm day and Kate had planned to have tea outside. Their neighbours the Armytages were coming, the old bishop from Killucan and Kate's new friend

Evie, who was married to the handsome fellow who had come into a place across the lake in Ballinea. It was a shame that Evie's brother Ed was still in Europe, Kate thought and then blushed at her own silliness. She hadn't seen him since last summer, for heaven's sake. She thought back to Maggie and Jim at lunch that day. She seemed to be the only one who couldn't get beyond the war and find someone special. Rose was already married and Nick would have Jeannie, she supposed. She had been there when Tony and Susan got together and now there was Maggie and Jim.

She allowed herself to think about Ed. He was so glamorous, she remembered, much taller than the local boys, with a wide smile and lovely even teeth. Ed had come to stay with Evie for a few days leave and been roped into a cricket game at Mount Conrath. The visiting team had been riled that the hosts had brought in this hired assassin who took four wickets and made thirty-six runs. Ed sought her out during the afternoon when he was eventually bowled out, polished off all of her egg sandwiches and made her laugh. When her mind sneaked back to that afternoon something twisted under her diaphragm. She knew she was being foolish. Ed probably never gave her a second thought. And fellows like Ed would need a lot of luck and there were already too many people in her life who needed it. Her friends thought her old-fashioned – a prude, even – but she could not be like the other girls on the base with all their romances and flings with one airman after another. Not like her little sister, apparently. Suddenly furious with herself, she slammed the smoothing iron over the tablecloth.

Kate poured the tea and cut the cake. Her mother sat in the wicker chair looking peaceful and contented. She popped the cork and everyone laughed as the bubbles frothed out of the bottle. 'Happy birthday Eleanor!' they chorused, raising their glasses.

'Absent friends,' the old bishop replied.

'What news of Ed, Evie?' Kate felt herself blushing as she asked the question.

'Actually we've had some good news – he was awarded an MC at Tenchbrai. It meant so much to my parents. Since he landed early on D-Day we'd heard nothing. But then you know what that's like, don't you darling?' Evie patted Kate's arm.

'I always knew Ed would be brave.' Kate blushed deeper. 'You know that Tony got the DFC? We shall be surrounded by heroes when they all get home, won't we?'

The weather turned the next day, and as Kate breakfasted with her mother the sky darkened to gunmetal grey and she wondered if she should put out the buckets to catch the drips. The door opened and Lilly poked her head around it. 'Willie's here with a telegram, mam,' she said.

'Oh Tony remembered your birthday after all, Mummy. I'll get it for you.'

The rain, which had started just after breakfast, had not let up all day. Kate crossed the yard. She needed to be in the barn. All the sunshine and happiness of the day before was gone. The iron bolt of the barn door was cold and she had to put her shoulder to one side of it to make the handle slide. The evening light filtered weakly through the dirty glass windows, filigreed with cobwebs, but it was enough to illuminate the old stalls, ghostly and empty now. Her breath misted in the stale air and miserably she remembered the warm breath of the horses that had lived in here, the gentle giants, Daisy and Dobbin, little Ben and Firefly. She ached for the living noises of them eating and rubbing against the stall walls, the gentle thud of droppings on the straw and the quiet jingle of their head collars as they tugged from the mangers. She longed for the sweet smell of hay, bran mash and leather oil. And for Tony to be there to wipe the smudge from her face again.

The names of the horses in Tony's childish handwriting were still on the wall under the blackened bridles, empty and skeletal now with twisted bits and curb chains hanging grotesquely as in a torture chamber. The saddles, dusty and hard, were stacked in neat rows like headstones. Kate raised her hand to caress the script and squeezed her eyes shut. When she opened them a blacksmith's anvil glinted from the corner, its pointed cone like a mortar. The one that had blown her brother out of the sky would have been much bigger. She pictured then her broken family in pressed uniforms collecting Tony's medal for him, just as he had predicted. Her chest heaved and a moan escaped from deep within her.

Twenty-four

CHANGI, OCTOBER 1944

E very morning Nick marched out to the airfield to swing his pickaxe for fifteen hours and fill swamp with rock. In September the monsoons came and the heat was unbearable. By now hundreds of destitute and dying men were drifting back daily from the railways, cramping the quarters and diminishing the scarce rations. Nick ate cat stew, dog rissole, grass, lily root, iguana, stingray and rat meat to keep himself alive. The medics played God and decided who needed food the most: a man qualified for an extra ration if the doctor could see the bones in his backside. Most of the wretches who made it back from the railways in the north were barely alive and died quickly and the line of white crosses in the prison cemetery lengthened every day. Nick was relieved when the brigadier stopped the buglers playing the 'Last Post' at the burials. Its mournful notes were corroding what was left of his will to live. Nick had felt like this before, in Aleppo and in Java, and he wasn't sure he could keep himself going a third time. He knew how easily a man could die when he gave up the fight: in the smallest of moments his breath would just stop coming. It was an effort not to stare at the groups of bedraggled men making the almost hourly trip to the graveyard to put to rest another shrunken corpse, and not to wonder when it would be his turn. Perhaps it would be easier just to give up now.

The camp became more and more crowded with the returning work parties from the railway in the north. To make room for them, 10,000 men were moved from the attap huts at Selarang and squashed into the old Changi jail, a concrete block built to house 600 civilian prisoners in peacetime. It had three floors with a central well of steel mesh and a series of gangways linked by metal stairways. Nick and his father were separated. Gerald and the other senior officers were housed in the warden's quarters and Nick shared a single cell with three others where he had one square metre of space he could call his own. The cells were suffocating, hot and claustrophobic, and at night the walls threw back the heat they had absorbed during the day. It was impossible to sleep. Nick's chest heaved with the lack of air and he imagined that each molecule had been through thousands of bodies already and there was nothing left in it for him. All night there was an uninterrupted cacophony of thousands of sick men snoring, grunting, groaning, puking and shitting. By morning the buckets in each cell were full to brimming.

Nick longed to be back in the hut that he had shared with his father. It was not just the space and being able to go to the latrine at night that he missed, but the amiable hours they had spent together tending the vegetables and playing chess. He had dysentery again. He realized that he had come to rely on his father over the last months, on the old boy's quiet resilience in this godforsaken place, and Nick was lonely and lost without him. He knew that it would break his father's heart if he gave up even though that was what he wanted to do. He had to survive. He would go and find the old man and see if he had any emetine for his guts. It would be good to talk to him.

A dull drone interrupted Nick's thoughts as he walked through the maze of packaging crates and makeshift fences towards his father's quarters. The noise grew until he could discern the unmistakable sound of machine-gun fire and the responsive boom of flak. A group of skeletal men gathered and all eyes searched the skies.

'There, there,' shouted one. 'B29s! Look it's the fucking Yanks! About bloody time.'

'Jesus, I hope they don't drop their shite on us.' The voice came from behind him but Nick did not have to turn around to know who had spoken. Sergeant Maloney had his gaze fixed on the incoming aircraft. Nick had seen many men wither, the flesh shrink from their bones and their eyes sink into their skulls in the years since he was captured, but he was shocked when he saw the sergeant. The man looked nothing like the sturdy fellow he had first met at the recruiting office in Vasey, a lifetime ago. It was as if all the fat from his body had been sucked out. Skin hung on his skeleton. His stick-like arms and legs were covered in sores and his head, bent back as it scanned the sky, was huge on his thin neck.

'Hello sarge,' Nick said, putting his hand out. 'You all right?' The sergeant looked at him in such a way that Nick was afraid he did not recognize him, or worse, did not want to.

'Jaysus, it's you,' the sergeant said. 'It's good to see you too. Really good. We didn't think you were going to make it, to be honest.'

'When did you get back?'

'About a month ago. Been in the hospital for a bit.'

'And the others?'

'Shorty is here. They hung him from a tree for the whole night and he refused to die. Typical.' The sergeant's cracked lips split into a weak smile, which quickly faded. 'Piper didn't make it. Cholera.' He paused and seemed almost embarrassed. 'D force had it rough, son. There's not many of us made it back. What about your dad?'

'Still with us,' Nick smiled weakly. Despite the funerals he watched every day he was finding it hard to process that Piper was gone too. 'Yeah, the old man taught me a thing or two.'

The sergeant cocked his head. 'He's been good to me,' Nick continued. 'I suppose I had a lot to learn – about him mostly.'

'Sometimes we have to find out things the hard way, don't we?'

'I should've been with you,' said Nick again, studying the ground between them.

'Now what would've been the point of that, for Chrissakes? You wouldn't have lasted a day up there. The whole lot of us should've got into that hospital bed with you and stayed there, that's the truth. Come on, Shorty will want to see you. This'll be a grand reunion. You know, if them's the Yanks,' he said nodding at the sky, 'this crap might be over soon.'

Nick allowed himself to feel a tiny prick of hope. The news from Europe, passed around the camp furtively by Mick Kelly and his boys, was good. The invasion in June had been successful and the allies were pushing towards the Rhine. And here were the American bombers. And perhaps, best of all, two of his friends had made it back.

As usual, Gerald was in the garden and on his knees. But there was something odd about his stoop: his head hung from his shoulders and the sinews in his neck pulsed as if he were grinding his teeth.

'Dad.' Gerald lifted his head in Nick's direction and for a moment Nick wondered if he had been drinking. His eyes were red, and had a dazed and faraway look. There was a sheet of paper in the old man's shaking hands and his shoulders were heaving.

'Hey, what is it?'

'Tony ... on your mother's birthday.' His voice cracked. 'My God, poor Eleanor.'

The next weeks throbbed with pain. Nick supposed that this was what was meant by having a broken heart. It did not seem possible that he would never see Tony again. What did *never* mean? Then a black panic gripped him as he thought he understood the answer. He was angry too. Why had the stupid boy volunteered for another tour when he could have been out of the war in some cushy instructor post? He had completed thirty-six sorties and won the DFC. What else did he have to prove?

Gerald avoided everybody after the awful news and it seemed to Nick that he could not bear to be with him either; his very presence must remind his father of what he had lost. The brightest star had fallen, after all. Nick understood that he would live the rest of his life with the crushing fact that he had survived and his brother had not. The decorated war hero, that luck-kissed happy boy, had been blown to bits doing the most courageous thing imaginable and what was left of him was buried somewhere in northern France. Nick, the man who still lived, had surrendered twice, and rotted away in a POW camp for almost the entire war.

And yet, through his despair, Nick craved his father's company. He wanted forgiveness. He wanted to be with someone who had the same pain. He believed his father's coldness was a punishment he somehow deserved. It increased his suffering, and that made him feel better.

Four weeks later, father and son sat on adjacent tea crates sharing a pipe of tobacco, watching the sun slide into the aubergine sea. There was nothing to talk about but by now they had become used to long silences.

Nick took a deep breath. 'Tony was always going to be a hero, wasn't he? He was born brave.'

Gerald slowly pulled his gaze from the lightshow of the tropical sunset.

'I'm sorry, Dad. I'm sorry I couldn't match up to him and now I never will. I mean ...'

For a moment, Nick wondered if his father had heard him.

'Tony never knew fear, son. That's a different thing. You see, it takes real courage to do a brave thing when you are afraid,' Gerald said. 'You've swum in waters where the strongest have drowned. You've done the right thing when it was easier to do the wrong. I don't think I could be more proud of you.'

He rested his hand on Nick's thin arm and squeezed it.

Epilogue

NORTHERN FRANCE, SEPTEMBER 1984

It is forty years today since we lost him and I don't feel like making small talk as we take the exit off the motorway for Wissant, a seaside village in the Pas-de-Calais. Back in 1948 the authorities could not tell me where Tony was buried but now, four decades later, the war graves people seem sure that he is here in Wissant, buried with the Canadians.

From the road one can make out the white ridge of the cliffs of Dover across the Channel on the horizon, a bright step out of the shining water to another land. It was such a short hop for him compared to those terrifying trips to Berlin and Munich. Ahead of us is Cap Blanche Nez, its cliff face chalky like its English neighbour, and on this warm autumn day it is honey-coloured, towering over a wide sandy beach. Mothers and children, some wrapped in beach towels and others making sandcastles, are dotted along it as the waves lap against sand left rutted by the receding tide. Behind us is Cap Gris Nez. It looks ominous beside its sunny sister.

It is hard to be anything but profoundly sad. Today would have been Mum's birthday, her eighty-fifth, but then she was never going to make old bones.

I sit in the back of the car beside my wife Jean. Kate's younger daughter, Charlotte, is driving and her husband, a military man, is map-reading. She tilts her head towards me when I speak because my accent is strange to her. I see the movement and sigh – I did not know my sisters' children at all as they grew up. This is my first trip back to Europe since I left for good in 1948. I had Dad's reluctant blessing back then to make a life for myself in Australia but now I wonder at the price of it, at what I have missed. This side of the globe seems so foreign to me. Not only does my family speak differently, I am afraid that we might have little else in common. And yet here we are, strangers really, searching for my brother's grave, a man they never knew. Perhaps family is more important than any of us thought. Perhaps we have survived all the splintering.

It is difficult to find the Commonwealth War Cemetery as new roads have carved across the old ones, blocked the route and sent us back on ourselves.

'There it is Nick,' Jean says, pointing to the copse of yew trees on the nearby hill. 'What a pity the new road goes so close to it.'

Charlotte parks the car and I emerge stiffly from the back seat, leaning on the car to steady myself, needing a moment to prepare. I flex each of my arthritic knees and take a deep breath.

The grass between the avenue of yew trees is mown short and sprinkled with the orange and vermilion leaves of the deciduous trees that stand amongst the yews of the graveyard. A gate with a well-oiled latch in the low wall encloses the cemetery. Despite the roar of traffic from the big road close by it is a quiet space. I am used to these war graves, given my long years working with the Returned Servicemen's League, but they never fail to move me.

The gravestones stand bright and straight. There are little flags, flowers and British Legion poppies in front of some, but otherwise they have a touching sameness. The boys buried here are all so young. Old men make war and boys pay the price for it. I am surprised at how small this cemetery is, given that it is the only Commonwealth War Grave Cemetery in Wissant and there was such fierce fighting here in September 1944 during the last-ditch German attempts to maintain the broken Atlantic wall. Thousands died, with the Canadians taking the brunt of it. The maple leaf on the flag flutters gently against a cornflower blue sky.

The front two lines of tombstones all bear the RAAF crest: *Per Ardua ad Astra. Through adversity to the stars.* How like my family's motto: *Ad Astra Sequor. Follow the stars.* God knows we have known adversity too. This will be where he is, I think. It is the end of a long journey that started in Dun Laoghaire when we were teenagers all those years ago. I take Jean's hand and we begin to walk along the rows. Charlotte and her husband follow behind us, giving us time and space to read the inscriptions. Only the thrum of traffic breaks the silence.

'Here's another one that came down in September 1944,' I say quietly. 'You see, Cap Blanche Nez had already fallen by the twenty-sixth,' I add, talking to myself, really. A familiar, desperate sadness washes over me as I remember that three days after Tony's Lancaster smashed into the ground somewhere around here the Germans had fled north. On the twenty-sixth, when Tony thought he was flying the easiest op of the war, only the big batteries of *Todt* and *Grosser Kurfürst* at Cap Gris Nez were still holding out. The Canadians had already relieved the rest of the coast. Tony and his crew were probably the last Allied casualties in Pas-de-Calais. We examine every tombstone and then go back along each silent line and do it again.

'He's not here, dear,' Jean says and looks at me anxiously. She knows what this means to me. 'Perhaps he is in the British one at Wimereux?'

'No, they said Wissant,' I say, unjustifiably irritated. 'I made them check as we were coming so far.' I cannot believe that we might not find his grave.

'I'm afraid they're still not very accurate about these things,' Charlotte's husband says, and the sense of it irritates me too. 'It may be that his grave is not marked. However, Wimereux really isn't that far. Why don't we go into Wissant and have some lunch and try Wimereux this afternoon?'

I realize that I am being humoured, that the search for Tony's grave and my journey may be in vain. As we leave, I look desperately behind me in case there might be a single tombstone hiding somewhere that we have missed. A frog hops across the path. I swallow hard.

We park the car across the stone bridge beside the Hôtel de la Plage. The shutters are painted candy pink and the building looks like something from a child's storybook. The hotel stands at right angles to an old windmill and together they frame a basin of water, which must have once fed the mill. Mallard and greylag geese strut on the far banks, preening their breast feathers with their bills. It is a charming scene but I am morose. My mind keeps going back to when I left Tony at the café by Flinders station, when I could say nothing to make him feel better.

'I think we need a drink,' Charlotte says. The man behind the bar has a rugged, pleasant face and his eyes are merry. His outdoorsy appearance is at odds with the heavy flowered wallpaper and the collection of warming pans it bears.

'Four cognacs please.'

'Very good for the cold,' the barman replies, misjudging the four sad faces in front of him. We sit outside on a little wooden balcony overlooking the mill race and the milky waters of the Channel behind it.

'I just don't understand it,' I say. 'They were certain he had a headstone. I came all this way because they said I'd find it.'

The barman appears with our drinks.

'Excuse me, how far is the British cemetery of Wimereux from here?' I ask.

'Perhaps thirty kilometres?' He gives a shrug.

'You see?' I say, glancing at Jean. 'He can't be there.'

'You are looking for someone?' the barman asks.

'My brother's grave.' My voice is shaky. 'He was shot down in a Lancaster in September 1944, today actually, the twenty-sixth. It's forty years ago today. They told me he was in Wissant but we've just been there and he's not there.'

'And your name is, monsieur?'

'Tottenham.'

'Ah,' the man says, letting out a deep breath. 'We have your brother with us here in the village with our people. He is not in the military one. We have been looking after him for you and waiting for you. Come, I will show you.'

The graveyard is about a kilometre from the village and stands on the top of a hill behind it. Cap Gris Nez is to the left and Cap Blanche Nez to the right. Four Commonwealth war tombstones stand together at the back of the cemetery, at its highest point. It is possible to see the cliffs of Dover beyond the sweep of the gentle hill. There are geraniums and ornamental grasses planted in front of the headstones. The nine names of the crew of Tony's Lancaster are engraved on three of them, three names on each one. At the bottom of the one on the farthest right I find him:

> *Flight Lieutenant*
> *A.B.L. Tottenham DFC*
> *Royal Australian Air Force*
> *26 September 1944 aged 21*
> *Rust not the sword of his glory with your tears.*

Postscript

It is 26 September 2014 – another anniversary, and thirty years after the pilgrimage made by Uncle Nick. My cousin Frances and I are having breakfast in Wissant. As we sip our coffee we pore over a sepia photograph, this one of our grandparents, Eleanor and Gerald, with my mother, Kate.

'Do you remember Grandfather?' Frances asks me.

'A little. Just before he died. He was making me a toy ... a doll, I think.'

The photograph was taken after the war, outside Buckingham Palace after they had received the medal from the king. They are all in uniform. My grandfather, head and shoulders taller than his wife and his daughter, is in the middle and holding the medal in its case in front of him. The women wear the peaked caps of the WAAF and sturdy lace-up shoes. My grandfather is sporting a beret at a jaunty angle but there is a terrible similarity in their faces.

Modern psychologists call it the thousand-yard stare, that limp, blank and unfocused look, as if life has been sucked out of them.

Frances and I arrive at the graveyard on the top of the hill looking over the village. Rose and Kate's daughters, on another pilgrimage to honour an uncle we never knew, there for our mothers who had never been able to visit where their brother was buried.

We have brought some heather from Ireland to plant on Tony's grave and when we finish scraping at the chalky earth and have carried a bucket of water from the cemetery tap to bed it in, we stand back.

'The target was Gris Nez – it seems strange that this could be the nearest graveyard, don't you think? I suppose they were looking for the V2 site, which Cap Gris Nez was protecting. That's why they had the film crew on board,' I say, looking over the fields between the graveyard and the dark cliff of Cap Gris Nez in the distance. 'I wish I knew where he came down.'

'We won't find anyone who would remember the crash now,' Frances adds sensibly. We head for Gris Nez, keeping its gloomy bulk in front of us as we negotiate the twisty roads away from the graveyard. A signpost points towards the sea: *Todt Battery Museum*.

'We should have a look at the museum, shouldn't we?' I suggest. We both feel the need to do more to mark the day. Seventy years.

The museum is in the old gun battery, an ugly concrete block perched on the top of the cliff. The exterior, at least, is not much changed from when it was active in 1944 – save that the gaping mouth, from which the 105-ton canon once pointed towards England, is empty.

In halting French I ask the busy curator whether he, by any chance, knows anything about a Lancaster shot down in the area in the last days before the Canadians relieved Cap Gris Nez. It is a long shot I know. The man stops what he is doing and looks up at us.